Herman

Heaven Forbid

Heaven Forbid

– A NOVEL –

Christopher Hope

MACMILLAN

First published 2001 by Macmillan
an imprint of Pan Macmillan Ltd
Pan Macmillan, 20 New Wharf Road, London N1 9RR
Basingstoke and Oxford
Associated companies throughout the world
www.panmacmillan.com

ISBN 0 333 72465 8

1 3 5 7 9 8 6 4 2

A CIP catalogue record for this book is available from
the British Library.

Typeset by SetSystems Ltd, Saffron Walden, Essex
Printed and bound in Great Britain by
Mackays of Chatham plc, Chatham, Kent

'With the passage of time, I'm convinced that my first years were a paradise. But I am undoubtedly mistaken. If there was ever a paradise, I must look for it earlier than all my years.'

E. M. CIORAN

For Dee

1. At the Villa Vanilla

When I was about five, I used to lie in bed and think about my past. Back to when it was just my mom and me. When we lived with my grandpa, when we had a deal. In the Days Before Raymond, in the Time Before Gordon. Before I was denuded, desiccated, discombobulated . . . before I discovered dynamite.

Every afternoon Georgie would swing me up onto the gatepost. The front gate was dark and wooden, and it faced Sligo Road. On the gatepost was a slab of stone, flat, good for looking down from, for seeing right down to the end of the road. A boy could sit there and wait for his mom to climb off that tram and come home from Consolidated Federal, where the ledgers were. Each afternoon she came home on the tram. It was red and cream, that tram, with a bell. She climbed off at Park Lake.

My grandpa told me he came to Parkside because it spoke to him of Ireland. The names of the streets were songs, and I sang them. Derry was the next street down; Wexford was the next street up. Then came Ballymurphy, then Mourne . . . Sligo Road ran down to

Erin Avenue, and across Erin was Park Lake, where the tram stopped.

Up the road from Park Lake was the zoo, and in the zoo was a cage of lions, big and yellow and tired and dusty. They walked up and down all day in their cage. On my birthday, my mom and me, we went to the zoo and rode in a little box on the elephant's back, with a pink umbrella over our heads, all the way from the monkeys to the seals. We passed the lions and she didn't even blink but at night she cried in her sleep.

My grandpa painted his house cream. He called it the Villa Vanilla. The shutters were yellow, the red tin roof had a curving lip. There was a palm tree in the middle of our lawn. I was at home in the garden but the garden was not my home.

My mom came walking up Sligo Road in the cool of the afternoon, wearing a big white hat and a frock with yellow daisies. I wore my Robin Hood hat with the feather and I waited for her to come home.

You could rely on it.

When she saw me she'd begin to run, wobbling on her high heels, holding onto her hat. When her skirt lifted I'd see her ankles, and her stockings gave her legs a buttery sheen, smooth to the eye but, when you touched them, rough as cement. Her best nylons – they cost the earth. She'd lift me off the gatepost (you could bet on it), she'd say: 'Hello, darling.' She'd kiss me, then she'd say: 'By golly. What a day. I've had ledgers in chunks. I don't care if I never see another blooming ledger – as long as I live.'

You could depend on it. Yes, siree.

I had a green hood with a tall green feather in it. I didn't have a tunic, but I had a hollow in my leg, right at the top. I didn't know how I got it, but she did. She'd push her fingernail right into the hollow – *push, push, push* – 'My golly, can you feel that? There! Know what it is? That's *pure* bone. That's where they put the needle in, when you were a baby. Again and again. We thought we'd lost you. How could you, Martin? To your very own mother. Some day I won't be here. Then what?'

'Then what?'

'Then you'll be sorry, won't you?'

'I will.'

'It'll be too late. You've only got one mother. Know what I mean?'

I knew what she meant. I was sorry even before it was too late. Hansel and Gretel got lost. Anyone without a fine sense of woodcraft got lost in Sherwood Forest. Except Robin Hood. He knew every leaf of the green-wood. James James Morrisson Morisson lost his mother at the end of the town, though he was only three. I knew how it felt. I knew every leaf in Sligo Road and if she ever got lost, I'd find her.

My room was next to her room. When I heard her cry the first time, I woke up and went through to her bed and climbed in and shook her.

Her voice spoke in the dark. 'What's the matter?'

'You were crying and crying.'

'Was I, darling? Fancy. Oh, Martin, just hark at them. Goll-ee. Isn't it a good thing you're right next door? It's when they ruin my sleep that I cry. That's the night-lions. Know what I mean? I'm not scared in the daytime. I'm as tough as an old boot. But at night . . . Who wants to be gobbled up by some mangy old night-lion you can't see? Before you've time to say excuse me. Or, kiss my foot. I've had night-lions in chunks. Know what I mean?'

I knew what she meant. She didn't like lions or ledgers or the past or the war or the dead or drunks. She had a soft spot for the little pig who built his house of bricks and cooked up the Big Bad Wolf in a cauldron.

'I'm glad he did. Imagine how you'd feel if that wolf turned up at your door, his tummy rumbling with his sharp digestive juices, just dying to gobble you up . . .' She shivered. She did a good shiver. 'It feels like someone just walked over my grave. Know what I mean?'

I knew what she meant. If you had the wolf at your door, huffing and puffing, you'd better not build your house from straw. If you didn't want to be dissolved in his sharp digestive juices you built with bricks. I was the bricks she built her house with.

She didn't like war.

'You won't catch me dwelling on what's dead and gone. Not me. Oh-o-o, no blooming fear. I don't want to see another war – not till my dying day. No *thank* you. I've had war in chunks.'

She didn't like Boers, she'd had Boers in chunks. For being ruddy hypocrites, the whole bally bang-shoot of them. They gave her the heebies, just thinking of them gave her the pip, and a cadenza.

She didn't like running balances. 'Running balances can be tricky. I know someone – he can do double-entry. Fancy that.'

She didn't like lightning. 'Never stand out when there is lightning in the sky, never ever use a telephone, or get in a swimming pool – or stand under a tree. A tree is the worst place to be near in a bad electric storm. Lightning loves a tree. A lightning strike can burn all the grass for miles around.'

What she did like were clothes and pearls and policemen and our deal, because we had a deal and we promised it was for ever. When the night-lions woke her, and I came to her, she pulled me into her bed and hugged me. The lions were tearing up the night.

She held my hand. 'Just listen to them. Aren't you glad we're in here and they're out there?'

I listened. They roared like a big yellow sea in the dark.

'I'll look after you.'

'Will you, darling? Keep an eye out? For ever and ever? Promise me . . .'

'I will.'

'How do you know what to promise till I tell you? Promise me – if ever you get lost – promise me you'll stay exactly where you are. Know why? Because I'll always remember where I left you. But if you move, I might never find you again. Know what I mean?'

'I promise.'

'Then let's practise. Say after me "My name is Martin Donally. I live at 99 Sligo Road, Parkside . . ."'

I said it.

'Repeat and remember . . .'

If I got lost I'd always stay exactly where she left me, and she'd find me. That was our deal. Repeat and remember. Tried and true. For ever and ever, world without end. Amen.

2. What a Boy Needs

I sat on the gatepost. I could see right to the bottom of the hill. I knew where to find her. She was always where I looked for her. I liked that. Coming up the hill, smiling. Behind me, somewhere, I could hear Georgie snipping roses, the sun was right over my head and the world was good. All I had to do was hold it there and things would be fine.

Good things came in the afternoons: sometimes rain, or the ice-cream man; my mom, always. You could count on it. She was kind, she had pretty legs, she wore big hats, her eyes were dark, she was frightened of lions. In the past, she'd been Monica MacBride, then she was Monica Donally – but now everyone called her the much-married Mrs Donally.

One day she said: 'I'm thinking of reverting. I'm sick of being Monica Donally. I'm going back to being plain Monica MacBride.'

'Can I revert too?'

She put her small finger in the corner of her mouth, turned her hand over and chewed her nail. And looked at me for a long time. She always did that when she was thinking hard.

'Golly – I don't know. Anyway, I'm reverting. And anyone who doesn't like it can kiss my foot.'

At night I lay awake for as long as I could, listening for the lions. I heard my gran's keys jingle as she walked past the bedroom door. She locked the door. I got up and unlocked it. My gran was very thin. She had a scar from a red Afrikander ox that had stabbed her with his long sharp white horn. Right in her middle. She had been driving from Curzon to Jo'burg and the Packard got stuck in a whole lot of cows and this ox stuck his horn though the window and stabbed her – just like that. It was a great scar, like a wide road. It ran all the way from her belly button to her breast and she let me touch it. She played the piano and she sang 'The Moon Has Raised His Lamp Above' with my grandpa, and their voices mixed like milk and honey. '*The moon has raised his lamp above, To light the way to see my love . . .*'

She wore a big bunch of keys on her belt and jingled.

'When we ran the Grange Hotel everything had to be locked – sugar and salt and liquor and eggs, pantry and larder and fridge and bar. Or they walked in the night. Grew legs and skedaddled. Lock it or lose it. To this day if I see a door I turn a key.'

Sometimes my mom woke me up in the morning and she'd be laughing.

'My mother passed in the night. She's locked us in. What ever would happen if we wanted to move?'

'I don't want to move.'

'You shall stay here for as long as you wish,' my grandpa said.

'Promise?'

We were sitting in the big green armchair in the living room, under the stain. I pressed back, feeling the tick of his fob watch. His cuffs went shooting out of his mustard-yellow suit like two white tunnels, smooth and starched. And in their buttonholes were soft milky pearls and on his finger a heavy gold ring with a peregrine cut into its black face and he was telling me what a boy needs:

'Fifteen years old. I came to Africa and lay alone in the veldt at night, listening for the enemy to cough or scratch a match. African spirits, Martin, to be sure, are small and hairy – that's the sooty sprites of Africa – veldt goblins and *tokoloshes*. Very kind to foreign fellows is your average African *tokoloshe*, ever ready and willing to warn a poor soldiering boy that someone's trying to kill him. That's when a boy learns what he needs. It's a bit of a fright to be freshly arrived in a strange land, and suddenly you're thinking: "Lord. Someone hereabouts is wishing me dead." It's discombobulating.'

'What does a boy need, Grandpa?'

'A boy needs every bit of help he can get. He needs

height. Elevation. He needs to be up where he can see what's coming. He needs light or the darkness gets to him. He needs fight. Above all, a boy needs bangs. High-explosive. Cordite, gelignite or – best of all – dynamite. Oh, we could have seen off the English – if we'd had more bangs. Shall we sing something, dear fellow?'

He wound his Supa Crystal Gramophone, blew dust off the shining discs, black wax in brown paper sleeves. He had Nat King Cole, Frank Sinatra and Bing Crosby. Paul Robeson was my grandpa's favourite singer of all time. Not counting Al Jolson and John McCormack. He dropped a record onto the silver stub. The songs went spinning into my head.

'Let's do Al Jolson, shall we? Giving the great line all the lean for which Jolson is justly famous . . . Ready? One, two, three. *Mamm-ee, Mamm-ee, my dear old Mamm-eeee . . .*'

My grandpa hated sportsmen. What a curve he got to his lips. He bent the word, he flicked it, it stung like a whip. 'Sports-*men*! Grubby-rugby-ites, Clickety-crickety-ites. Socks and jocks men. Bags of golf-wallahs. The white-hatted, green brimmed, brown-shoed bowling brigade. Oh, Martin, my dear, the barbarian is at the gates. And how do we know? Easy. Never mind his sword, look at his shorts. Lord save us. Let's cleanse the mind and have a story. Which shall it be tonight, Martin?'

' "The Swiftly Flowing Stream".'

'Again?'

'I'll be you, and you can be the man who nearly drowned.'

'Very well, my dear, I'll be starting.'

He went and lay down on the green carpet, which was the swiftly flowing stream. I started walking round the room, because I was on my way home from Mass one Sunday morning many, many years ago in Waterford and I passed the stream. My grandpa lay on the green carpet and waved his arms and coughed because he was nearly drowning in the swiftly flowing stream. He kept shouting: 'Help, help! For Christ's sake, help!'

I came along, my hands in my pockets. I was being him, walking along the riverside, whistling 'Poor Old Joe'. *'I'm comin', I'm comin', though my heart is full of woe . . .'*

The drowning man was going down for the third time. He gurgled. He was a fine drowner. I jumped into the stream. My gran sneaked in sometimes when I was in the water and we were swimming for our lives and she'd say: 'For Pete's sakes, Dan, what sort of example are you setting the boy rolling about on the floor like that? And you in your suit too.'

'I am being saved, Mabel.'

Then my grandpa played his da, who was a terrible man for the drink. He was waiting when I got home; he saw water streaming from my one and only Sunday best black suit. My grandpa was good at playing his da, very fierce, reaching for his desk ruler, which was his da's small black cudgel. Beating the daylights out of me for ruining my Sunday suit while I lay on the carpet, kicking and screaming – but softly, because if we made too much noise it upset my gran.

Then, after I'd been beaten, I ran away from home.

I loved this bit. I opened the door and stepped into the passage, looked back, waved, and my grandpa wrapped his hankie around his head. Now he was being his poor old mam, waving goodbye to me from behind his chair, which was the window of the MacBride hovel, back in old Éire. Her silver hair was shining. She waved and wiped a tear from her eye. I stepped aboard the Union Castle liner that carried me to Cape Town to fight for Kroojer and the Boers, and left her behind for ever.

When we got to the boat bit, my grandpa always started singing 'Mother Machree'.

'*Sure I love the dear silver that shines in your hair, and the brow that's all furrowed and wrinkled with care . . .*'

I waved, she waved back and my grandpa's voice got just the right sob:

'*I kiss the dear fingers so toil-worn for me-e-e-e, Oh, God bless you and keep you, Mother Machree.*'

I often cried at this bit. It was such a good, sad song.

But it was fine now. After years and years away, my grandpa was going home to Waterford, to the hovel in the hills. His ticket was booked on the *Pendennis Castle* – a city afloat. He read me the ads – there was a string orchestra and the first-class smoking room was lined in white linen, making it one of the coolest places in the tropics . . .

'Such luxury, it's a wonder anyone ever gets off.'

But I knew he'd get off. He'd step ashore in old Éire, he'd drive to Waterford.

'I shall run up the path of the MacBride hovel.'

'Yes, Grandpa.'

'My old mam will be at the window.'

'Holding out her hands, all toil-worn . . .'

'Holding 'em out to her own dear lost son. My goodness, what a hugging and kissing and a song and dance there will be. Forty years it's been. We're all ready – but for one small fly in the ointment.'

'We need to keep an eye on Uncle Kei.'

'Clever boy. We need to keep an eye. Uncle Kei is the fly. It is his predilections.'

He smiled his very slow smile, he lifted his cane, he spelt it out on the blue sky. 'Pre-di-lic-tions . . . urgings, predispositions, secret and shameful yearnings against which the man is powerless. Hence the need, continually, to keep an eye.'

'I'll keep an eye. You go home to your old mam.'

'Bless you, dear fellow. But Kei's predilections are not easy to spot.'

Words he spoke, he sang, he drew. My grandpa gave away words every day. They tasted fine and I swallowed them:

Pe-ri-pa-te-tic – so full of clicks you might have been talking Xhosa.

With a pencil he drew a big 'T' and next to it a big 'P'. 'Know what that stands for? "Tee-pees"? *Tall persons*. Grown ones. Watch out for them. You're small; it's a tall world. Being young and short by destiny, a boy better watch his back. Yes, sir. This is Injun country.'

I sat in his lap counting three buttons hard against my back – God the Father, God the Son, God the Holy Ghost. I listened to the tick of his fob watch and the rise and fall of his breath.

'What's to be done about said urgings? That is the question.'

'Don't know, Grandpa.'

'Great minds think alike. Darned if I know either. I am quite discombobulated by Uncle Kei.'

At the back of the Villa Vanilla was a long white wall. It stood up high and kept us from whoever lived behind us. I never saw anyone behind us. A mulberry tree stood in front of the corner. You pushed through the long branches of the mulberry tree and there you were, in the corner, between the high white back wall and the garage wall. It was a secret place. No one went there, only me. You had to be small to squeeze under the mulberry branches. A big log lay against the wall, white and smooth. I was at home in the garden but it wasn't my home. My mom said so.

My place was somewhere right, where you could sit and lean against the wall and be very, very quiet, where you could tie down the sky, right there, between the red roof of the Villa Vanilla and the sharp tip of the palm tree, with, sometimes, the clouds in the sky, hanging there like washing. I sat there to make sure everything was right. I knew where I was, nothing changed, nothing moved – at least not for now.

I started on the words – 'Peripatetic . . . discombobulate . . . predilections . . .' Then I had a burst of 'Mother Machree' '*I kiss the dear fingers so toil-worn for m-e-e-e-e . . .*' I had to get the words right. If I got them exactly right then maybe we'd just go on being where we were.

3. Gumpf

Auntie Fee was my favourite aunt – she told me so I wouldn't forget. She said there was nothing she wouldn't tell me – only I wasn't allowed to tell anyone. When Auntie Fee wanted me to do something she looked like she was going to cry.

'I love you to bits.' Her big green eyes went *blink, blink*. 'And if you don't love me right back – ' *blink, blink* went her green eyes – 'I might cry. You wouldn't like that, would you?'

'I wouldn't.'

'Give me a kiss, then. I wouldn't either.'

The hair on her cheekbones was shiny and soft, her dark hair on her head was springy. She had cat's eyes, quick eyes that jumped on you sideways while she was telling you something. To see what it did to you. Was it helping? Was it hurting? You never knew which she was hoping for. She was so kind. It was scary.

She was married to my uncle Jack. He was an ex-fighter-pilot ace. He had a dimple in the middle of his chin, blue eyes and wavy black hair with a white line down the middle of his head. Uncle Jack's real name was Horatio but no one called him that. And he was married to Auntie Fee. Her real name was Fionnuala but only my grandpa called her that.

Auntie Fee didn't read me Christopher Robin, or Jonathan Jo with a mouth like an O, or Peter Rabbit, or *The Little Engine Who Could*.

'Gumpf, pure gumpf.'

She read me Robin Hood. I liked Robin Hood because he could blend and merge and vanish in the depths of Sherwood Forest. In his suit of Lincoln green, invisible among the mighty oaks, he felt the breath of his pursuers hot on his neck. Robin always outran his pursuers.

Auntie Fee said: 'They'll get him one day. You wait.'

She shook her head when it said in my book that Robin Hood and his Merrie Men laid out a mighty feast on the greensward and supped till midnight.

'*Sward*? I'll give him sward. Sward my eye.'

She liked the Sheriff of Nottingham. She said he didn't have a black heart and Robin of Locksley hadn't any business loosing an arrow through it.

'Absolutely not. Damn cheek. You do not go around shooting sheriffs.'

When Robin lay in Locksley Hall, and turned his face to the casement, and loosed a shaft through the window because he knew that he was going to die, Auntie Fee smiled.

'It's all very well running round in green briefs, very

high and mighty. But just wait. Till the iron enters the soul. Hoo, boy!'

She was sorry for the giant in *Jack and the Beanstalk*. Jack was too big for his boots. If anyone should've been shot through his black heart it was that Jack. She liked it that the Giant had a voice that chilled your blood. She liked it when the Giant said he'd grind Jack's bones to make his bread.

'So would I. Silly boy. I'd grind his bones to make my bread any day of the week. I'd have made a very good ogre.'

She liked *The Three Billy-Goats Gruff*. When she got to the smallest Billy-Goat Gruff nearly getting eaten by the troll, she said: 'Serves the blighter right. I think those silly goats had it coming. Trit-trotting across his bridge. Drive me mad, it would. Trit-trot, trit-trot . . . Give me the troll any day of the week. You can talk to a troll. What's to be said to a lot of goats?'

When she was telling stories she looked at you like the Giant looked at Jack. It was true – Auntie Fee would have made a good ogre, if she hadn't been my aunt. A good troll. She had a voice so soft and sweet and melting that it chilled the blood.

'There's nothing I won't tell you. Nothing I can't remember. I'm as wise as Solomon; I'm as old as the hills. I'm an old fossil, I am. Do you know what's a fossil, Martin? Something so old it has turned to stone. Something that remembers every wrinkle.'

She didn't like stories about Ireland, and saving people from drowning.

She said: 'Irishry? Hmm ... my Eye-rish-ry, more like.' And she lit a Goldflake cigarette.

'There comes a time when the iron enters the soul, hot and hard it comes. And not just in fairy stories.'

My grandpa liked stories about people who got on. Auntie Fee liked stories about people who had gone to pot. She'd point up at the stain on the ceiling and I'd push back into the deep green chair.

'Follow my finger,' Auntie Fee said.

I followed her finger and there it was – the stain on the ceiling. Dark and sad. It still looked wet. The cracks between the floorboards went racing into the distance, shooting like arrows for the stars, running like roads across the face of Ireland.

'What's that?'

'Cousin Caítlín's map.'

'Dead right. Cousin Caítlín on the ceiling, Cousin Caítlín twice removed, who came from overseas, and who went to pot. See – there's Waterford, where your grandpa came from. Screw up your eyes, Martin, and you can almost see the MacBride hovel ... That's Dublin, and there's County Cork, and the Mountains of Mourne. You could drive around the country, from that map.'

'Why didn't she cry England – where she came from?'

Auntie Fee said: 'England's bigger. So she stuck to

Wales. You don't want to cry big places. It's bad enough crying Ireland. It's a titchy place. Imagine if you did Russia?'

Auntie Fee stroked the back of my neck. Her voice got nicer, softer, sweeter. It was very scary.

'I don't want you ending up like that. Imagine crying a country – a biggie? Like Egypt – or even Mesopotamia. Can you imagine how much crying that'd take?'

'How much?'

'Oh, weeks.'

'Let's have Cousin Caítlín.'

Auntie Fee sighed, shook her head and lit another Goldflake.

'Cousin Caítlín was a funny, lovely country girl, with coal-black eyes and a love of horses. She came from the Welsh Borders. A good rider. Surprisingly fair for a half Welshwoman. The Welsh tend to be small and dark and Celtic. Not tall and blonde, with deep grey, slate-grey, almost charcoal eyes. She was blonde and black, fair and dark, your cousin Caítlín. She wasn't stuck-up either.'

Auntie Fee always sounded surprised; she expected people 'twice-removed', and from 'overseas' to be stuck-up.

'Thinking they know everything about everything. And as result they are – what, Martin?'

'Clots, Auntie Fee.'

'Are they ever. And often Pommies to boot.'

'Cousin Caítlín was a cut above.'

'Very much a cut above. Cousin Caítlín sailed across the sea in a Union Castle boat, from Southampton to Cape Town, and then she went by train from Cape Town to Johannesburg. Then she went down to Curzon and stayed at the Grange – Grandpa's hotel. Cousin Caítlín said of it, "My, my, this is a jolly little place."' Auntie Fee snorted smoke. 'Imagine. A jolly little place . . .'

When Auntie Fee's smoke was sucked into her mouth it was blue, when it blew out of her nose it was grey.

'Caítlín came, she stayed, she conquered, just like old Julius Caesar. And just like poor old Julius she got stabbed in the back. Cousin Caítlín had a fling . . . and it was fatal, fatal!'

Her voice shivered the air over my head. I loved that cry. It made me hear the horses they rode, my uncle Matt and Cousin Caítlín, when they had their fling. I heard the hooves in the veldt. That was the thing about words, you could do what you liked with them. When my aunt said 'fling' I saw a woman in a wide yellow skirt turning, and her skirt getting wider and wider around her, like ripples.

'Uncle Matt was as handsome a devil as ever wore uniform. Caítlín didn't sit around. She set her cap at Matt.'

The only caps I'd seen were the caps my uncles brought back from the war. Army, air force, navy. My uncles wore them when they sat out in the garden or went down to Park Lake and lay on the grass, and if they didn't cover their faces with newspaper then they laid their caps over their eyes and said things like 'Gosh, I'd love a zizz.'

How did you *set* a cap?

Auntie Fee said: 'Don't you know? Fancy that. I thought everyone knew. It means to get off with someone. That's what Caítlín did. She gave him the eye. She was the panky to his hanky. Know what I'm saying?'

I didn't know what she was saying. But I knew Cousin Caítlín came from the Welsh Borders and met our Matt, and was hanky to his panky, and it had been 'fatal, fatal!'

'Mattie made about as much sense in love as he did trying to be a priest. Which is a big fat zero. But she had a fling with him. She gave him the eye, make no mistake. And a lot more besides.'

I saw Cousin Caítlín handing over to Uncle Matt one of her coal-black eyes, dark as the water of Park Lake. But I reckoned she couldn't have done that because she needed both eyes to do what she did.

What more besides had Cousin Caítlín given my uncle? Being panky to his hanky?

Auntie Fee said: 'Put it this way. He took whatever was on offer. He's always been greedy that way has our Matthew, believe you me. She gave and he got.'

One day Matthew and Caítlín were out riding in the

veldt, and her horse put its leg into a meerkat hole and she fell off and hurt her back, hurt it so badly that they had to put her to bed, because she was 'quite, quite unable to move' . . .

'And there she lay . . . frozen all over.' Auntie Fee always leaned back and closed her eyes. 'She couldn't move. Imagine. Not a muscle, from her nose to her toes. And Jacob, the chef from the hotel, fed her with a teaspoon. And they couldn't send her back to Wales because the war was on, and they couldn't keep her in the hotel because – apart from the pain and suffering of it – Martin, those rooms are for letting . . . and Daddy runs a business there. And Jacob has to cook for all the guests and can't be spending his time with a teaspoon feeding soup to a sick woman. Can he now? And so they brought Cousin Caítlín, silent and still, up to Jo'burg, to Sligo Road, and put her to bed in the room above the living room and there she lay, and a nurse was found to feed her with a teaspoon, like a baby . . .'

It made me shiver to feel how cold Cousin Caítlín must have felt, frozen all the way down her body, from her nose to her toes.

'One day your uncle Matt came home on leave. Now they hadn't told him about Cousin Caítlín and they hadn't told him she had been brought to the Villa Vanilla. Believe it or not, your uncle – the same who was once going to be a priest – he sat in this very room, in this very chair, and must have thought himself very private. And he canoodled one Denise Egan. She was your uncle Matt's little bit of fluff . . .

'Just imagine. In the room above poor Cousin Caítlín lay, quiet and cold, and from the room below, this very room, the sounds of their canoodling – ' Auntie Fee flapped her hands like flying birds – 'arose into the air, and passed through the floorboards, and flew into the ears of Caítlín. Frozen as her body might be, there was nothing wrong with her ears, Martin. She heard the lot.'

'And she cried, didn't she? Cried and cried . . .'

'Buckets. And her tears slid down her cheeks and onto the floor and slipped through the cracks in the floor-boards and fell at the feet of my brother Matthew, and at the feet of his bit of fluff.'

'And Uncle Matt?'

'And Uncle Matt – what?'

'Didn't he see?'

'See? Uncle Matt? Never.'

'But there was the stain.'

'There was. And the tears dripping from the ceiling and the pool on the floor. But Matt was far too busy doing you-know-what with you-know-who. Love is blind. Your uncle Matt is the blindest man I ever knew. And that Denise Egan – she was an articled clerk, you know. A real thickie. She was with Bowman and Brewster, who had offices in Jeppe Street.'

'And afterwards?'

'Afterwards, when the war was nearly over and it was

safe, Cousin Caítlín was shipped back home to the Welsh borders, where the doctors were better. There is just the stain left now.'

I looked up at the stain.

Why had no one come along and said to Cousin Caítlín 'That's enough tears for one day' and dried her eyes?

'They never do,' Auntie Fee said. 'She can thank her lucky stars she only had Ireland to cry. That's the thing with crying. Once you start, you never know where it'll end.'

She got out the atlas and we looked at all the countries we didn't ever want to cry.

'Imagine doing Australia?'

I said: 'I'd be discombobulated.'

'What was that?'

I said it nice and slow, tasting it: '*Dis-com-bob-u-lat-ed* . . .' It was like going horse-riding in your mouth.

Auntie Fee said: 'I heard you the first time. Who told you that? I think I'm going to cry, Martin.'

'It's just letters, from Grandpa.'

'Just letters. What do you mean, *just* letters?'

I showed her. I drew TEEPEES. I drew them like my grandpa did. Except I drew them in the sand with a stick, and he drew them with a pencil on a piece of paper.

'Gumpf, and more gumpf,' Auntie Fee said. 'What else has your grandpa been telling you?' I told her about height and light and fight and dynamite and she said: 'Well, if that isn't the giddy limit.'

She went straight to my grandpa. 'Honestly, Daddy, putting such *twak* into the child's head. Martin won't thank you. One fine day.'

'Why's that?'

'He'll be for the high jump.'

'For picking up a word, here and there?'

'It's not allowed.'

'Why ever not?'

'It's a well-known fact, Daddy. Ask anyone. You're not supposed to learn anything when you're small – not till you go to school. That's when you're allowed to learn. When the teacher tells you. It's the rule.'

'Well, I don't care for that rule.'

'*You* may not care, Daddy. But *you* won't be the one having his bottom beaten, or his mouth punched, when that mouth pops open and out comes "discombobulated". You won't be the one sent to the headmaster's study for six of the best. It might be fun for you, but think of Martin. I foresee difficulty.'

My grandpa smiled. '*Difficulty.*' And he sang: 'Mrs D, Mrs I, Mrs F-F-I, Mrs C, Mrs U, Mrs L-T-Y . . . *Now you try, Martin* . . .' He picked me up and kissed me. 'What's life too long and short for, boy?'

'Shorts and sports.'

'Clever man.'

I knew Auntie Fee was thinking: 'Gumpf, gumpf and more gumpf.'

'It's all fine and well for you, Daddy. Encouraging him. What about Martin? What happens when he's out in the world I dread to think.'

She put me to bed and she whispered in my ear, her lips ticklish: 'Forget them, or there'll be tears.'

'Tears – like Cousin Caítlín?'

'Buckets, oceans. Would you like having to cry China?'

'No, Auntie Fee.'

'Me neither, I love you too much. Well then, will you promise me something?'

'I promise.'

'Wait till I tell you what to promise me. Promise me you're going to forget those words your grandpa keeps putting in your head. Pure gumpf. What happens if they're rattling around in your noggin when you go to school? No words allowed, till they tell you which.'

'Will they know?'

'Of course they will. In two ticks.'

'How?'

'Easy. They'll take one look at your head. If it's bigger than it should be, they'll know. They'll just give your *kop* a shake. If it rattles, you're for the high jump. Better forget them, now.'

I felt the tears begin to squeeze out of my eyes.

'Good heavens, what's that for?'

'I *can't.*'

'No need to shriek. It's easy. When you go to sleep put your ear on the pillow and let one fat word slip out. One a night. Till they're all gone. Try, Martin. Try "discombobulate". I hate that word.'

I tried. In bed I pressed my ear to the pillow, I closed my eyes. Once, I felt something warm running out of my ear. But it was only a little water from my bath, warm and wet on the pillow. I lay listening for the night-lions. Sometimes I saw maps on the ceiling and sometimes I heard my grandpa's voice. It sang in my head like wind in a tin can, like bubbles under water. '*Now you try, Martin* . . .'

Sometimes I cried a bit but I had to stop because you never knew where it might end. In the morning maybe I'd find Mexico, or America, on the floor.

4. Building the Country

I sat on the gatepost. I was wearing my sailor suit and my hood. Uncle Charlie was a sailor in the war and he gave me his kitbag when he came home from the navy. It was white canvas and smelt of salt and tobacco. I liked it but I didn't know what to do with it. I was trying out the words my grandpa gave me. Words were good; if you put a lot of words together you got a story. Stories stayed the same. If they didn't stay the same they didn't work.

Georgie was in the flower beds, cutting off the heads of dead roses. I could hear his shears. Jonathan Jo was a gardener too, with a mouth like an O. Alice had lots of gardeners in Wonderland, but they were only playing cards. We had Georgie. He came from Zululand. He had very big muscles in his neck and a good, strong back.

General Smuts said the country was built on the back of the black man.

When it got really hot, Georgie would pull off his heavy tunic and his back would run with sweat as he pushed the mower over the thick kikuyu grass that stretched in front of the wide red veranda. The palm tree waved its hairy head in the blue sky. I climbed on Georgie's back and hung there, with my legs round his waist, and he'd push the mower with one arm and hold me fast on his back with the other. It was a strong back.

Anyone could see that General Smuts was right.

Georgie wore the garden. He had his feet in the grass, leaned a hand on the palm tree, lit his skinny cigarettes and sat down on the ground and stretched out, and sometimes, when he did the watering, he seemed to be asleep with his eyes open, moving the hose very, very slowly and staring. He was a big starer.

My grandpa said: 'You're drowning that poor dahlia.' And he'd start singing: '*I'm a lonely little petunia in an on-ion patch . . . an on-ion patch . . .*'

Georgie would start waving the hose. '*And I cry-yi-yi all day . . .*'

The spray would hang in the air for a moment and then splatter on the grass. Like lace, like jewels.

My grandpa said: 'That Georgie is pure water in the desert. A well that never runs dry. He overflows. A less desiccated man I never met. Which is to say – ' *waggle, waggle* went his eyebrows, like they always did when he was telling me a new word – 'never dry, parched, or thirsty.'

My grandpa in his silver suit went walking in Sligo Road. People came to their gates to watch him go by.

They wore baggy khaki shorts, matching socks and white short-sleeved shirts, open at the neck. My grandpa lifted his walking stick with its silver head to the clouds. He tipped his dark brown fedora to all he passed.

'They reckon you're a wild man,' my gran said.

'I like to dress, I will not be denuded.'

He saw my eyes.

'That's to say – stripped, my dear – being without a stitch, stark naked, unclothed, reduced to the bare skin. To the very buff. In a word, DE-NU-DED.'

My gran said: 'Dressing is one thing – they might manage the dressing. But the doffing and perambulating . . .'

'D'you hear that, Martin? There's a good one. Peram-bu-lating. Which is to be walking up and down. Like being peripatetic. Only more stately. Wandering to and fro with a flourish, and tipping the hat. Smiling and doffing . . .'

My gran said: 'It's not the doffing *per se*, Dan, it's who you doff to. Washerwomen and gardeners and every black biddy who walks by. What happens come the election? Tell me that. If the New Lot win they'll sweep the servants off the streets. Who will you doff to then?'

'The New Lot haven't a hope. Have they, Martin boy? You tell your gran. Not a snowball's hope in hell. Djann Smuts is going to win, rest assured. And Dan MacBride will go on tipping his hat to the women he passes, black and white. General Smuts tells us "This land was built on the back of the black man." I say so too. I salute them. To do anything else wouldn't be kind.'

He picked me up and folded me to his chest where, always, my nose hit a silver button. I loved the curve of his black boots, the way he shot his cuffs. I saw on his crisp starched sleeves, like pinned butterflies, the winged goddesses – shaped, he said, from a nugget of West Driefontein gold – which were his cufflinks.

Each afternoon we perambulated and my grandpa doffed. We knew every house and every face. One day I saw my grandpa shocked rigid the way Auntie Fee sometimes got shocked rigid and couldn't speak. We walked past a house near the end of Sligo Road and we saw a man pruning roses in his garden. He wore short white pants and short grey socks and his black shoes shone. For the first time ever my grandpa didn't doff, because we had a catastrophe instead.

'A catastrophe of the first water, dear boy, a clear and present danger, a lamentable omen of our future, right there in the person of that man. What did I say he was?'

'A catastrophe, Grandpa.'

'You said it, boy. A disaster, walking or otherwise. Next time you go past his place with Georgie, watch his face for signs of looming sadness. Let's turn now and walk back again. Take a close look. Forewarned is fore-armed.'

'Yes, Grandpa.'

I saw a man with pink legs, like rubber, and pink cheeks and hair like licked ice cream. The man looked at us. I saw he had dreamy eyes, Chinese eyes. Blue, slanted.

'That is Hendrik Frensch Verwoerd. A Walking Disaster, on our very own doorstep. God moves in mysterious ways.'

I liked the thought of the man with creamy hair. I didn't know why. Maybe because he was in Sligo Road and everything in Sligo Road seemed good. Sligo Road had these jacaranda trees marching down to the lake at the bottom of the road. I wanted them to be oaks, like you got in Sherwood Forest, but my mom said you couldn't have everything. Sligo Road had travelling Sammies, selling snakes and silks. And the ice-cream man on his bike. Sligo Road had the sports-and-shorts brigade. Next door was Rosa Snippalipsky who walked on her hands. Now Sligo Road had a Walking Disaster, with his ice-cream hair.

When I went walking with Georgie we never passed Dr Verwoerd's house. When we got close, Georgie would lift me onto his shoulders and we'd cross the road, which was a very big river, and we were henchman, Little George and Martin Hood, and there were crocodiles everywhere. He was very good in rivers. But he never passed the house, even though Georgie could do more things than anyone. He did the garden, he did me and he did Little John, and on Friday nights he stayed in his room at the back of the house and a whole lot of people came to see him, and went away with bottles clinking in their bags. Sometimes I heard him singing: '*Wine on beer makes you queer, beer on wine makes you fine.*'

'He's a shebeen king,' my grandpa said. 'Why in heaven work for us? He makes a mint, that fellow.'

'He can't be a *king*, not in a shebeen. Shebeens have queens,' my mom said.

'Tell that to Georgie. He can be whatever he likes.'

Next time we went past the house Dr Verwoerd was there and Georgie wanted to cross the road but I wouldn't climb on his shoulders. I held Georgie's hand, I held him there and watched his face for signs of looming sadness. He didn't like it.

'Why don't we ever walk past that man's house?'

'In case he puts the spooks on us,' Georgie said. 'He's a b-a-a-ad man, Martin. Let's go. Before he attacks.'

That sounded funny. Dogs attacked, and soldiers of the Sheriff of Nottingham attacked Robin Hood 'deep in his greenwood bower'. But how would the Verwoerds attack Georgie? What would they attack him with?

Georgie said: 'Some people, they just attack.' He clicked his fingers. 'Like that.'

'Why?'

He just nodded his big head. And flicked his eyebrows at Dr Verwoerd, like my mom did when she was keeping her beady eye on someone, and we crossed the road and went on down to the lake.

In the lake was an island and on the island was a fountain, and it turned different colours, but only on Sundays. In the park there were willows by the water and oaks and bluegum trees, tall and dark and cool. There were lots of barbers under the bluegums. They set out their stools and they hung their leather strops from the branches and sharpened their razors. We weren't supposed to talk to them, but we did. Our friend was Amos. He was there on Sundays. He had a blue cloth and a white basin and shiny scissors and a big stool and he always said: 'How are you, young Martin? Do you want a trim?'

We collected acorns, the cups were smooth, you pushed your tongue into them and sucked and they stuck there. For ages. Georgie could make the cups whistle, but I couldn't. The willows were washing their hair in the lake, people gave bread to the ducks and the ducks were always greedy for more.

The children came with their nannies but none of the other nannies would sit with us. They grabbed all the shade under the weeping willows. They didn't like Georgie being there because he was a man. Georgie and I made a place for ourselves under the oaks by the playground. When everyone else went home, it was our turn. We were trusted allies.

There were three swings. First Georgie pushed me,

then I pushed Georgie. When we were on the swings we had to be on the lookout. In case the Ghost Squad saw us.

'What's the Ghost Squad?'

'Bad men. Policemen. They'll jump out from behind a tree. Oh yes.'

There was a slide and a red merry-go-round. And there was a yellow rocking horse with black handles for ears and six black seats. It was very old and the yellow was peeling. You pulled bits of paint off and chewed them. The slide dropped you fast and got so hot it burnt the backs of your legs as you went down. I got on the red merry-go-round, and Georgie pushed really fast and showed me how to jump on, jump off, then lie down on the grass and the whole sky went spinning round at the back of my eyes, right down to my knees. The world went on turning and you got up and fell over.

I rode home on Georgie's back. At the bottom of Sligo Road was the blue van with a wooden counter. Miriam leaned on the counter and the big kettle breathed out through its hooked nose. Birds came for the crumbs on the counter. We always stopped there – only we weren't supposed to. But we did, always.

Georgie always said: 'Hey. She's still here.'

'Will she always be here?'

'Till she gets moved on.'

'When will that be?'

'When the police catch her.'

'I want her to stay for always.'

'She can't. That's why she's called the Café de Move On.'

Miriam said: 'What'll be, my boys?'

'Doorstops and apricot are what this chap needs,' Georgie said.

Big slices of white bread and apricot jam and tea, always. And Georgie said: 'Wipe those crumbs from your chin, Martin. In case your mom sees.'

Georgie knew what a boy needed. He lifted me onto the gatepost, where the slate was warm and grainy, and I was in heaven. A boy needs height. The ice-cream man's bell came floating up Sligo Road. Georgie also heard it because he swung me off the gatepost. The bell came in waves, *crash-BANG*, and as it came closer it said: 'Hurry UP.' It gave me just enough time to run to my grandpa, who put his hand into his pocket and held out a pile of tickey coins like silver seeds in his palm. The ice-cream man lifted up his brass bell and banged it down like a hammer on the hot air. It was hard to pick just one tickey out of a sticky pile; it was so flat and thin, like tin. The bell was louder. 'HURRY UP, HURRY UP.'

His icebox was bolted to his bike and sat on a single wheel; STOP ME & BUY ONE! it said in curly golden words on the white icebox, painted all over with blue igloos and icebergs. He sold frozen suckers and tubs and Eskimo pies. If he went past you, he never turned back. If you didn't buy one he didn't stop.

I ran, the tickey tight in my fist. I squeezed through the wooden slats of the garden gate and shouted to the barelegged man with his fat white cold sidecar.

'Stop, please – stop.'

The ice-cream man stood up on his back-pedal brake and took a long time stopping and the cart squealed. Then he swung back the heavy lid of the icebox, dropping it smack on its back, and cold steam jumped into the jacarandas.

I gave him my tickey, he gave me an Eskimo pie, wrapped tight in red and gold paper. Georgie was waiting. He always got the first bite and then he swung me high onto the gatepost. I could see Rosa Snippalipsky next door, walking on her hands. Her red hair hung down and brushed the grass as she walked and there were green bits of grass in her hair, like jewels. The grass grew round her fingers like rings.

I saw Mr Jinnah, the Snake Sammie. He brought his brown basket of yellow cobras into our garden now and then, and if you gave him a penny he whistled to his snakes and made them dance.

My grandpa said: 'Mr Jinnah, you've more coil to your mind than one of your snakes.'

Mr Jinnah lifted his cobras, one in each hand, holding the backs of their necks like puppies, kissed them under their soft chins and said: 'Mr Mac, you've more wit in your finger than an entire boatload of Irishmen.'

My gran said: 'Hold him tight, Mr Jinnah. If that serpent so much as sets foot in my garden, I promise to send Georgie after it with a spade.'

I saw Mr Moosah, the Silk Sammie, who came with his box of silks. 'The finest shantung from the fairest East.' Mr Moosah flicked his wrist and a square of silk jumped into the air, floating there like green smoke; it was a colour you could taste.

I spent a lot of time on the gatepost. I didn't go to school.

'You're too young,' they said.

Rosa Snippalipsky went to school and she came home every afternoon carrying a brown suitcase. She always stopped at the gatepost and said: 'Hello, Robin Hood' on account of my hat. It had a big green feather that waved. I looked down on lots of people, like the cater-pillar looks down on Alice, very high and mighty. Nar-rowing my eyes, like Robin Hood. Squinting keenly into the oaks of Sherwood. Even though they were jacaran-das, marching all the way down the pavement. Robin's eyes were green, like the oaks. He had sensitive nostrils. My eyes were brown, like my mom's. But I narrowed them anyway. I hoped my nostrils were sensitive. I planned a feast beneath the oaks, we would sup on suckling pig and roast venison from the forest, we would cavort on the greensward.

I asked Rosa if she wanted to cavort with me. She said you didn't get greensward in Jo'burg. You only got kikuyu grass, down at the lake. She couldn't cavort. Cavorting was not something anyone did.

'And people don't "sup". Maybe in books they sup. But not in Jo'burg. Proper people have *supper*.'

I wanted a doublet of Lincoln green. It made you practically invisible. It said so in my book. I had a bamboo bow. I had brown eyes. I had enemies everywhere. My mom said she very nearly lost me once. She didn't say how.

From the gatepost I watched when the big white Packard came through the gate. My grandpa was driving and next to him were my uncles, all in the wide front seat. Uncle Matt wore a round yellow rosette, and I knew they had been out on the campaign trail. Uncle Matt was standing for a seat in Boksburg North. I didn't know how you could stand for a seat. Uncle Matt said he would walk the seat he was standing for. He was going to fix the New Lot, good and proper. He was going to show them his teeth. He was going to eat them for breakfast. I looked at Uncle Matt's teeth; they were big and white but they didn't look very sharp.

My grandpa said Uncle Matt was fine, only he needed pepping up. At breakfast time he used to pep up Uncle Matt.

'Carry the fight to the enemy, Mattie. Rationality takes on the Walking Disasters. Us versus Them. If we want a new world, we better damn build it ourselves. *Homo sapiens* takes on the cavemen. Triumph – or die in the ditch.'

One day my grandpa took me on his knee. 'I have a mission for you. Top secret. The Verwoerds have asked you over. Go, my boy. When you're in the garden of the doctor, make a note. Remember! What does the doctor wear? Say? Eat? No matter is too small. Does he have a cat? Is he armed? Report back to me. But Martin – be careful. They shoot spies.'

'I wish you wouldn't put ideas into his head,' my mom said.

'Shall we ask your mom if you may go?' my grandpa said.

'I can hardly say no – now. Can I?' she said.

Georgie walked me down Sligo Road to the Verwoerd house, but they wouldn't let him in. 'No, no, John.' They waved him away. 'Just leave the little boss. Come back later.'

I was scared. I said: 'Georgie's supposed to stay.'

'Is that so, John?' they said to George. 'Well, if the little master says you stay, you can stay. But you must sit out on the pavement. OK, John?'

A lot of people from my street came to the Verwoerds that day, and they all had to leave their nannies outside the fence. The Verwoerd boy was Willem; he was much bigger than me. There was another boy called Barrie, he couldn't talk very well, he just grunted and said: 'Wazza-matter, hey?' Rosa Snippalipsky was there and she walked on her hands, and Barrie asked her if it was definitely true she was a Jew and Rosa said it was. There was a big girl with freckles called Dora Devine, who wore pink pants, and twins called Cruickshank who always cried at the same time, even if only one was hurt.

We played games that the Boers used to play when they were in their ox-wagons trekking across Africa, fighting savages. We started with *kennetjie*. It was very hard to get right. You had a long bit of broomstick, brown, like the truncheon on a policeman's belt, and a short bit. And you flipped the small bit into the air and hit it across the garden. After that we hooked our fingers together and did finger-wrestling. Then we played 'knifey-knifey'. I had to stand with my feet apart, and Barrie threw a knife into the grass, next to my foot. Then it was Rosa's turn but she said she'd only do it standing on her hands, and she did, even though Barrie said she could bleed to death if he hit a vein. But he didn't. Then we played 'Boers and Savages', and I was a savage and Rosa Snippalipsky was a Boer wife and Ted gave her a white bonnet with long white strings that tied under her chin and didn't fall off when she walked on her hands. The Cruickshank twins were also supposed to be savages but they cried every time Ted lifted his broomstick and shot them. Dora Devine climbed into the tree and wouldn't come down, and Barrie said she could be the lookout since she was in the tree already, and she sat up there showing her pink pants. But not looking out much. And every time Barrie shouted 'Here come the savages!' Dora started crying and said: 'Where? I can't see nothing!'

I hated her crying, so I said out loud: 'Desiccate!'

Dora stopped crying. 'What?'

'It means – be dry!'

'No – what did you call me?'

Barrie came over. 'Wazzamatter?'

Dora said: 'He called me a dizzicut.'

Barrie said: 'Wazzadizzicut?'

'It means stop crying, be dry,' I said.

Dora started screaming: 'I'm not a dizzicut. I'm not, I'm not!'

Barrie said: 'Look what you done! What you call her names for? You want me to call you names? Like Pongo? Bum! Pigface! Hey, hey, hey?'

Dora got on the ground and screamed into the grass, then she got up and her mouth was full of sand. She was still screaming: 'I'm not a DIZZICUT!'

Barrie started pushing me. 'Hey? Hey? Wazzamatter, Pongo?'

I got worried. I went to the fence. Georgie sat on the pavement across the road. Waiting. I waved at Georgie and he waved back.

'Don't worry, Martin, I'm still here.'

Then Mrs Verwoerd rang a bell and we had to go

inside. There was ice cream and jelly on the table. Dr Verwoerd said grace with his fist pressed to his head, the way Protestants did. We ate *koeksusters*, which were golden and sweet and rubbery and the juice ran down your chin if you were at all slow in swallowing, which I was. Then we ate milk-tart. Afterwards Mrs Verwoerd did the washing-up. She dipped her arms into the soapy water and the suds hung on her elbows.

'Look at my lace sleeves.'

It was clever.

Then Mrs Verwoerd took us to the gate and gave us back to our nannies.

Georgie said: 'Want a ride, Martin? Jump on. Hold tight.'

He went down on one knee, I climbed high into his shoulders and rode him home. I pressed my cheek into the flat space between his shoulder blades, my arms tight round his neck, feeling every step he took shaking though him. He was good. You could see why the country had been built on the back of the black man.

When we got home, my mom said: 'What did you see?'

I said: 'Mrs Verwoerd does the washing-up.'

'I might have known.'

'Can I do the washing-up?'

'Certainly not. That's what Georgie's for. Go and play in the garden.'

My grandpa was in the garden talking to Mr Snippalipsky, who was leaning over the fence. My grandpa put his hands on my shoulders.

'Mr Snips, this boy has just supped at the dread doctor's table. And lived to tell the tale.'

'No lies, hey,' Mr Snippalipsky said. 'What's he like, Martin?'

I said: 'They do their own washing-up.'

My grandpa laughed. 'Let them stew in their own juice. And wash their own dishes – if that's what they want.'

Mr Snippalipsky said: 'Dishes sounds fine. First it's dishes. But dishes are just for openers, Mr Mac. For starters. Next thing, it's no gardeners. Then no maids. And before you know it – no Snippalipskys. That's what happens when the All-White Brigade gets going.'

'No need to tell me, Mr Snips. I know what happens. I was the last Catholic Mayor of Curzon. Until they closed me down.'

'I run the last Jewish music hall in Jo'burg. D'you know what happens to people like me, when the Pure White Brethren come calling?'

'They'll have us Holy Romans before they have you Jews, Mr Snips.'

'It'll be the first time the Jews came second, Mr Mac. Still, we'll go down fighting, hey?'

'Better not go down at all. My son Matt is standing in Boksburg North, d'you know that? Safe seat.'

Mr Snippalipsky looked at the sky. 'What do you

think about the Indianapolis 500? I heard it on the wireless. Mauri Rose came in the winner, top speed 119 miles an hour.'

'You've lost me, Mr Snips. I don't see what motor racing has to do with the New Lot.'

'Think about it, Mr Mac. This is 1948. Half the century's gone. It's passed. The world goes on. Somewhere else a man goes whizzing around the racetrack at 119 miles an hour. But not here. Not us. We're stuck in reverse. Going nowhere – fast.'

I moved off from under my grandfather's hands. Behind me I heard him saying: 'Never known a boy more prone to vanishing. He's the ghost of the garden.'

I went to my place behind the mulberry tree. I narrowed my eyes. It was very quiet in Sherwood Forest, it was just as well I knew every leaf . . .

5. Playing Politics

Life was too long for shorts, too short for sport. On account of the Big Fight and the coming elections and the need to stop the New Lot, or die in the ditch. In the mornings, Uncle Matt used to say his manifesto out loud for my grandpa, so he could pep it up:

'We promise freedom for all, before the Law, and a just solution of the native problem . . .'

I lay on the floor, pushing a small green wooden truck between the table leg and the wastepaper basket, and listened to Grandpa and Uncle Matt playing politics. Giving the 'Nats' what-for. The words went bang, like firecrackers. You spat them out. There was 'your common-or-garden-Nat', 'your brain-damaged-Nat', 'your Nat-in-need-of-a-kick-in-the-pants' and 'your Nat-we-are-going-to-eat-for-breakfast'.

I took any bits I wanted from Uncle Matt's speeches and walked into the garden and tried out the words that tasted best:

'Vote South Africa, Vote Smuts' got a good chew as it went by.

I liked 'freedom for all Europeans', it was rich and dark; 'before the Law' had a good round brown sound, but 'a just resolution of the native problem' felt sticky in my throat. Like going down the slide in the playground at the lake. I climbed the steps to the top of the slide and sat down and pushed myself over the brow and my legs squeaked, my pants stuck, then I shot down the slippery silver slope of 'the native problem', rolling 'problem' off my tongue, making the 'em' ring like bells in my nose.

My grandpa said we were going to 'walk' the elections.

'Malan's chaps are cocky, even so,' Uncle Matt said.

My grandpa smiled his shining smile. 'Let them dream on. If wishes were horses, beggars would ride. Just think, Matt – if they ever kicked out Our Djann. Why, man, what then? No servants. No Georgie to do the garden; no Indians, like Mr Gandhi, selling fabrics in a thousand country general dealers; no Catholic MacBrides like you and me, Matt. No Jewish Joel Snippalipsky to bring in the dancing girls. Who'll make the country run? Malan's men. The All-White Brigade? Nationalists? That'll be the frosty Friday. We're in Africa. This country was built on the back of the black man. Our Djann is right.'

Once, my auntie Fee said: 'People say Smuts is going to lose, Daddy.'

My grandpa went as pale as pale, he pointed to the door. 'Fionnuala, leave my house.'

But no one ever had to leave my grandpa's house; you

could say anything you wanted at the Villa Vanilla – it was a free house.

In the evenings we piled into the Packard 'to do the meetings'. I liked the Malan meetings best. The neighbours thought we were off to a party. My grandpa wore a red rose in the buttonhole of his salt-and-pepper suit. Uncle Matthew wore a double-breasted brown suit with a yellow silk rosette on his lapel and Uncle Charlie wore his sailor suit because it drove Malan's men crazy. He looked like a Limey and they hated Limeys. Malan's men had never gone to fight in the war and hated Churchill. They had spent the war, my grandpa said, knitting tea cosies for Mr Hitler. Uncle Jack wore his blue 'demob' suit. It had baggy knees and he said he knew how an elephant must feel with knees like that. Georgie always came with us, dressed in a fine salt-and-pepper suit like my grandpa's.

'Martin can ride in the cubbyhole,' Uncle Matt always said, taking out my grandpa's yellow driving gloves and handing them to him.

'He's too big for the glove compartment,' Uncle Charlie said.

'Confound the child. Martin, stop growing,' Uncle Matt said.

And I squeezed into the back seat, between the armrest and Uncle Charlie.

My gran never came. She said: 'What shall I do if they throw you in the clink, Dan?'

'Bail us out, Mabel.'

My grandpa drove and we all sang: *'She'll be comin' round the mountain when she comes...'* When we arrived at the hall, we had to get through the crowd outside. We formed a line, my grandpa out ahead, leading the way, then my uncles, then my mom and me. The policemen wore brown caps and jackets and brown holsters and brown belts. They were the brown edges of the meeting. Uniforms made my mom strange, she always smiled at the men inside them, and said sorry about thirty times and looked pink. Any uniform did it, she wasn't fussy – policemen, bus conductors, doctors.

'Monica, be ready to butter up the constabulary if they take an interest,' my grandpa said.

It was very dark and growling outside the hall. Big men booming like the night-lions, tearing up the dark. And what set them off, always, was Georgie, in his suit. The picture of elegance. The big men wore shorts, they had big angry bellies pushing the air out of the way when they walked, even their knees were angry.

My grandpa always moved Georgie up front when we marched inside the hall, and I loved the noise it made. We marched down the aisle, with my mom smiling at the policemen. The moment Malan's men saw Georgie sitting down in the hall they began shouting: 'Kaffir out, Kaffir out!' It was very exciting, it was why you played politics, it was why life was too short for sport. Then the police drew their truncheons and charged. Malan's men ran away. Or they got hit, or they started fighting with other men. The thing was to stand perfectly still when the hitting started.

'Otherwise the cops can't tell you from the Brainless Brigade,' my grandpa said. 'It's all perfectly normal.'

The policemen looked like moths, dancing under the weak streetlights, landing on people every now and then, and hitting them. It was all perfectly normal, my grandpa said. People came to the meetings to talk about the election, but what they wanted was to fight.

When the fighting began, the police suggested that Georgie be locked in the car 'for his own protection'.

And my grandpa said: 'Well done, George, we riled 'em. Now you can take forty winks, before they kill you.'

Mother always said: 'My godfathers. Who'd have thought there'd be so many people.'

It was always like that. You could rely on it. It was all perfectly normal, even when they wanted to kill Georgie, even when Malan's men got hit by the police. Even when they bled. That was the pattern. First they had a go at Georgie; then the cops had a go at them. Then Georgie was locked in the car. Then they bled a bit, in public.

'They *expect* a few smacks on the noggin,' my grandpa said. 'That's why they come to these meetings. Good clean fun. Battle scars.'

When Georgie was locked in the car, everyone settled

down in the hall. Dr Malan came onto the stage and all Malan's men shouted: 'Hooray, hooray', and stamped their feet like horses.

'Hark at the herd, the All-White Brigade, the Walking Disasters,' my grandpa said.

Dr Malan wore a black suit and a black waistcoat and put his hand on the big black Bible that stood on a stand on the stage and started the meeting with a prayer. All the men took off their hats. And my mother was the only one there to have her hat on, a pink hat with artificial cherries on the brim, and a crisp straw look I loved. She bowed her head because she felt about prayer the way she did about uniforms.

They weren't our prayers. Malan's men did not pray like Catholics, they never went on their knees, they never joined their hands together at their breasts; they just lowered the heads and frowned and pressed huge fists to their foreheads, and they looked very worried, like they were trying to remember something very urgent. Like they were on the lav. But a prayer was a prayer, my mother said, 'and so deserves respect'. And she stuck her elbow into my side and made me bow my head too.

Then Dr Malan spoke, he had his Bible and he had his fist. He banged the stand. He said NO! and NO AGAIN! As well as NEVER! And NEVER EVER! As well as NEVER IN A THOUSAND YEARS! It was loud and slow, like cracks of thunder, then the bangs got louder and faster, like an engine backfiring, and when the bangs got louder all his men clapped and whistled. *Bang, bang, bang . . .* like Guy Fawkes Night, like the storms that blew up over Sligo Road, when the blue sky turned to charcoal and the lightning ran down the sky's face and the thunder cracked. Dr Malan banged and flashed. He banged his fist on the stand where the Bible lay, or he stamped his black boot on the bare boards of the stage. The air got thick and warm, the people in the hall started clapping their hands and murmuring, like a wave, like a prayer, like it was going to rain. But it stayed dry. Only Dr Malan got wet, on his face, he wiped the water from his forehead and sat down. Everyone stood up when he sat down, like they were going to pray again, only they didn't. They waved their fists; they were very angry but being angry made them feel good.

There were a few people who shouted things at Dr Malan, and my grandpa said they were 'suicidal communists'. Then the fights started, and the cops came rushing into the hall with their truncheons and hit the fighters again until it was quiet.

At the end of the meeting there were questions.

My uncle Matt stood up and started speaking; we couldn't hear him because all around us men in the hall jumped out and pointed their fingers at Uncle Matt. They were screeching: 'Out! Out!'

We knew what Uncle Matt was saying. 'What will the doctor do about the native question? Only General

Smuts knows how to solve the native question. Isn't it time we accepted that this country is built on the back of the black man?'

Dr Malan was banging his fist, he was pointing his finger at Uncle Matt and we knew what he was saying. 'No. Never . . . Not in my lifetime . . .' He always said that and all his men banged and yelled.

Uncle Matt was supposed to sit down then, but he didn't and Dr Malan waved his arms until his men got very, very quiet and he leaned forward and he pointed at Uncle Matt.

'And who might you be, young man?'

Uncle Matt stood up very straight. 'I have the honour to contest the seat of Boksburg North for the United Party in the forthcoming . . .'

I had to cover my ears it got so loud then. Everyone jumping and shouting and the cops tapping their truncheons and my mom saying: 'My golly . . . some people . . .'

My grandpa shouted: 'Well done, fellows! Time to skedaddle.'

And we skedaddled. The policemen held our arms as we walked down the aisle. Uncle Matt said: 'Are we being arrested?' The cops said no – we were being escorted for our 'personal protection'. Once, a fierce fat man punched my grandpa in the chest. He didn't hit back; he stopped and said: 'You're a boor and an oaf, sir. Kindly get out of my way.' And the fat man looked surprised and sat down.

My mom blinked her eyes and looked amazed and said to the policeman: 'Really. *Some* people. Thank you, Sergeant. I'm really sorry. I hope you've not been too put out. Who would have thought?'

Outside the hall, Georgie was waiting in the dark car and flashed his teeth like torn election posters. All around us there were men running and men fighting and police and men punching each other.

'My godfathers,' my mom said sometimes, 'I think they'd kill us, given the chance.'

'That they would,' my grandpa said. 'It's a blood sport. It's all they know. Hitting people till they're senseless. But I reckon we'd have a few moments' grace if things turned nasty.'

'Why's that?'

'They'd murder George first.'

And that is how it was, when we all went out 'to do the Malan meetings'. It was a pattern; it was all perfectly normal. The policemen pushed us through the gangs of big square men. We got back to the car. Georgie didn't get killed. Everyone shouted when we drove away, even the ones who were bleeding. As if a bit of blood made the whole world friends.

In the car my grandpa sang: '*Sure I love the dear silver that shines in your hair . . .*' I tried it and he said:

'You want to get the real McCormack wobble in the voice. That's what brings a lump to the throat. A million miles – aching miles – between you and home. Oh, it's splendid stuff. Brings a sob to the heart.'

I tried it again. '*I kiss the dear fingers so toil-worn for me-e-e-e . . .*'

'Magnificent, my dear. John McCormack would be proud of you.'

We did the Jan Smuts meetings too; the halls were the same, only the nights were different. Only Georgie didn't want to come inside with us when Jan Smuts spoke.

My grandpa was amazed. 'Why not, man?'

'I'll wait in the car, Boss Mac. Lock me in.'

'Why would you be wanting to sit alone, locked in the car?' My grandpa scratched his thick grey head. 'As if you were the great big bogeyman – as Malan and his henchmen impute. Our Djann speaks for people like you, Mister George. And people like me. Civilized people.'

'I'm scared, Boss Mac.'

'You poor benighted man, think what you're saying. How would Our Djann feel if a black chap had to be locked in a car – for his own protection? That sort of thing happens with the other side. Not with us.'

So Georgie came in with us. But he walked slowly and he didn't like it and he had to sit in a special row at the back, with all the other servants.

'It's for his own protection,' my grandpa said. 'The police insist.'

Our Djann walked onto the stage. He was taller than Dr Malan. He looked like a lamp-post, thin and silver, and he always began the same way. 'Now listen here – I haven't got much time . . .' His white hair and white pointed beard and little glasses all caught the light. It was very quiet when he started speaking. It was a lot like church, which was ever so important even if you weren't sure why.

Jan Smuts wasn't thunder and lightning like Dr Malan, he was clouds, lots of clouds, floating. In the middle of what Jan Smuts was saying my grandpa clapped and shouted out: 'Yes, sir.' And Jan Smuts would lift a friendly hand in the air as if to say: 'I hear you, Dan MacBride.' My grandpa wiped his eye, he said he was very moved, he said Jan Smuts was almost a saint.

'A rare genius.'

Auntie Fee said: 'Whist, Daddy, the General's speaking.'

Our Djann's music was warm and silvery and sacred and everyone felt terribly glad Jan Smuts was looking after us. And on our side.

But there was a pattern. It was never quiet for long. Because there was the other side. Some big man at the back would yell: '*Oom* Jan, we're sick of the blacks and coloureds and coolies. *Oom* Jan, you're nothing but a *kaffir-lover* and *coelie-creeper* and a coloured comforter. *Oom* Jan, you're nothing but a bunch of rubbish. Get out.'

My mom clicked her tongue. 'Ex-cuse me.' I knew she was shocked rigid. And flabbergasted. To think anyone could speak to the Prime Minister like that. She always looked pink when she was shocked rigid.

The police came and took away the big man who'd been shouting, and he asked was he being arrested and they said no, it was for his own safety.

'Trust someone to spoil it,' my mom said. 'Honestly, some people.'

The hall was planted with Malan's men, my grandpa said. 'The Brainless Brigade. The All-White Wonders. Hitlerites, political pygmies. Give them the greatest man this country's ever seen – a saint, a political genius, a philosopher – and what do they do, the sports-and-shorts men? Heap abuse on his head. Curses on his name.'

Auntie Fee said: 'The cops are doing a bit of head-bashing themselves.'

'I should hope so,' my grandpa said.

Jan Smuts was practically a saint, and shouting at him was like spitting in church. How could he do his best for civilized people if blithering ignoramuses kept yelling at him? 'Mother of God, I've seen nothing like it. These fellows are barbarians. They do not deserve to eat the soil he walks upon. Never in my life have I seen such hooligans.'

He always said that.

My uncle Matt stood up then, and said to Jan Smuts: 'As candidate for Boksburg North, I commend you, sir. For your loyalty, your integrity and for trying to solve the native problem.'

Our Side cheered like mad, and the Other Side yelled things.

'The cops have collared a bunch and they're shovelling them into the Black Maria,' Auntie Fee said.

'Good show,' my grandpa said. And he'd turn and grin at Georgie in the back row and Georgie would pretend not to see.

When it was quiet again, Jan Smuts made that soft rolling of his hand in the air as if winding up an invisible spring, as if to say it was really nothing at all . . . and Matt was quite right. Then he walked slowly off the stage and everyone yelled themselves hoarse for him to come back. We always hoped. We waited. My grandpa said that Our Djann was a busy man and we should wait a bit more. We always did but he never came back.

Then a policeman walked onto the stage. He cupped his hands round his mouth and shouted: 'Listen carefully because I won't say this again.'

'Charming,' my mom said. 'Who does he think he is – Lord Muck on Toast?'

The policeman said: 'Owners of servants present in the hall must escort them to their cars immediately. For their own safety. The police cannot take responsibility for servants left behind. Strays found wandering about the hall will be locked in the cells overnight, and may be claimed at the station during office hours.'

My mom said: 'What about Georgie? Hadn't someone better check? We wouldn't want to lose him.'

Uncle Matt fetched Georgie from the special pew at the back of the hall and took him out to the Packard and locked him in.

'Better safe than sorry,' Uncle Matt said.

Then we all sang 'God Save the King'. My grandpa sang more loudly than anyone, even though he was a rebel and an Irishman and a republican. 'Because it hurts the Nazi brigade to hear it.'

And we were still singing when we went out into the night. Malan's men, outside the hall, tried to drown us with their version: '*God damn the English King – down with the foolish thing . . .*'

Georgie was in the back of the car, with his eyes just over the window ledge. They were wide and white. He was frightened, the same as always. Sometimes he had to lie on the floor. If Malan's men saw him they'd try to turn the car over. Then the police would run at them, and hit them, and there'd be fighting all around the hall.

It was all perfectly normal.

We drove home, singing: '*Little Brown Jug, I love*

thee . . .' and even Georgie joined in, especially in the bit that went *'ha, ha, ha, hee, hee, hee . . .'*

My mother turned pink. 'Heavens above, don't encourage him. I don't think that's a very suitable song for a servant.'

She turned to me and took my hand and squeezed it. 'Stay very close, I don't want to lose you. Once was enough, thanks very much.'

'Did you nearly lose me?'

She looked at me, tapping her teeth with her long pink nail, her eyes goggling, like they did when she was thinking hard. The way she looked at the policemen in the political meetings, like she was summing me up.

'He'll have to know, Monica,' my grandpa said.

'I've put all that behind me, Daddy. That door's closed. What's past is past. Martin agrees with me. Don't you, darling? What's gone is gone.'

'What's gone?'

She kissed me. 'You're gone – to bed. We've had quite enough excitement for one night, thanks very much.'

6. Rabbit Scoff

On Saturday morning we went to town. I wore my sailor suit and my mom spent a lot of time making my hair into a quiff. She lifted it and patted it and gummed it. It was like a hill on my head. We climbed on the tram in Erin Avenue, next to the lake. From the top of the tram you could see the curly lawns that were greensward for feasting on. My mom paid fourpence on the tram for herself but she paid nothing for me because I was too young.

The sun lay down in the water, and it pulled the water over itself like a sheet. I saw the barbers under the bluegums, with their scissors and their soap, their faces shining. The lake looked back at you and blinked as you went by. The willows always washed their hair in the water. The rowing boats went round and round the fountain, which only worked on Sundays. The willows caught the sun in their branches. The tram shivered when it started again.

Sometimes my mom got her elbow and jabbed me with it, in the side, and opened her eyes really wide and jiggled them. 'Well, bless me. Lady Muck on Toast.' Mrs Verwoerd, in her black dress, was sitting down with her boy, Willem, who had bare feet, and no hair because it was all shaved off. We clanged up the long hill, passing the zoo, where the lions were – who went roaring in the night, when my mom cried, and thanked her lucky stars I was there to take care of her. To save her from their sharp digestive juices.

'We're fine, so long as we've got Our Djann,' my grandpa said. And my mom was fine, so long as she had me. That was our deal. You could depend on it.

We got off the tram in Jeppe Street and my mom took my hand because she knew the drunks were ready to bump into us. We waited at the lights to cross the street. My mom spotted a man, fast asleep across the pavement.

'Lift your feet and step over him, Martin. My god-fathers, dead to the world – at nine o'clock in the morning.'

We stopped off at Mrs Minniver's Gowns. She tried on a balloon dress and turned in the mirror. 'What do you say, darling? Does it do anything for me?'

She liked navy-blue and pink and white bows; she liked gloves with buttons. She had a lot of rules – you should never wear brown by night, or beige indoors.

'They simply do not go.'

At Cranford's the drapers she liked a bit of lavender taffeta. 'Lilac or pink? Which is more "me", darling, would you say?' At Le Chapeau, she bought a black hat with a small black veil that turned her face to tiny diamonds. 'I know a certain someone who thinks veils are so mysterious.' In Silver Firs Footwear she tried on a pair of shining black high heels. 'Can I get away with patent leather? D'you reckon?' She turned this way and that, making a small round red mouth at herself in the mirror. 'For delivery,' she'd say at all the shops. 'Plenty of tissue paper, please. In case I ever travel. Tissue paper's good for packing. It doesn't grow on trees. I save it all.'

And she did, in the great big built-in cupboard in the passage, outside her bedroom. Boxes and boxes of paper. From Pickles, CTC, Stuttaford's, Greaterman's, Anstey's.

We held hands, we ran across Commissioner Street to Anstey's. We pushed through the glass revolving doors. Over our heads the brass canisters whizzed, and the escalators climbed like snakes, right through the air.

The floor-walker wore his black jacket and black tie and pointy collar and he said: 'Good day, madam, good day, young sir.'

Maisie, the manageress, wore a black dress and a white pinafore. 'Hello, madam,' she said.

And my mom said: 'A table for two, please.'

I smelt the tablecloth, it was like creamy dust. The side plates had golden rims. The sandwiches were thin and sharp, lying in a field of sliced lettuce.

'Please use your side plate, Martin.'

My mom ate very tiny ham sandwiches, spread with Colman's English Mustard, and the lettuce the sandwiches lay in was cut very, very thin so it was a wet green field you wanted to walk on. But you couldn't walk on it so you ate it instead. I finished the ribbons of lettuce, always, and afterwards the side plate was bare and it had a gold and cream flower on its face.

'Rabbit's scoff,' my mother said, 'this child could live on rabbit's scoff.'

She sighed and shook her head and lifted her hand to her wide-open mouth. She took my hand and pressed it on my leg. 'Do you feel it? The bone?'

'Yes.'

'I'd only just got home from the hospital with you – and I had to hand you back again. The trouble you caused. The doctors and nurses worked night and day. My godfathers. You were so ill. They had to give you blood, but they couldn't find a vein. They put the needle in so often the flesh never grew back. That's why you have a big hollow there. They had to give you so much blood, I thought you'd blow up like a balloon. You were so tiny. So thin. And so *fussy*. Your father's was the only blood you'd take. Imagine. They tried mine. "He won't have yours, Mrs Donally," says this doctor. Rabin was his name. Jewish, of course. I was very put out, I can tell you. "Well, thank *you*, very much, Dr Rabin," I said. Really the cheek of it.'

She nibbled sandwiches and poured her tea from the silver pot and wiped her red lips with the white napkin, such a small perfect press of the lips, such a lovely pink print, I loved her even more, with Maisie hovering, saying: 'More hot water, madam?' She didn't notice Maisie. She was seeing it all again, right in front of her eyes. 'I still can't believe it. The doctors and nurses working their fingers to the bone. Honestly, Martin, what on earth did you think you were up to?'

I said I didn't know what I'd been up to.

'You just kept slipping away. That's what. No matter what they did. You simply wouldn't try. Day and night, you hovered, you teetered. What if you'd . . .?'

'What?'

'We had to drag Father O'Keefe out. In the middle of the night. You've been given the Last Sacraments, Martin. D'you know that? At your age. It's not normal. Only very old people get the Last Sacraments. Normally.'

She finished her sandwich, she wiped her lips, she lifted her little finger and sipped from her cup, she gave that laugh of hers that said she was flabbergasted, shocked rigid, a little high laugh, like a pony's.

'What did I do?'

'Mmmuh! We won't go into that. All I will say is that you were a very sick child. And I hope you know it. And then, if you'd – after the trouble they took – if you'd . . .

Well, if you had – I wouldn't have known where to look.'

I was sorry. For not taking her blood. Sorry for the fingers of the doctors and nurses. Sorry I'd got Father O'Keefe out in the middle of the night. But I was glad too, pleased with this other person, who'd been me, who'd made a fuss. I liked him, I was proud of him, I wished I'd known him. This other me, hovering and teetering . . . and jolly nearly doing something so bad my mom wouldn't have known where to look.

She poured another cup of tea. Her chin drooped to her chest. 'There. I've told you. I don't want to talk about it – ever again. I still shudder to think of it.'

My mom could do a good shudder, her shoulder moved like the wind under her pale apricot cardigan. As she took a sip of tea to warm herself, her pink lipstick left a kiss on the cheek of the cup. One on the napkin, one on the cup. Always so dainty, my mom with a teacup, her little finger crooked, her little lips on the cup. She dabbed her lips with her napkin. Little neat dabs.

'When I think of those doctors and nurses, and how hard they worked . . . I wouldn't have known where to put my face.'

It was a pretty face, with a pointed chin and dark hair, and wide brown eyes which got big and glowing when she got upset.

'From that day to this, I've said to myself – I've had it

with losing people. I've had it in chunks. I've had it – '
she lifted her hand to her forehead – 'right – up – to –
here. I couldn't have coped if I'd lost you too.'

She got tears in her eyes. I hated that, I got hot in the
middle of me, and frightened. I'd do anything to make
her stop.

'But you didn't – I'm here.'

She didn't seem to think much of that.

'I'll look after you. And I'll buy you finest shantungs
from the Silk Sammie, one day.'

'Thank you, darling.'

'And pearls.'

'Real ones? I love real pearls.'

'Real ones.'

She'd smiled and taken my hand and squeezed it and
we'd sat there squeezing hands and being happy.

7. Lightning

The brass plaque with its curly letters, VILLA VANILLA, would catch the sun. Everything was as it always was, at about half past two, on a Saturday afternoon, and we were going racing. Through the slatted gates came the hot tarry tacky Saturday afternoon smell of Sligo Road. I was always ready first. I waited at the gate while everyone else got ready. I watched white men go by in grey suits and black hats and brown shoes, or in white flannels, flapping at their ankles. Or in white shorts. The sun caught the backs of their heads and shone on the bone, where their hair was shaved as short as short could be. They were on their way to rugby or bowls or tennis or golf. The afternoon was huge and hot and high. There was nothing else for them to do after Saturday lunch.

Georgie came out into the driveway and opened the garden gates. With one hand he snapped up the latch that held the gates closed, and then with his ankle he flipped the bolt that pegged the gates to the ground, pushing both open at the same time, one with his elbow and one with his hip. It was lovely to watch. The right-hand gate would swing until it hit the concrete post that stopped it, then bounce, then lie back against the post again, shivering. Then he cranked the Packard. He always did. You could depend on it.

I was waiting for my mom and my grandpa and my uncles to put on their hats for the races. I watched the bikes. Large black men, on bicycles slung with flags and shining like mirrors, rode slowly by. I liked best the bikes with long whip aerials on the handlebars, and small green flags of Zion flying in the bright air. They rang their bells, they laughed. The men on the bikes were off somewhere fun; they were dressed, they were polished, they were shining. They never wore shorts. They wore suits and pink socks and brilliant shoes.

My grandpa came out. He wore a silver suit with silver buttons and a silver watch and his silver hair was bright in the sun. He liked bikes.

'You get more style on a passing Raleigh, with three bells, chrome spokes, some black and red bunting flapping on the cross bar, a good aerial clipped to the back of the saddle than you get in an entire stadium of rugger-buggers. Believe you me.'

He opened the car doors and hooted and we all piled in. I sat up front with my mom, in her huge blue hat and her long white gloves and the smallest dark curl showing under the brim of her hat, and I was glad because I thought if she looked that good how could anything bad happen? On the back seat my gran sat between Uncle Matt and Uncle Charlie. She wore yellow, and kept saying: 'I feel like the cheese in a sandwich.' She wore yellow gloves with three bone buttons on the back of each hand, like tiny pearls. I know because I counted. Uncle Jack and Auntie Fee drove behind us, in a little blue Anglia, and my mom kept saying: 'Well, go-lly. Isn't my sister posh – in her own car. What will they think of next?'

We pulled out into Sligo Road, and on up the long hill to Parktown, and my grandpa was singing: '*Never mind the weather, as long as we're together, we're off to see the Wild West Show . . .*' We sailed up Parktown Ridge where the giant houses of the gold magnates sat like forts behind huge walls of hot brown rocks.

'On our left and right are the mansions of the abysmally rich . . .' Uncle Matt said.

He always said that.

The gardens of the abysmally rich were like green rivers and they went spilling down the rocky hill in giant steps, stopping off on the way down to make a tennis court here, and a swimming pool there.

'Must be worth a mint,' my mom said, when we got to the top of the Ridge.

She always said that.

From the top of the Ridge I looked down on the trees that ran from the zoo to the lake and I knew that under that thick green cover lay Parkside, and that was where

I lived. I couldn't see the houses for leaves, it looked like a huge forest. We passed an empty field with three fig trees, and two black donkeys with burrs in their ears; next to the road two black men with blankets around them were bending over an oil drum full of grey-red coals; the smell of cooking meat floated in through the open window of the Packard.

My grandpa sang: '*We're off to see the Wild West Show, the elephant and the kangaroo-oo-oo . . .*'

At Turffontein Racetrack a thousand people in colours like confetti blew in the air and the horses thundered. My mom put down five bob, either way, on a mare called Hot Chocolate and she won by a short head from Mr Magic and Lady Be Good, and picked up ten guineas.

'We're in the moolah. Spots are on you, Monica,' Uncle Jack said, 'the bookies will be weeping into their champagne.'

And then everyone drank gin slings.

My mom said she fancied Long Tom in the next race. A thousand people in colours cheered and laughed, and the horses went round the track like tanks, with Grandpa dishing out cash all round, saying: 'Give Martin a flutter too, won't you, girl.'

And my mom went off and put down five bob, either way, on Long Tom and won ten quid, and gave me a florin which I put in my pocket and Uncle Jack said: 'You're in the dosh now, Martin. Lend us a shilling.'

And Auntie Fee said: 'Shame on you. It's his money. Leave him alone.'

Everybody drank gin slings again, and my grandpa said: 'There's a good thing. Isn't it now. What's the point of going to the races and not having a flutter on the gee-gees?'

My grandpa fancied a horse called Midnight. 'He has a heart as big as America. The stamina of a lion.'

No one would back what my grandpa fancied. But he didn't mind.

'If we could look into his heart, his soul, Martin, my dear, what would we find? Molten power. If we had half his spirit, how blessed we'd be.'

My grandpa stood at the railings, his glasses pressed to his eyes. 'Come on, Midnight!'

Midnight lost. It was the same as always.

Afterwards we drove home singing:

'*The Camperdown Ladies sing this song, doodah, doodah,*

The Camperdown Racetrack, five miles long, oh doo-dah day.

Going to run all night, going to run all day,

I bet my money on the bobtail nag, somebody bet on the bay . . .'

When we got back to the Villa Vanilla, Georgie opened the wooden gates.

It was the early evening with the sun making powdery

golden lines on the high blue sky. We sat in the garden. It was what we always did. It was fine.

My grandpa told me his plans. He didn't need to. I knew his plans, he'd told me so often but I liked it. When he told me where he was going I knew where I was.

These were his plans:

Lead the Life of Riley.

Make a few bob at Turffontein.

Keep an eye on Kei.

Visit his old mam.

'But first and foremost we'll defeat the White-As-Snow Brigade. Come, Matthew, let's go to work.'

They went inside to do Matt's speech and we sat on the lawn.

My mom said: 'Poor Daddy, he takes it all to heart. I just hope he doesn't get hurt. When I think how he helped his Boer friends . . .'

Auntie Fee yawned a big yawn and she tapped her mouth with her fingers.

'You're not going to tell him the story about our dad, are you? Again? That's not the father he needs to be told about.'

'You think you're so smart, Fionnuala. It's all very well for you. You've got someone, you've got Jack. We've got – only ourselves.'

'Oh yes? What about you-know-who?'

My mom said: 'Auntie Fee's being silly. You do want to hear the story about Grandpa falling out with the Boers, don't you, darling?'

'Poor Martin,' Auntie Fee said. 'He's heard it a dozen times.'

'Poor, my foot, he loves it.' My mom sat down and started her story.

'When the Boer War ended, Daddy joined the British Mounted Police. But being a policeman reminded him of his own da, who beat him, so he left. He wandered about, all over the show. One day, he rides into Curzon. A little *dorp*. Daddy got a chair from the bar and sat in the street, outside the Grange Hotel, which was for sale. And what did he do – he counted customers. He was doing some research. He could have been a fine account-ant, your grandpa. And when he got to a certain number – he had it. Across the road and into the Standard Bank he went, and there, without so much as an excuse me, or a kiss my foot, he sweet-talked the manager into lending him three hundred pounds. A lot of money in those days. And he bought the pub. A boy fresh from the war. It was following his bent, he said. All he could do was breaking horses or keeping a pub.'

I let her voice wash over me, I knew the way from there. How the people of Curzon liked him because he had fought the English, because he poured a good tot of brandy. How he built the school and the rail siding and got the train to stop in Curzon. How they sent him to talk to the English government, because they couldn't speak English. How he got to be mayor ten times.

And then it all fell in the water.

'One day, Curzon got its first Calvinist minister, the dominee. And the dominee said to the *volk*: "You think this bloke's OK because he isn't a bloody Englishman? Let me tell you, brethren, he's worse than an Englishman, he isn't even a Christian. Dan MacBride's a damned Catholic . . ." And that was the end of it. Oh, it trickled on, for a few years. But your grandpa was dead in Curzon. The New Lot had come to town – Malan's men, the All-White Brigade. So Daddy came to Jo'burg. Which was lucky for you and me. He took us in. When we had nothing – except each other. It was horrible. We were alone – lost—'

Auntie Fee always said: 'Excuse me while I pull out my hanky.'

My mom always pretended she didn't notice.

'And if that weren't bad enough then I nearly lost you. Honestly, Martin. When I think back . . . to what you went and did. After all I'd been through.'

I said: 'What had you been through?'

'Tell him,' Auntie Fee said.

'Why should I?'

'If you don't someone will.'

'Then I'll know who to thank,' my mom said.

8. Cherubim

On Sunday mornings we went to Rosewood parish church, and Father O'Keefe talked about angels. You could be sure of it. In the Middle Ages a thousand angels could dance on the head of a pin. The Angel of the Lord declared unto Mary, and she had a baby. Adam and Eve were driven out of the Garden of Eden by a cherub with a flaming sword that could turn this way and that. Keeping them out of the Garden. Adam and Eve got their marching orders, they were lost for ever. They couldn't go home. Even if they were ready to say their names and addresses. 'We're Adam and Eve. We live in the Garden of Eden, Paradise . . .' They could say it till they were blue in the face. No one would come looking for them. And even if they found their way back to their garden, the angel was there, with his fiery sword, turning this way and that. For ever.

'If you want to know how long for ever is,' Father O'Keefe said, 'think of the longest time you can think of, and it won't even be the first half of the first second of for ever.'

'Listen carefully,' my mom said.

Everyone had two angels, a good one on your right shoulder and a bad one on your left shoulder. They whispered in your ear and tried to steer you towards good or evil. You couldn't see them, said Father O'Keefe, but sometimes you could feel them.

All my uncles sat in a row and smelt of soap, with Uncle Charlie at the end. He looked like a bookend, my grandpa said, and he kept us all upright. Georgie came too, and he wore my grandpa's suits to church. My grandpa said it was only right. Most people dressed so badly it was a sin.

'Imagine – hearing Mass in shorts. We'll show them a thing or two. I'll bet the Good Lord loves a nice bit of tailoring. Georgie wears his clothes wonderfully well.'

'*Your* clothes, Daddy,' Auntie Fee said.

'No difference, Fionnuala. Georgie is a study in elegance. And elegance in these denuded times – stripped bare, impoverished, poor and naked, remember, Martin, my dear? – is a virtue. If you want to know what lies in store – God forbid – if the New Lot ever take over this country, look at the way they dress.'

'Politics isn't a fashion parade, Daddy.'

'Don't you believe it, my darling.'

Sometimes Father O'Keefe came to our house in Sligo Road and sang 'Sipping Cider' in a barbershop quartet, with my grandpa and Uncle Matt and Uncle Charlie. Father O'Keefe blinked his tufty grey eyelashes and

opened his red lips wider and wider when they got to
'*through a straw-aw-aw . . .*'

One fine day Father O'Keefe said he wanted a quiet
word. He said Auntie Fee couldn't come to church, it
wasn't allowed. My grandpa called us, and Auntie Fee
was crying.

'I'm ex-communicated.'

My grandpa said he'd never sing barbershop with a
priest again.

'Our Fionnuala's married to Jack, who has been
married before, so she's not to come with us to Mass
any more.'

Auntie Fee didn't come after that. My mom said it
was kinder not to notice.

When we got home from Mass, my mom was ready.

'Did you hear? Buckingham Palace has announced
that the Princess Elizabeth has been delivered of an
infant prince . . .'

'Hoo, boy,' Auntie Fee said, 'Monica Donally, you
are a one.'

Father O'Keefe had another quiet word. He said it
was fine having Georgie with us when we came to Mass.
Only he'd have to sit in the last pew, at the back of the
church. OK? That was the custom. Servants had to go
in the pew purely for servants.

My grandpa said: 'Bugger me, Sean, this country's
built on the back of the black man. I am not putting him
out there, in limbo-land.'

So we went to Mass and we all sat at the back with Georgie.

Auntie Fee said: 'Thank heavens for small mercies. I'm glad I'm not in church. I don't have to see you lot sitting in the servants' pew.'

Georgie asked us to stop sitting with him. 'I feel funny, Mr Mac. It's better you sit up top. In the pew that's pure.'

My grandpa said: 'A pure pew? Sean O'Keefe's an eejit. So are you, Georgie. Where – this side of Heaven – will you find such an animal? Pews are never pure. Wait for the election, and Djann Smuts in his glory. We're going to sweep away pure pews and all this nonsense.'

Auntie Fee said: 'Georgie sits at the back when we go to hear Smuts.'

'That's different, it's for his own protection,' my grandpa said.

From then on Georgie sat alone at the back. My grandpa would turn and wave at him to come and sit with us, in the pure pew, but he pretended he didn't see.

Then Georgie stopped coming. He still put on his Sunday suit and he still opened the gate for us, and my mom said: 'It's kinder not to notice. I'm sure he has feelings, just like the rest of us.'

When we swept past Georgie she would look the other way, so he'd think we weren't noticing, and talk to me.

'Martin, how about that story of Adam and Eve being

chased out of Eden by an angel. Once they saw that cherub, they just knew they'd had their chips. That must have been some cherub. I wouldn't like to meet *him* on a dark night, with his sword, flaming like that.'

Auntie Fee asked how that smarmy old beggar Sean O'Keefe was these days, and my mom said: 'We had such an interesting sermon about Eden. I never knew that angel was posted there until the end of the world, which could happen any second. The last trump will be played by angels.'

'You're doolally,' Auntie Fee said.

'I'm not. Martin knows what I mean, don't you, darling?'

'I know what you mean.'

'Thank you, darling. I'm pleased *someone*'s on my side. Angels are very important. Angels came to Mary, and she conceived by the Holy Ghost.'

Auntie Fee said: 'Angels? My foot in a jam jar.'

'I believe it,' my mom said.

'You would.'

'What's that supposed to mean?'

'You know what I mean. How did *you* do it? Don't tell me – I know – an angel dropped by and – *bingo*. Next time you looked, you had a bun in the oven?'

'Don't be coarse.'

'Why won't you ever say what happened?'

'Why should I?'

'You know why. *It* wants to know.'

My mom looked at me. Auntie Fee looked at me. They looked at me as if I were a long way away.

'There'll be floods and boils – at the end,' my mom said. 'At the final trump.'

'Boils my eye,' Auntie Fee said. 'You can believe that gumpf till you're blue in the face. Not me.'

'Oh no? Just you wait. It's in the Bible. It's all there, Fionnuala. If you read the Book of Revelations.'

'I couldn't care two pence. You've got a weakness.'

'Have I just? For what?'

'Marrying.'

'Hussy.'

'Once you started, you never blooming well stopped. Remember Bing?' Auntie Fee started singing: '*I'm dreaming of a White Christmas, just like the ones I used to kn-oo-w . . .*'

My mom screamed at her and covered her ears. Then she looked up at the sky and said to me: 'They say Danny Kaye has made a triumphant return to the British stage . . .'

'I'd rather talk about someone who sang like Bing Crosby,' Auntie Fee said.

My mom started crying and pretending not to. My gran came in then, and said: 'Girls, girls, girls. Do simmer down. What ever must Martin think?'

I didn't know what to think. Except that it was funny to hear my mom called a girl.

She said: 'Well, all right. But if Fee doesn't believe what the Bible says then I, for one, am very, very sorry for her. She'll be sorry too – when the angel blows the final trump, and the world's destroyed by fire and brimstone, and everyone gets boils.'

Auntie Fee said: 'Never mind the final trump – what about the present moment? *Someone* is looking at you, Monica. *Someone* is absolutely *dying* to know why you don't like me to sing like Bing. *Someone* will have to know, some day soon.'

'But not now,' my mom said.

'It's looking at you, Monica, its ears are out on stalks.'

My mom wasn't listening. She got her hard-as-nails look, her tough-as-an-old-boot look, she put her arms round me. 'Oh, darling, what *must* it have been like? In that Garden. I can just picture it – Adam and Eve, out on their ears, and this blooming great cherub with his sword. Turning every which way to stop them getting back into the Garden. My godfathers. One minute you're in Eden, the next you're out on your ear. Stark naked. I'd have been flabbergasted, wouldn't you?'

'One day, you'll be off,' Auntie Fee said.

I said: 'Off where?'

My mom sent her eyes shooting sideways at me. 'See what you've done, Fee?'

'Tell him about his father.'

My voice went up, I couldn't help it. 'What father?'

'It's looking at you, Monica. It is not a fool. Sooner

or later it is going to want to know why they call you the much-married Mrs Donally.'

My mom tapped me on the shoulder. 'Imagine, Martin, poor Mr Gandhi has been stabbed. All India is in shock.'

'You think you're smart, Monica MacBride,' Auntie Fee said, 'I'll bet you heard that on *British Movietone News*. At the bioscope. You go every night, don't you? With that bloke.'

'What bloke?' My voice was all shivery.

They didn't hear me, they were over my head like clouds, talking.

I went outside to my place behind the mulberry tree. I sang in my head: '*Ol' Man River, he keeps on rollin', he just keeps rollin' alo-o-o-ng . . .*' I sang it over and over and over. I wondered about poor Mr Gandhi being stabbed. I tried out my name, in case I reverted. 'My name is Martin MacBride, and I live at 99 Sligo Road . . .' It wasn't the same. I liked Donally. I hoped my mom wouldn't revert. If she did, who would I be? Where would I be then? 'You've only got one mother,' my mom had said, and that was right, so I wanted to keep the one I had.

9. The Glorious Dead

One night Auntie Fee came to see me and we were on our own and she took me on her knee and kissed me and said in my ear: 'Can you keep a secret? Don't you dare ever say I told you – promise?'

'Promise.'

'Very well. Once upon a time, before you were born, there was the war. You've heard of the war. What a time that was. Everyone went dancing every night. We danced the waltz and the foxtrot. And the hokey-cokey – hands, knees and boomps-a-daisies . . . We danced at Club 400 – on top of Chrysler House. And at the Wanderers. We danced at the Langham and Old Ed's. We danced all night. We had top bands – John Massey and Eve Boswell. In those days people were kind. It was the war, you see. And in wartime people look to each other. And, boy, did we dress. You never went out without stockings. Most of us wore waist-nippers. We had a gay old time. But tight times too. You get the picture?'

I got the picture. War was dancing and looking out

for each other and waist-nippers and top bands. Tight times. Gay times. War meant wearing stockings all the time, and doing the waltz and the foxtrot.

'We were proud of Our Boys. Our Boys wore red tabs on their shoulders, to show they were going to fight the Germans. Malan's men didn't want to fight the Germans. They tore the red flashes off the shoulders of Our Boys. Our Boys gave as good as they got but it didn't hurt because they were only sewn on.'

She forgot about my forgetting words, looking into the smoky air at the end of her nose, looking back to the war.

'Pilots were top-hole, terrific, tremendous, titanic. Your mom and I preferred pilots. Don't ask me why. I don't know why. But we did. It was such fun – till it went to pot.'

Auntie Fee looked into the air, straight ahead of her, and in the air she saw Our Boys. In her stories everyone was still dancing.

'In Jo'burg, we never had blackouts. We burnt the candle at both ends. Bright lights, big bands. Such fun. Like it was going on for ever. Then, *bang*, one day, it just stopped. They were gone – Up North. "Taking the Dak", they called it. The Dakota. You never knew when it would happen. One fine night you'd be dancing at Old Ed's, or on the roof of Chrysler House, and suddenly he'd say: "I'm taking the Dak, sweetheart. Use my old Anglia, won't you. No good to me now." Or you and the bloke might go and have a last coffee at the Doll's House, and he'd say: "I mayn't have much time left. Marry me. Today, tonight." You'd wake up next morning and find you'd promised to marry him. Your mom did that, a lot.'

Auntie Fee began with the names: 'First came Mick James. I think he fancied me did Mick, but your mother spotted him first. They got engaged and she wore a big sapphire on her finger. Not that it did her any good. Mick took the Dak one day and he hadn't been in North Africa two ticks when he was shot down. Lay there, in the wreckage, till he died. Legs were broken, you see. Such a shame, he was a lovely dancer . . .

'Then came Teddy Collins. Number Two. Now Teddy, he had an eye for the popsies. A nice-looking man, Martin. We went dancing at the Langham, often. I can see him now. Tall, with coppery hair. A real charmer. Between you, me and the gatepost, I never did trust Teddy Collins. Too smooth. Your uncle Jack told me he was in Cairo with Teddy. They'd be having a few snorts at Shepheard's hotel, and Teddy would sing out: "Shufti – bints at three o'clock." That was Teddy all over. Always on the lookout. He went missing in action. So they told your mother. In Libya – or was it Mesopotamia? Who knows? What if he did a bunk? Pretended he croaked. I wouldn't put it past Teddy Collins. What if today he's off somewhere fancy, married to someone else, which is tantamount to living in bigamy?'

Auntie Fee would jab her finger at the sky.

'Anyway that was Mick and Teddy – gone to heaven. Then came Number Three. He had very fair hair. Sometimes they called him Bing. He sang: "*I'm dreaming of a White Christmas . . .*" absolutely beautifully. He never took a spot. That was strange. He drank orange juice. He'd say: "If I can't get merry on a glass of this, I'm not worth the paper I'm written on." That was your daddy Dennis. He was a good sport. He took your mom to the Club 400 for strawberries and cream. Ciro's for the Palm Court Orchestra. He took her to Old Ed's and the Wanderers Club. Very swish. Somewhere different every Saturday night. They did the foxtrot as to the manner born. I wish you could have seen them. Anyway, your mom gets married to Dennis. Third time lucky, hey. Then your dad takes the Dak Up North. He's on bombers, Wellingtons. He sticks his neck out. Then you get born. And you're no sooner born than you start dying. Your dad comes home on leave and you do nothing but perform. Some leave that was. But here's the funny thing. You don't die, then Dennis goes back Up North. He's not there two minutes when – *bang*.'

'*Bang?*'

'*Bang-crash*. Had his chips. Number Three – gone to join the Glorious Dead. Your mom was going to marry three chaps, but she didn't. She only married one – and he croaked. But that didn't stop them calling her the much-married Mrs Donally. She hated that.'

'Am I an orphan?'

Auntie Fee looked misty. 'An orphan's got no mom and dad. You still have your mom, so you're only half an orphan.'

If we saw an aeroplane flying in the sky, Auntie Fee would put her arm round me and point. 'Follow my finger. That's your daddy, on his way to heaven, off to join the Glorious Dead. I wonder who he's dancing with now? Don't be sad, Martin.'

I wasn't sad. I was really pleased I had a father, his name was Dennis Donally and he was dead, and I had been nearly dead once when my mom almost lost me, and I felt close to him when we talked about the Glorious Dead. I liked talking about it. Auntie Fee didn't like talking about it too much. I wanted to know what he looked like and what he said and what he did in the war. She said I had better ask my uncle Jack.

Uncle Jack was very good because he'd been in the war – but he hadn't joined the Glorious Dead. His pink cheeks were shiny, and his black shaggy hair was shiny too. He liked to wrestle and he liked to think about Life.

'Hello, Martin. What about trying a half nelson on your uncle? Do you read me? Over and out . . .'

When I beat him, he said: 'Well, I don't know. Bloody amazing. Where do you get your strength from, sonny boy? You're a feisty little tyke with a kick like an ostrich.'

He looked up at the palm tree in our garden and he said it had gone all shaggy in the head, 'like a hairy flag pole'. And he shook his own shaggy, shiny head because he was thinking about Life. He got very pink and his eyes were full of light when he thought about Life.

'Your dad and I, we joined the SAAF in 1941. His number was 205428V. Six below mine. We trained as air-gunners and transferred to flying school. Dennis wanted to be a fighter pilot. Your auntie Fee talked Dennis into bombers. Fighter pilots had a lifespan of about a week. When we went Up North we didn't know what we were doing half the damn time. Even our gear was makeshift. If you saw two SAAF officers dressed alike you shouted "Snap!". I flew Spitties. Here I am today, right as rain. Dennis flew bombers and – *wallop*. Life is a right royal bugger.'

Uncle Jack wore a white scarf sometimes. It was his lucky flying scarf. Every pilot had a lucky something. He'd been with Number One Squadron. Spitties. The Squadron's lucky thing was a Turkish carpet, got from a Certain House in Beirut. The carpet caused a spot of bother. A 'tinc-ture' of trouble. (I liked *tincture*, it tasted of sherbet.) That carpet was a right royal bugger – like Life.

'The madam of a Certain House asked for her carpet back. She'd lost a precious something on that very rug.'

'What?'

'Part of herself. A highly personal part.'

'What part?'

'What she meant we can only guess at.'

'Did you give back the rug?'

'Are you mad? Of course we didn't. It was the squadron's good luck. Where we went, it went. Madam could whistle for it.'

I thought of madam whistling.

Uncle Jack gave me a photo of a plane. 'Wellington bomber. That's what he was flying when he bought it.' He gave me a photo of a man in an air force cap. The cap was big and tilted over one eye, so you couldn't see much of his face, which was white and curved. 'A snap of Bing. I miss him.' He punched me softly on the jaw. 'Good luck. Keep it clean. Don't tell your ma I gave it to you. She'll have my guts for garters.'

I spent a lot of time looking into the picture of my dad but my dad would never look out at me. He was turned away, he was inside the picture, he was behind his cap. Uncle Jack also gave me an old box-Brownie camera that didn't work but had a viewfinder which made the world melt, as if you were looking at it through an ice cube. It had a leather case, with a camel on it, and it smelt good.

Uncle Jack lit a cigarette, tapped the loose ends of tobacco and spat a few bits off the end of his tongue. 'We were in Egypt together, your dad and me. Western desert. We had just plastered El Waq. That was on Dingaan's Day. Anyway, soon after, the Spitties went up and took a shufti. Jerry was moving his armour. We saw tank emplacements. I'm talking bloody huge. Ginormous tank parks. Rommel, of course. What a fellow he was. We always said we'd win the war if Rommel was on our side. The bombers were told: "Get your arses airborne." Keerist. The Wellingtons pasted the place. But they walked into one hot party. Jerry was throwing up everything he had. Your dad radioed they'd got his gunner. He was heading home. He didn't make it.'

Uncle Jack gave me a green book and a brown book, full of very thin writing.

'Here you are, sonny boy. These are your dad's logbooks. Look, that's his name, on the cover. See? It says "Donally D.H." Inside are his flying hours, the different kites he flew, his training reports. All the usual air force bull. The SAAF sent them to your mom after he went west. She sent them back. Didn't want them. Somehow they ended up with me.'

'Where is he now?'

He gave me another little photograph. 'I sent a pal of mine to get this snap. I gave it to your mom but she didn't want it either. Here it is – plot number five, row F, grave nineteen.'

There was this dry field, some stones and lots of white crosses all the way down the field, and humps of sand under the crosses. I could taste the sand.

'They lost him. I kid you not, the desk-wallahs actually lost the man's grave. There was a hellavuh fuss. I mean, you give your life for your country – then they go and lose your grave. "Where is he?" your mom wanted to know. They couldn't tell her. They got the numbers wrong, they got the wrong cemetery. So I sent my mate looking, and he found it. It's not much, it's a grave – but at least it's his. Your dad's in a little desert place called Ramallah, east of Jaffa . . . That was Palestine – before it got to be Israel.'

We had to lay the photo down in the light and stare hard, it was small.

'If you look hard you can just see his name: "Lieutenant Dennis Hubert Donally . . ." They've only given him one "L". The stupid bloody palookas. Can't spell, can't count – typical bloody pen-pushers. Anyway, it's yours to keep.'

Uncle Jack looked at my face and he said: 'Soldiers don't cry, except into their beer. Put up your mitts. Let's spar a few rounds.'

We did and he won and he said it was an absolute bastard – when you thought about it – Life.

'You're sailing along. Tail's up. Then, suddenly – *wham!* Everything's changed – for ever. What to do then?'

I waited for him to tell me but I saw that Uncle Jack didn't know what you did then – and that made me really worried. If he didn't know, how was I supposed to know?

I looked again at the picture. 'Plot number five, row

F, grave nineteen.' I didn't like it that they had spelt his name wrong.

Uncle Jack said: 'It doesn't matter now.'

It did to me. I was going to go to Palestine, as soon as I could, to write my dad's name properly. If the desk-wallahs couldn't get it right, someone had to, hadn't they?

I put the logbooks and the camera and the pictures of my dad and the grave into Uncle Charlie's kitbag and I put it in my cupboard. They were my treasures. Sometimes I looked at the picture of my dad. I liked the bit of him I could see; I was sorry the cap was in the way of the rest of his face.

10. College Men

Auntie Fee leaned back in the green chair, her Goldflake cigarette firing up and the smoke coming out of her nose like trains, and bits of smoke flying like birds at twilight, past her eyebrows and up to the ceiling. Blue when she breathed it in, grey when she breathed it out. Auntie Fee was remembering the Glorious Dead. She looked into the air at the end of her nose and the boys came back. Still dancing, still burning the candle at both ends, still gay. Before they went west, pranged their kites, copped a packet, bought the farm, flew off to heaven to join the Glorious Dead. Up and down her voice went, climbing into the smoke from her cigarette. Her eyes watched me; they were soft and sharp, they waited, wanting to see if it hurt, and if it hurt she was happy because she could make it better.

'In those days, the first Sunday of each month had a special rhythm. First thing in the morning, Daddy went to the graveyard. "Dancing with ghosts", he called it. He went to visit his brother, Michael – Mick. Mick is the only one in his family Daddy ever clapped eyes on again, after running away from Ireland. "We took a lot of casualties, one way and another", Daddy always said. Meaning he ran off to Africa. Meaning his elder brother, Matthew – shot by the Black and Tans. And his second brother, Charlie – hung by the British. Michael – Mickey – Mick – was his youngest brother and Daddy loved him. About ten years after the Boer War he'd made a bob or two at the Grange. So he sent for young Mick. Paid his fare to South Africa. Mick must've got here in about 1913. And he took to the life. Worked the bar, trotted horses. He and Daddy lost a lot of tin at Turffontein.'

'How much?'

'How much? Mountains. Then the war came – the Great War – and Mickey decides to sign up. Daddy thought he was mad. An Irish boy, with his life ahead of him. But nothing was to be done. Mick would be a soldier and fight for King and Country if it blooming well killed him. So off he sailed to France. And it killed him. In the trenches. Bled to death. I wouldn't like that. And so Daddy raised the memorial in the Curzon cemetery. It's white marble. He wrote on it "In Memory of my Beloved Brother, Michael". He couldn't say "Died for King and Country" because the MacBrides were fierce Fenians. So he put "Died for his Beliefs", though Daddy will tell you straight the only thing young Mick believed in was whisky and women. So why go and die in France? But there you are. I like Mick's memorial. It's a fine stone.'

There was no one in the grave my grandpa went to see in Curzon cemetery. But he still went. One day I'd go to my dad's grave in Palestine. I'd put up a really tall stone, I'd spell his name right and there'd be no chance of his getting lost again.

'Next – after seeing to Michael's needs – Daddy would walk and talk his way through the town: "Good Morning, Mr Mac," says Mr Gandhi, outside his Emporium. "Morning, Mr Gandhi," says Daddy, lifting his broad white hat to Mrs Gandhi, who never says a word because her hubby does the talking. Daddy and Gandhi would talk racing, who'd won what on the gee-gees. And all the time everyone's watching. Curzon's like that, everyone watches all the time. And your grandpa doesn't care. He talks to the world and his wife. White and black, coolie and coloured. English and Boers. Jolly sure. There's no one he didn't talk to. Mr Klein, the blacksmith; even Mr Schevitz, the chandler.

'Talking and walking. Down Long and into Broad Street. Past the shops, the school. Past the shunting sheds and the grain silo and rubbish tip. And behind him, growing longer with the minute, comes a very odd lot. Tramps. Hobos, bums, knights of the road. Boys off the boxcars, poor whites, *bywooners*, remittance men, loafers. Wanderers and wastrels passing through Curzon.

Trekkers. Hitching lifts. Riding the rails. Moving from the warm beaches of Durban to the goldfields of Jo'burg. And back again. And why this crew of *takhaars*? Derelicts? Because, this was the first Sunday of the month and your grandpa was making his special collection. Marching down Long Street, at the head of his band, coming up to the steps of the Grange, waving his walking stick like a drum major, and your gran would see them and say: "God help us, not again, Dan."

'And he would say: "Mabel, some of these fellows are scholars. I have a high regard for college men."

' "Con men, more likely," Mommy would say.

' "Plain hungry men, Mabel. If once you've felt it, you never get over it, you ache for ever. My poor old mam, my brothers, my sister – I tell you we were poorer in Waterford than the poorest black chaps. Not even the water could be relied on. How can I, with a kitchen stuffed with provisions, deny fellows who lie in the shunting-yard, with bellies growling? Who may have been on the road for days. Who have done nothing amiss in life but lose their way. Who, but for the grace of God, might be me – Dan MacBride. Or you. Or anyone else. Which of us may not one day stray or fail or falter. Find himself far from home. And being lost, who would not wish a kindly word, a good table, a square meal?"

' "They'll not set foot in my house," Mommy would say.

' "They never do," he said. "We'll lunch *al fresco* –
which is to say, on the stoop."

'And the big table on the front veranda of the Grange
Hotel was laid with hotel cutlery, and hotel plates, and
white starched napkins stiff as boards, signed with a big
GH. The salt cellars were made ready, the cut-glass
cruets of vinegar and oil, the sauce bottles and the little
balls of butter in their silver dishes. And down they sat
– Daddy and his College Men – tramps, travellers, poor
whites, ex-stokers, winos, old soldiers – getting their
bellies filled on the first Sunday of every month.

'And every so often Mommy said: "Thank the Lord
the wind's not in our faces," and would be running in
and out with vegetable soup, liver and onions, blanc-
mange and stewed apricots, washed down with water or
milk. Daddy kept hard drink away. "Dossers and tinkers
and methylated-spirits men build a thirst," he said, "it's
tramping the roads that does it. Moving between the
Rand and the Coast, like migrating birds. It parches the
tongue. That's fair enough. Slake a thirst, by all means.
But they do the bottle to death, and it's bad for their
brains, clever men like these."

'We all had to be there for the College Lunch. Daddy
would sit at the head of the table, and he'd say: "Fionnuala, kindly ask the gentleman on your right to pass
the rhubarb." His friends loved it. They thought it was
Christmas. They combed their hair, shook the dust out
of their collars and sat down and filled their faces like

there was no tomorrow. That's how it looked, that Sunday, the first Sunday of the month, August 1944.

'Your mom and I were in the bar, nattering to a couple of old Boers. You were there too. Daddy poured her a brandy and splash, and said: "There you are, Monica, but don't take long, the College Men are here." And you were sat down on the corner of the bar counter, and those Boers were feeding you lemonade and peppermints.

'Daddy and I went out to the table, he said grace, the College Men began baying for their grub. Just like any other lunch. I remember Daddy saying: "Aha, here comes the tureen. Gentlemen, will you take soup?" It was Mulligatawny that Sunday . . . when suddenly this taxi comes trundling down Long Street. The tramps goggled. All the way from Jo'burg, you could see by its number plates. It must have cost a fortune. I knew who it was – Demiopolous, from the Greek Café at the Parkside Shops, driving right up to the hotel steps. He gets out, looks at the table, at the College Men, and pulls out this letter: "This is for you, Fee . . ." he says, even though it isn't and he knows it isn't; it's addressed to Monica Donally, clear as crystal. It's that horrid brown colour, y'know. And it has *The War Office*, in black letters back and front and it says "Private and". But I've no shame in these matters. Your mom's still inside, with you. So I open it and read it – and can't remember exactly but it says something like – "Dear madam, It is my sad duty to inform you that Lieutenant Dennis Hubert Donally has been posted as Missing, presumed Lost . . ."

'Daddy's watching me, so are the tramps – and we all know. Then Daddy says: "Who'll teil her?"

'I went straight into the bar. You were drinking with the Boers. They were shouting: "What a little soak this boy is. What a little *dronkie.*" I left you with the Boers. I took your mom into the little sitting room, where the round table is – you know the one? – and I gave her the telegram from the War Office, and she read it. Then she asked me what she should do. I told her something your daddy Dennis liked to say – "When you feel your worst, look your best."

'She listened, poor thing. She went upstairs and changed into a cream cotton frock with big blue buttons. She'd bought that dress for her honeymoon. It had a flowing line. But this is what I remember – you know how fussy she is about what does, and does not, go? Well, she wore brown patents . . . with blue and cream. Brown. It didn't go.

'Then she said: "We'd better go and help Daddy." And that's what we did. Poor old Demiopolous just goggled. I don't blame him. All these tramps, tucking in. Your mom, in her pretty dress, passing the potatoes. Demi shut his mouth. If your mother wasn't saying then Demi wasn't saying. It turned out it was your uncle Matt who sent the taxi. He was on weekend leave from the army when the telegram came to the Villa Vanilla.

There were no phone lines to Curzon in those days, and so he went over to the fish and chip shop and said to Demi how much to drive to Curzon. Demi said a fiver. Matt didn't have it, so he borrowed it from Georgie. What would we do without Georgie? Anyway, we were thankful to Demi for coming. Daddy broke his "No booze" rule. He gave Demiopolous a glass of brandy because he was driving. And another for the road, and all the College Men watched, with their tongues hanging out.'

Auntie Fee smoothed her skirt and sighed, pushed her cigarette into her mouth and stuck out her chin so that, from underneath, she looked like Popeye the Sailor Man. Her eyes went misty, she was tired because the telling of the story made her feel good, but remembering made her sad.

'Daddy usually said goodbye to his friends in a formal way and called them lucky men, with the road before them and the wind in their hair. This time he just said: "Lunch's over, lads," and wished them good winds, full bellies and Godspeed. And your mom just went on smiling and looking pretty. Most times tramps stick like glue. They burrow in like ticks. We'd find them, days later, sleeping in the coal shed, hidden behind the servants' rooms. Even up the gum tree. There was always someone left over. Like crumbs, they got into the cracks. But that Sunday they melted away like the morning dew. Your grandpa never gave another College Lunch.'

'Not even once?'

'Never-ever-ever-ever again.'

'What about the tramps? How did they eat?'

'You don't have to feel sorry for them – tramps find a way.'

I did feel sorry for the tramps, and for Demi who drove the taxi, and for my mom and my grandpa. Most of all I was sorry they never had another lunch. I hated that – I didn't know why. Just to say 'never-ever-ever-ever again' made me shiver.

11. Keeping an Eye

On Sunday afternoons we drove down to Curzon in the Packard, with the top down. Mr Leeuwenhoff kept an eye on Uncle Kei during the week. But he wouldn't spy on the Sabbath, said my grandpa, 'being devout – that is "living according to his beliefs", "pious" and "religious"'.

So we did Sundays ourselves.

Telephone poles flew like matchsticks past the window. My grandpa sang: '*And when I die, don't bury me at all, just pickle my bones in alcohol . . .*' Curzon stood up out of the veldt: smudgy, sleepy, dusty, smelling of horses and motor oil and leather. We drove down Broad Street. There was the chandlers, Schevitz and Sons. We turned into Long Street. There was the Grange, plump and pale. Like a fat lady built of milk, said my grandpa. To me it looked like a good white bed, with windows. We passed the Standard Bank. Across the road was NIC LEEUWENHOFF – ATTORNEY, in curling golden letters above the door. A black man was shining the golden letters. His ladder marked the spot where, long ago, my grandpa sat on a chair and watched the Boers nipping into the bar of the Grange Hotel and decided to buy the place, though he didn't have a brass farthing. The man had a red cloth, which he spat on. The sun shone on his head and dust from the street ran along the lines under his feet like the veins in leaves.

'Why does that man work on Sundays? No one else is working.'

'He doesn't count.'

Sunday was strange because no one worked, except some people did, only they didn't count. Sunday was strange because no one drank. Except some people did. The Grange was cool and quiet, and smelt of floor polish and old tobacco. The front door was locked because no one was allowed to drink. But the back door was open because sometimes they did. And they had to get into the bar somehow, said my grandpa.

'This being disconsolate Calvinist country, Sunday is sober. Sunday is sacred. Sunday is also full of drunks, dying for a spot, but fearful of someone seeing them wetting their lips. Sunday is stuffed with sinners aching to sin. A day of rest, when you may beat your servant, or your wife, or your horse, so long as you're not caught doing it. Always remember, my dear – you may do anything you please in this land – so long as *a*: you do not enjoy doing it and *b*: no one sees you.'

A few Boers still came to drink and my grandpa called them his loyal customers. The bar was long and dark, and smelt of old beer. The tiny glass they used to measure the drink was called a tottie. It got rinsed in a copper bowl and poor people who couldn't afford anything else called for a 'totwash', which was the rinsings in the copper bowl. It cost a penny a wash. The Boers gave me tiny shots of lemonade in the totwash glass.

'What a little soak. What a *dronklap*,' they shouted.

I asked Auntie Fee if they were the same Boers who'd been there the day my mom got the news.

'I can't say for sure,' Auntie Fee said. 'All Boers look alike to me, and they all shout.'

They sat at the bar. Big dusty men with dark pipes bubbling beneath their noses. Not like before, said Auntie Fee, there were stacks of Boers before my grandpa was the Roman Danger. A lot of Boers had got scared of the Roman Danger, after what the dominee said. A lot had gone over to Malan.

'Isn't that too typical for words?' my mom said. 'Anyone who is frightened by a Roman candle is a sissy.'

My grandpa said it was war. They hoped to bleed him dry.

'The plan of the Brain-Dead Brigade is to boycott the bar, to ruin me by dying of thirst. They know a weakness when they see it. A hotel in these parts doesn't sell rooms, it is not a place to stay, a hotel stays afloat on its booze bill. A hotel is a licence to sell liquor.'

On the wall of the bar was a big painting of a lady. My grandpa said she was called *Aphrodite Risen from the Waves.* One of my grandpa's College Men painted her. He wrote his name just under the lady's foot: Zac Fuerwegler. She was just in and just out of the sea, and she had water on her shoulders. She was not wearing anything, only a bit of foam. She had blonde hair, and blue eyes big as searchlights. She was under the clock on the wall, and across from the billiard table. The table had a big light over it, and long green fringes hanging from the light, and a big notice on the light that said NO LEANING OR SMOKING OVER THE TABLE – BY ORDER OF THE MANAGEMENT.

'Look at Aphrodite's eyes,' my grandpa said. 'They follow you round the room. She watches the drinkers. Keeps 'em off the table. That baize costs a fortune to replace. And she keeps the language down. The Boers are terrible swearing people, but they don't believe in swearing in front of a lady. Especially a naked one. She's denuded, my dear. Remember "denuded"?'

I did. Only I wasn't saying so, not out loud, in case Auntie Fee heard, so I just nodded.

Behind the bar was the pantry and in the pantry was a ladder. If you climbed the ladder and sat on the top step, you could be there without anyone seeing you. And if you leaned forward and pressed one eye to the hole, right in front of your nose, you could look down into the bar. Had Mr Fuerwegler made the hole? Or had he found a hole there, and painted around it, for the lady's eye? If you looked through her eye you saw the farmers pulling at their glasses with frothy lips, where the beer stuck the way the sea foam did to Aphrodite. Or the shaving cream did when Amos the barber dabbed my chin. You saw the big light with the fringe that hung over the billiard table. And the farmers knocking the balls from one side to the other. And the blue smoke from their pipes climbing in rings above their heads. You saw the door of the Gents, where they walked in and out, buttoning their flies.

You could see Uncle Kei, whom we were keeping an eye on.

Uncle Kei was my gran's youngest brother and 'never amounted to anything until Daddy gave him a leg-up' my mom said. Uncle Kei was so quiet in front of my grandpa you thought he couldn't speak. He went on sucking his chalky fingers and looking down on the sawdust floor. Uncle Kei knew we were keeping an eye. He didn't like it. He said we were to stop. My gran told him we would stop keeping an eye just as soon as he stopped his predilections. She was very kind to Kei.

'What can I do? He's my own dear brother?'

Uncle Kei was short. He had blond hair in a wave on his forehead. When we came down on Sundays, he only ever said: 'So, how is it, then, you lot?' and went on mixing brandy and water for the Boers, writing what they owed on a Castle Lager blackboard, in yellow chalk. On top of the blackboard it said MR CREDIT IS DEAD. I wondered if Mr Credit had bought it Up North.

Uncle Kei didn't play politics. He never said much, except 'You people are on a hiding to nothing, these new Nationalists are going to run this town.'

'Kei has all the backbone of a doormat,' my grandpa said.

'He's good with figures,' my gran said.

'That he is,' my grandpa said. 'Quick figuring and pliable, with the political affections of a harlot – he's perfectly fitted to be a grand man of business.'

'He doesn't get on with folks. He doesn't have your common touch.'

'Touch is a problem, Mabel. Touching is what he shouldn't do. All I ask of Kei is to run a decent bar, keep his hands out of the till. And off the guests.'

All over Curzon posters of Dr Malan were tied to lamp-posts. My uncle Matt went with a big pile of posters of Djann Smuts and he tied them to all the lamp-posts that didn't have Dr Malan on them. Our Djann and the doctor stared at each other across the street, and waved in the wind. A van came to Curzon, and it had a loudspeaker on the roof. A man in an air force cap played the gramophone.

'A lounge lizard,' Auntie Fee said.

'A communications officer in the war,' my grandpa said.

'Can we please not talk of war? I've had it in chunks,' my mom said.

'A lounge lizard in a lorry,' Auntie Fee said.

The man in the van started playing his record. Uncle Matt started singing, in time to the music from the Commando's loudspeakers: '*Hitler has only got one ball, Göring has got none at all . . .*'

My mom said: 'Do you mind, Matthew? This child picks up anything he hears. Next thing, he'll be singing it at home. That's *all* I need.'

Uncle Matt said OK, and he changed the words to: '*Malan has only got one ball . . . Ver-woerd has none at all . . .*'

My mom laughed and covered her ears. 'Shame on you.'

The posters flapped from the lamp-posts – and when they got torn they flapped even better. The New Lot tore ours down and we tore theirs down.

Uncle Matt stood in the bar and practised his speech. A few Boers watched him, and Aphrodite watched him too.

'It is said by our opponents that we face three dangers in South Africa today – the Black Peril, the Roman Danger and the Jewish Menace. No, no, no, my friends. One evil, and only one evil, stalks our beloved land. The Nationalist Danger. And its chief henchman, architect of division and discord, is Dr Malan.'

'Good, Mattie boy,' my grandpa said. 'Hit those "D"s – Dee-vision and Dee-scord.'

Fewer and fewer Boers were drinking in the bar of the

Grange Hotel. Auntie Fee said they were scared off by Uncle Kei. 'He's so creepy. I wouldn't buy a drink off him.'

'It isn't Kei that's creepy,' my grandpa said, 'it's the times. They won't come near me, my old friends. These boys, who were brave as buffalo when the enemy moved up his big guns, run scared now, scared of the dominee, scared of the Romans, scared of the Jews, scared of the Browns, scared of poor whites and rich whites and non-whites, scared of Indians, scared of the world. Boys who were happy to die for their freedom are getting ready to assassinate it. Men who fought the English to a standstill for the right to breathe the free air of their own republics run now for the wagons. What a scandal, what a catastrophe – for us, for them, for the country. Once they were Boer warriors. Look now what they have come to. Brandy and soda soldiers, ready to ruin an Irishman who keeps a pub. That's the limit of their new Boer war. Sweep the servants off the streets. Start a booze strike. It is sad, it is pathetic. Condemned men readying themselves to vote for the noose.'

Uncle Kei said: 'Because they're scared, they do strange things. It's only natural, Dan.'

My grandpa said: 'It's my future they're running away with. I'm not having that. Rally the troops. Hold them in the countryside. Sally forth. It's Our Djann – or bust.'

His eyes were shining, his face was red, his moustache

was black. Everyone nodded. They looked and they nodded – I knew that look, it was tall, it was deaf – they nodded, they didn't listen.

'It's your funeral,' Uncle Kei said.

12. A Pike of My Own

My grandpa said a war needed a war chest. He got out the Packard. We were sallying forth.

'Height, light, fight, dynamite – and funds. We're off to Crossly Hall to raise some dosh.'

My mom said: 'Sally forth, then. I'm not visiting that sniffy Jean Crossly-White. Plain Jean Buys as she was, when I knew her at school. You'd think she'd done something special marrying old Dick.'

My grandpa said: 'Crossly Hall is the biggest private home in the country, after the Prime Minister's house.'

'I don't care if it's bigger than Buckingham Palace,' my mom said.

'Do come, pet,' my grandpa said.

'Dick Crossly-White is a drunk, Daddy.'

But she came, and she wore her little half veil. 'I'll show that Jean Buys.' Auntie Fee wore a yellow hat and Uncle Matt was in his election suit. My grandpa sang 'I'll take you home again, Kathleen' in his round, brown voice. His yellow gloves played a taradiddle on the steering wheel.

Crossly Hall was very big, it was as big as Curzon, it was so big you couldn't see the end of it.

My gran said: 'Fifty-six rooms, each fit for a king.'

'A baronial hall,' Auntie Fee said, 'of hand-carved sandstone.'

'So what?' my mom said.

'Italian masons shipped in for the job,' Auntie Fee said.

Two long lines of tall trees, stiff as soldiers, stood in the driveway and we drove between them with Auntie Fee saying it really was quite something and my mom saying she wasn't impressed.

'Teak from Java,' my gran said.

'Stinkwood chairs from Knysna,' Auntie Fee said.

'Doors of Japanese oak,' my grandpa said.

'Floors of Oregon pine,' Uncle Matt said.

My mom made a little mouth, gave three little yawns and tapped her lips. 'Excuse me for breathing.'

'Red roof tiles from Marseilles,' Auntie Fee said.

'Sixteen fireplaces,' my gran said. 'Delft tiles, with sailing ships.'

'Kiss my foot,' my mom said. 'Just let that Jean Buys say one thing to me and she'll get jolly what-for.'

We sat waiting in a big room with lots of old spears all over the walls. My mom pinched me. 'I wouldn't want to meet one of *those* on a dark night.'

'Pikes. Nice sharp pointed weapons.' My grandpa put

his arm round me. 'As a builder of houses, what do you say to this place?'

'Please, Daddy – don't,' my mom said. 'I have enough trouble with him and his houses as it is.'

'Nonsense. Every boy should have his own pike.'

There were photos all over the room, all of the same man. He was riding a horse. Shooting a buffalo. Holding a cricket bat. He was shaking the hand of Djann Smuts. He was catching a big fish in a river. Shaking hands with Dr Malan. He was flying a plane.

Auntie Fee said: 'It's not just Kei who's got pliable principles.'

My grandpa said: 'Old Dick's all right.'

Auntie Fee said: 'He's only all right because we need his dosh. Let the Nats get in and Dick will be in bed with them before you can say Jack Robinson.'

Mr Crossly-White came in, looking more creased than his pictures, and very tall. He had a mole on his chin with three white hairs in it and he smelt of peppermint and brandy. His hair was fat and red.

He said to my grandpa: 'Glad you could come. This is a battle, Dan. A field marshal needs to consult his generals.'

'Blooming heck,' Auntie Fee said.

Mr Crossly-White gave my mom a kiss on the cheek. 'Hello, Monica MacBride, long time no see.'

A woman came in then. She wore a hat that wound

around her head; she had a long black cigarette holder and in it she put a long black cigarette and lit it with a long white match.

Mr Crossly-White said: 'By the way – do you know Jeanie?'

My mom smiled. 'I'll say.'

Mrs Crossly-White breathed out smoke like a dragon. She looked at my mom. 'God. It's been years.' Mrs Crossly-White looked at me and she made her mouth into the shape of a red mouse with white teeth. 'This must be Bing's boy. Is he as wild as his dad?'

My mom cleared her throat, she turned pink. 'Ex-cuse me.'

'Hoo, boy,' Auntie Fee said.

Uncle Matt said: 'We want to rally the troops, Dick. We want to fight the New Lot, run them out of Curzon.'

Mr Crossly-White waved his arms. 'Spot on, Mattie man. Let's talk tactics. We need cash, for our campaign chest. I vote we have a gala. A fiesta, rally, giant jamboree – rolled into one. What does Curzon do well? It does maize. Mielies. Nowhere does it better. Curzon – the town where maize is monarch. Let's call it "Big Mielie Day". We'll turn the Hall into a huge playground. We'll have an airfield. We'll offer people flips in my planes. We'll really push the boat out. My pals from the Stock-Ex will chip in.'

'I have such fond memories of Bing,' Mrs Crossly-White said.

'Me too,' Auntie Fee said. 'Dear old Bing.' She began humming: '*I'm dreaming of a white Christmas* . . .'

My mom turned to her. 'Shut up,' she said. 'Just you shut up.'

'Did I say something I shouldn't?' Mrs Crossly-White blew smoke out of her red lips.

'I need some fresh air,' my mom said.

'Why don't we take a stroll round the ancestral acres?' Mr Crossly-White said.

Mrs Crossly-White said: 'I've seen it all before.'

'Ex-*cuse* me,' my mom said.

We went walking outside and Mr Crossly-White took my mom's arm. He said he hoped the fresh air helped. She looked pleased and said: 'Well, yes it does, thank you very much, Dickie. I always forget what a lovely home you have.'

Mr Crossly-White waved his hands. 'Good for a fiesta – not so? Loads of space to get lost in. We have a chapel, a coach house, an eighteen-hole golf course, a polo field, a stable block, a couple of aircraft hangars.'

He showed me a little stone house with a big steel door in the middle of a field. 'Know what that is, Martin?'

I said was it a garage.

'A garage it certainly is not. That, Martin, is where I will be buried, after I die. That's my private mausoleum. All Crossly-Whites must be buried on the estate, according to the terms of my father's will. That's my last resting place. A tomb of my own. Only the buggers made it too short – I'm six three in my socks. So I'm having it redone. I don't plan to crouch for all eternity . . . I mean, why the bloody hell should I?'

After we'd seen the ancestral acres, we climbed into the Packard and my grandpa was very pleased.

'That's a new one, Martin – "mau-so-le-um". A private little house, for being buried in.'

' "A field marshal needs to consult his generals." What hooey,' Auntie Fee said.

'Doesn't know he's doing it. He's half cut most of the time is old Dick,' Uncle Matt said.

My mom said: 'Fancy making jokes about being buried.'

'Dick has a soft spot for you,' Auntie Fee said.

'What *do* you mean?'

'At school he did. Everyone in Curzon knew. He still does, I'll bet. *She* saw it, in a flash. If looks could kill.'

'Damn cheek. What does Jean Crossly-White know, anyway?'

'She knows the score. The much-married Mrs Donally's in town – so lock up your hubbies.'

'Mrs MacBride, if you don't mind. I've reverted.'

I said: 'Am I wild, like my father?'

'You see?' my mom said. 'That's what I get for going to Crossly Hall and being nice to Jean Buys. Thank you very much.'

We drove home and there were shadows; they lay on

the veldt like the silk the Sammie brought, the finest shantung from the fairest East. Dark blue, mauve, thick as smoke. Was I as wild as my dad? How did you get your very own pike? Might Uncle Kei have one of his predilections? Would Mr Crossly-White fit into his mau-so-le-um? If the New Lot won the war would they come for us first, or for Mr Snippalipsky?

13. Visitors

I sat on the gatepost watching for my mom. She didn't come. She didn't come again and again. Georgie lifted me down and said maybe she'd be coming later. I asked why she didn't come and he said he didn't know. I asked if she'd forgotten and he said he was sure she hadn't forgotten. I asked him where she was and he didn't say anything.

I went to my place against the backyard wall, pushed past the branch of the mulberry tree and sat down in the middle of the log. My back was against the wall and my eyes were closed. The sun was high and warm. Georgie's shears cut the head off another flower. I opened my eyes. I put things in their right places. The tip of the red roof of the Villa Vanilla was in the middle of the patch of blue sky. The jacaranda that grew outside the front gate stuck its finger in the eye of the sky.

I started singing in my head: '*Mona Lisa, Mona Lisa, I adore you . . .*' from my grandpa's gramophone collection. Singing in your head is not the same as talking to yourself; it's better, but you have to be careful, it's not something you want to let people see you doing, even if they can't hear you, because your face scrunches up when you're singing in your head, and you lift your shoulders with the music.

I had just got to the part that goes *Are you warm, are you real, Mona Lisa? Or just a cold and lonely lovely work of art?* when I looked up and this boy was leaning over the wall. He was looking right down on me. He had horrible black hair and a horrible thin nose and he was very, very white.

'What're you doing?'

I didn't say anything.

'How old are you?'

I stopped singing. The trouble with singing in your head is when you stop. Then there is this huge buzzing nothing blowing up bigger and bigger like a balloon between your ears and it is noisier than your singing. I was angry; I was frightened; I was thinking: 'No one knows this place, this place is MINE. Go away.'

'My name's Raymond. I'm bigger than you.'

How long had he been looking down on me – while I'd been counting and singing? He'd just got his eye over the wall, that was all, but that was enough.

It was horrible to know he'd been watching me.

'Why d'you talk to yourself, are you a mad boy? Why don't you go away?'

Go away. *Go away?* How could I go away from my own place? I got up. I stood on the old round smooth tree trunk lying next to the wall; its bark was the colour of chocolate and it was worn white as milk, and it had a couple of bald bumps in the middle. I stood on the tree trunk, stretched up, grabbed the wall and lifted myself until I got my eye up to the top of the wall.

'I'm as big as you are.'

'You're standing on something.'

'I'm not.'

He tried to look but he couldn't. The log was too close to the wall.

'I know what you're doing.'

'What?'

'You're standing on something.'

'It's *my* garden.'

'What're you standing on?'

I wouldn't say and he couldn't see. He could look at me, but he couldn't look down on me. We stood there. My arms were getting sore, holding me up high. Then his head went away, and I let myself fall and landed on the log. I sat down. I was shaking a lot. I needed to make sure everything was the same. I checked the hollows in the smooth log. I sat right in the middle so the white wall was perfectly against my back, and the tip of the roof of the Villa Vanilla was here, and the top of the jacaranda was there. I counted to twenty-one very, very slowly. I listened to my breathing. I could hear Georgie's shears snipping deadheads off the roses. I looked up and the boy was still gone.

When I lie in bed, thinking about my past, there is 'Before Raymond', when I was happy. And there is 'After Raymond', when everything in the garden went to pot.

When my legs would work again I went out of my secret place, and Georgie came along and lifted me up onto the gatepost and I hoped my mom would come. She didn't come and she didn't come again. I was singing: '*Macushla, Macushla, your fond voice is calling* . . .' and she was right there, coming up to me on the gate.

She said: 'Hello, darling.' She sounded the same but she was different. She kissed me. 'This is Gordon.'

He was tall and thin. He had blue eyes and a curving nose, like a beak. His voice was strange. Loud. Sing-songy. High. It came out of his nose, right over his moustache. It was black.

'Hello, young Mor-ton. Hello, *boet*.'

'Gordon's from Port Elizabeth. D'you know where that is, sweetheart?'

The man said: 'Everyone knows PE – it's the friendly city – Pee-eee.'

That's how a man would sound, if he were shot by Robin Hood. 'PEE-EEE!' he'd cry and fall to the floor, an arrow through his heart.

'Is he always this quiet?' the man said.

'Quiet.' My mom gave her little 'ex-cuse me' laugh. 'You should just hear him. Mostly, Martin can talk the hind legs off a donkey. When he wants to. Can't you, darling? He knows words like you wouldn't believe. Say something for Gordon, darling.'

I pulled my Robin Hood hat down over my ears.

'He's wearing a sailor suit,' the man said.

'I like it,' my mom said.

'It looks a bit odd with that hat.'

'I'm not responsible for the hat. You chose the hat yourself, didn't you, darling?'

I had never heard her ask a question like that. She wasn't really talking to me – she was talking to *him*.

'He's being a bit shy. Aren't you, Martin?'

He laughed. It was terrible. His laugh was in his nose, pushing the air out – 'Eeoch-eeoch. Shy? We'll soon shake that out of him. Won't we, Mor-ton? Won't we ma-an? Shyness is for girls. In my book. Ask any girl.'

'He's not normally this shy – are you, Martin?'

I began to feel cold around my middle.

The man reached up and, suddenly, my head went cold.

'Gotcha. How's that feel, Mor-ton?'

In his hands he had my hat. And he was bending it. I went on getting cold. I didn't know I said anything till it was out.

'De-noo-ded.'

'There's one of his words,' my mom said.

'My, oh my. That's a big one for a small boy. Hey, *boykie*?'

He waved my hat in front of me so the feather brushed my chin. I tried to grab it but he pulled it away.

'Shame,' my mom said. 'He's very fond of that hat.'

'Just teasing. I stand corrected.'

He put my hat back on my head. It sat there, heavy, like a stone. He lifted his hand with his fingers snapping like a bird's beak. 'D'you know what I call what you've got on your head, *boykie*?'

I thought he was going to take it again. I reached up to my hat and felt my feather.

'With that big feather – I'd call it a "bahm-teckla".'

'He's still teasing,' my mom said. 'Aren't you, Gordon?'

I said: 'This is my Robin Hood *hood*.'

'Oh is it now? I beg your pardon, Mor-ton. I stand corrected. How very silly of me not to have seen what it is. It's your Robin Hood *hood*.'

And then they were gone. Then his thin voice, sharp, brown, like rusty wire.

I could hear his laugh, floating back through the garden. And my mom laughed right back.

I went on sitting on the gatepost. I wanted to go on sitting there for ever and ever, world without end. Amen. I started singing 'Old Man River' and I got to the bit about '*You and me, we sweat and strain . . . body all achin' and racked with pain . . .*' and I couldn't sing any more.

Georgie came over and swung me up onto his back. 'Want to go to the park, Martin?'

I was busy thinking. Gordon was strange. It was more than his words. I could work out words like 'Martin' and 'bum-tickler' but the sound of him I couldn't work out.

'Did you see that man, Georgie?'

I hoped he'd say no. I hoped the man hadn't happened and I had just made him up.

Georgie nodded. He still didn't say anything but I heard him, all the same. He was saying: 'What does it mean? You tell me, Martin.'

I didn't know but I was cold.

14. Border Country

I needed to speak to a girl. Rosa Snippalipsky was a girl.
I went next door. She was in the living room. As soon
as she saw me, she turned her hands outwards, making
webbed feet, and flipped herself upside down, and her
hair ran on the floor like a red river. She was very good
that way.

I went and lay on my back on the sofa, let my head
fall down to the black and blue carpet, and we stayed
like that, nose to nose.

'Are you shy, Rosa?'

She shook her head and her hair moved like snakes.
'No, Martin. Why?'

'Girls are shy. Shyer than boys.'

'Says who?'

I opened my mouth but nothing came out. I was
drowning in all that I didn't know how to say. I got
right under a big wicker chair. I was flat on the floor,
watching her walking on her hands. We didn't say
anything. That's what I liked about Rosa, you didn't
have to talk to her while she walked on her hands. I

liked the way she put one hand down, and then another, and the thick carpet grew around her white fingers like blue and black grass. I liked the way her red hair followed her around the room.

I opened my mouth again, I said: 'Gordon.' That's all.

She blinked. Her eyebrows were sweet and true, like good yew bows. She looked worried, she looked kind, she saw I was in deep trouble. When she spoke her voice was reaching out a hand to save me. Like my grandpa saved the man who was drowning.

'Who's Gordon?'

'He's from PE.'

'Where's that?'

It was useless. PE was some place no one came from. It was no good. She didn't know his name, or where he came from. In her world there weren't any Gordons. In her world there never would be.

'They say PE's the friendly city?'

'Why's it friendly?'

I got even deeper under the chair and put my head down on the carpet and I could feel Rosa walking around. The carpet bent a little when she came close.

Mr Snippalipsky came home. He was very fine, he smiled, he kissed Rosa, he sat down on the white sofa, he cracked his knuckles and kicked off his shoes, and he said: 'I'm very, very tired of bump and grind. How-oh-how I wish Gaiety Girls were a tiny bit less gay.'

And then he saw me under the chair. 'Good Lord. We have a visitor. Hello, Martin.'

Rosa asked him if he knew PE.

Mr Snippalipsky said: 'Certainly I know PE. I hope you will avoid that part of the world, my dear.'

'It's not for me, Daddy, it's for Martin.'

'If I were Martin, I'd stay right where I was. Safely under a chair. Right here, in good old Jo'burg. Certainly I know PE. It's on the East Coast. Border Country. A land where ball and bullet are king. Brains are not much regarded. Its associated settlements are East London, King Williamstown, Grahamstown. Popular with English chaps. Once upon a time they came to Africa to settle and fight the Xhosa Wars. No more natives to shoot these days. So balls it is. Rugby, cricket, tennis, soccer, bowls – any ball will do. As long as they can hit it or kick it or beat it. They do that day and night. Balls. That's PE.'

Mrs Snippalipsky came in then. She was very dark and her arms were brown and she carried a chocolate cake, so dark it made me shiver.

'Martin is asking about PE,' Mr Snippalipsky said.

'He shouldn't go near the place, full of rugger-buggers.'

'Do you hear Mrs Snips backing me up, Martin? Rugger-buggers, cricket wizards, bags of golfers. Your grandpa would be appalled if you went to PE.'

'I'm not going.'

'I'm glad to hear that, Martin.'

Rosa said: 'But he knows someone who's from there.'

'That's different. We probably all know someone from PE. We won't hold that against him. That's not Martin's fault. Would you like your tea and cake at the table, Martin, or are you happy under the chair?'

'This is my famous Sachertorte, a Viennese confection,' Mrs Snippalipsky said, 'dark chocolate and firm, sweet apricot jam in the middle. Everyone – climb in.'

We drank tea and ate Sacher cake and licked the jam off our fingers. Rosa said: 'You don't have to go, Martin.'

It got later. I thought, maybe, I could just stay on and they'd get used to me and not ask me to go. Then I thought I couldn't. There was me over here and the Snippalipskys over there. There was a big piece of glass between us. I was on one side and they were on the other. Rosa walked on her hands a bit. I watched her – it was magic. She was so – *firm*. She knew where she was. She knew who she was – Rosa Snippalipsky. She lived with her mom and dad, in her house. Her dad did Gaiety Girls and her mom did chocolate cake. And they always would. Rosa didn't need to know where PE was; she didn't need to know who Gordon was. She didn't need to worry about places on the Borders. She'd never have a Gordon walk into her life and say: 'Is that your bahm-teckla?'

'You don't have to go.'

But I did. My mom would think I was lost. She'd come looking for me. We had a deal. I'd stay where I was and she'd find me. I lived at number 99 Sligo Road. I was at home in the garden, but the garden wasn't my home. Also, it wasn't for ever, nothing was for ever – except keeping an eye out for each other, me and my mom.

15. Home

I liked it under the chair in Rosa's house, and I had this idea – it sang in my head: *'If you want a home – build your own.'*

I did that. I started low down, close to the ground, making caves. Caves in corners. Behind chairs and doors. Caves in cupboards. Beds were very best for caves. I crawled to the wall, pushing myself on my stomach over the smooth floor, like a snake. I liked caves. Caves are fine but they can be tricky. You come to the end of them pretty soon and you can't do much, stuck under a bed. Except pull in your legs and push your nose into the corner. Breathing in dust and darkness.

Also, you got found.

'Will you please come out from under there?'

After caves, I did tents. A blanket over a table was all it took. You got inside and it was fine. But the walls were thin. Everything shook when someone came along. Someone always came along. Even if you held your breath, they'd know you were there and come along and bend down and shout through the walls: 'For Pete's sake, what d'you want to be cooped up in there for? Go and play outside.'

So I started my shacks. Easy to build. I got old sacks and branches and cardboard boxes; corrugated iron was good. I did a lot of shacks. They were easy to build but they were too thin. I knew what had happened to the three little pigs. I knew how it felt when Gordon lifted off my Robin Hood hat and left me feeling the cold wind huff and puff.

That's when I fell in love with bricks. There were piles of them in Sligo Road and Wexford Street and Erin Avenue for all the new houses going up. I watched the men building walls, and licked my lips. It took a thrower and a layer. The thrower would toss the brick into the air, in a lovely curve, a loop like an eyelash. Somewhere between the ground and the sky the brick stopped, just for a second, and got snatched out of the air by the layer. He laid one brick on another, with an oozing layer of cement in between that dripped over the edge like jam, and with a lazy flick of his trowel he sliced off the sliver of cement. Like I did when Mrs Snippalipsky gave me a slice of her famous Sachertorte, and I pressed the hard chocolate halves together. The apricot jam fattened, and I sliced it off with my finger.

Just the *look* of the bricks made me weak – all clean edges, sharply cut as the sandwiches we ate at Anstey's. I collected them, took home two dark brown shining bricks and slept with them. Like new pound notes, like perfect toast, I loved them all – yellow hairy face-bricks, rosy bricks, steely-purple bricks.

My mom was flabbergasted.

'The backyard's a shanty town. There are hovels everywhere. Little *pondoks*. Mother of Mercy, this child will be the death of me.'

'Martin the shanty-king,' my grandpa said.

My mom said to me: 'Why've you got bricks in your bed?'

And I said: 'I adore them.'

'You can't. Not bricks.'

'Why not?'

'Because only God can be adored.'

Maybe – but I adored bricks. You could rely on them, until they got tall. They didn't like to be higher than you were. They stopped fitting. They fell on you. There is something about a house you build when you're small that doesn't like it. The thing won't hold. About five or six or seven bricks up, just as the room is coming along nicely, the walls wave like curtains and the windows collapse, the doorway drops and the roof falls in.

'Crikey Moses. This child will kill himself, one day.' Auntie Fee smiled at me.

Let them fall, I said. I'd build another, and another. I thought: 'If I go on doing it, I'll get one of them to stand up, one day.' While I built I'd be counting, or singing something nice and sad like '*Poor Old Joe – whose heart was full of woe . . .*', or speaking something from Uncle Matt's election manifesto.

'Martin the master mason,' my grandpa said. 'Wherever you look in the garden he's thrown up another dwelling.'

Georgie gave me a lot of little tiny bottles. He taught me the names: brandy and gin and sherry and peppermint liquor. I took them with me each time I built a new house. I made shelves for my bottles.

My uncle Matt said: 'Martin's got a collection of miniatures. Rum, gin, Scotch, you name it. He's running a bar. Next thing, he'll be lending us money, just like Georgie.'

'Martin the shebeen king,' my grandpa said.

My mom said: 'Please – don't. It's bad enough him building hovels all over the show. I wish you wouldn't, Martin.'

'Why?'

She looked sad and twisted her hankie in her hands and said: 'You're just not supposed to. I can't think why you started.'

When the night-lions woke her and I climbed into bed with her, she held me tight and her tears were very wet and she said: 'I don't know what I'd do without you. I just wish you wouldn't build those places . . .'

I wanted to say I'd stop but I couldn't. I was at home in the garden but the garden wasn't my home; I was at home at the Villa Vanilla, but it wasn't for ever. My houses were home. I did them myself. I was in them when they stood up, I was in them when they fell down, they were mine. You could creep inside them and be hidden. No one could see you – till they fell down. Why did they shout when my houses fell down? They were my houses, weren't they? They fell on me, they didn't fall on anyone else.

They passed over the roofs of my houses, like clouds. I heard them talking about what Gordon didn't do.

'Why doesn't he come racing?' My grandpa was discombobulated. I heard it in his voice.

My mom gave her little 'don't ask me, Daddy' kind of cough.

'What Gordon doesn't do is legion. I'm flummoxed, pet. Doesn't race, doesn't wager a bit of tin on the gee-gees. If you're going to go to the races, you'll be having a flutter – surely?'

'You'll have to ask him, Daddy. He's Presbyterian. He just doesn't.'

Soon my mom didn't come racing with us any more.

Gordon was there, often, in the garden, and I'd duck into one of my houses. He did something to the garden. He had this shadow all round him and when it touched something, it went dark. When he looked at us, we went all wrong. Nothing we did was right.

What was most wrong about us was Georgie.

Gordon just looked at Georgie and you knew how

not right he was. When Georgie walked out of the front gate in his suit, Gordon stared and stared, and a little vein went up and down near his ear. He'd shake his head and go: 'Christ Almighty . . .'

Georgie knew he was being looked at, and he would go very, very quiet and bend lower and lower as he cut off the deadheads. There were so many things that were not right with Georgie. It was not right for him to be the gardener and the nanny and the cook and the shebeen king and the bank. It was not right for Georgie to be a walker, in a fine silver suit.

I heard Gordon saying: 'Dan – correct me if I'm wrong – I understand you borrow money from him?'

'He's family is Georgie. We all live together and help where we can. Something odd about that?'

'Mostly, one borrows from a bank. No offence intended. I work in a bank.'

'Dammit man. *He* is our bank. Without Georgie, we'd never be liquid. He's a giving fellow.'

I heard Georgie snipping slowly. He was on his knees in the flower beds, keeping his head down. His snipping got faster.

Gordon spoke to Georgie in round slow words. 'Boss Mac says you lend money, Georgie. D'you fancy lending me some?'

Georgie went on snipping.

'Do you only lend to the big boss, hey, Georgie? Where do you get your money from, Mister George?'

'Georgie's a shebeen king,' my grandpa said. 'He brews and sells hooch.'

'Lending out the profits?'

'He does.'

'I'm not sure it's legal.'

'Legal is not a country we've been to much. Not this family.'

'I mention it only because of the cops. The Ghost Squad. When they catch him flogging booze they'll have him for bloody breakfast.'

'Anyone laying a finger on that boy will have me to answer to,' my grandpa said.

Georgie was saying less and less but he was very useful. When a house fell on me, he'd come along and pull the bricks off and say: 'What are you doing down there, Martin?' He showed me how to make kites. We split bamboo and tied it with string. We cut green tissue paper from a Mrs Minniver's box we found in my mom's cupboard. Georgie made glue with flour and water. I ate it off the tip of my finger. My mom saw me and said it would stick my insides together. But it didn't. We made a kite and flew it in the park and it stuck in the oaks. It was green and almost invisible to the human eye, among the oak leaves, like Robin Hood in Sherwood Forest.

'Too bad. We'll make another,' Georgie said.

Very, *very* useful.

Sometimes my mom dressed me in my sailor suit. I

didn't like it but then I heard Gordon say: 'Walking about in a big collar, with blue piping, He looks like a Limey bunny boy.'

'Oh, Gordon, he does not,' my mom said. And this door slammed in her eyes. She was as tough as nails when the door slammed in her eyes and she wouldn't move.

Gordon said: 'Only jesting, Monica. The boy can take a joke, can't he?'

'Shame on you, Gordon.'

'For Pete's sake, I apologize. OK?'

I asked Georgie what a Limey bunny boy was. He said he didn't know. Anything Gordon knew about Georgie didn't know about.

I asked my uncle Jack.

'That's a pooftah-wallah, when it's at home, Martin boy. Who said that to you?'

I didn't tell him. I couldn't say Gordon's name out loud, I tried not even to think it. I didn't mind being a Limey bunny boy. Or a pooftah-wallah. If Gordon didn't like it, it was OK. I built a lot of houses and I ate glue off the kite paper. I said to myself that when I grew up I'd borrow money from Georgie every day, and wear a sailor suit from morning to night.

One day my mom said: 'Gordon likes you.'

I pulled on my Robin Hood hat, I checked that the good green feather stood straight up. I checked my back. Like a sensitive deer, Robin of Sherwood turned his fluted nostrils to the sky and sniffed the wind, sensing danger everywhere. I did my magic, I made my spells, I walked and talked and sang in my head. I built houses. I tried to block him out. I cut him into bits in my mind and waited for him to fall apart. He didn't. I dreamed that maybe he'd go away. He didn't. He got into all our safe places. He was like smoke, like water. He was everywhere.

How could Gordon like me? I didn't know what she meant. But I felt bad. Then I saw what she meant – and I felt worse. What she meant was that she liked Gordon.

16. The Price of Eggs

Georgie was my nanny. Everyone had a nanny. Nannies did kids. But nannies were girls. No one else had a Georgie and every day he walked me down to the park.

Once, I asked my mom if I could have a girl nanny.

'But why? You've already got a nanny.'

'He's a man.'

'Well, he'll have to do. Nannies don't grow on trees, you know.'

'Georgie says Dr Verwoerd's going to attack us.'

'What a thing to say. That's just Georgie talking. We don't know how their minds work, do we? Anyway, I can't worry about that right now. What has Dr Verwoerd got to do with the price of eggs?'

Every day we went to the park. Georgie went down on one knee. He swung me up on his back – he was deep and brown and strong, like a river – and we were off, down Sligo Road.

'Hold on tight.'

I held on very tight.

My mom said: 'Remember – Georgie's not to go on

the swings; promise me he won't, or we're for the high jump.'

Georgie changed his size when we went outside the gates of Sligo Road. At home he was tall. But when we got out of the walled garden at Sligo Road, out in the open, Georgie was short, like me. I pushed my head into the hollow in Georgie's back. His big broad head sat well above the square neck of his white tunic, and his legs below his shorts were full of muscles. He bounced when he walked. I forgot he was a man. He could be a camel or a horse or a kangaroo or a cat or anything. He was bareheaded and barefoot and barefaced, and I never knew anyone who looked better in less.

We passed piles of bricks and Georgie saw me looking and licking. 'Not now, Martin. Later. When we come home.'

We crossed the road when we passed Dr Verwoerd's house. Everything was the same as always. We had tea and doorstops at Café de Move On. I asked Miriam if she'd be moving on, and she said: 'I am never moving on.'

We went to the playground and Georgie sat on a swing.

Rosa Snippalipsky was there. 'Nannies aren't allowed on the swings. You can't get on the swings with yours, Martin Donally. If you do, someone will tell.'

'I don't care.'

'You've got a man nanny; you *can't* have a man

nanny. If he gets on the swings you'll be for the high jump.'

'I don't care.'

'Bet you do.'

'I don't.'

But I did.

She popped her legs over her head and walked on her hands. I could see her pants, they were pink. Some kids started singing: '*What's the time? Half past nine. Hang your broekies on the line . . .*'

Georgie jumped off his swing. 'Never mind, Martin. Let's go and see Amos the barber. Time you had a shave.'

The barbers were thick under the bluegums. The barbers sat you on a high stool and gave you a little round mirror to hold while you were having your hair cut. The men having their hair cut had big white sheets wrapped round their shoulders, and some of them had lots of white soap on their chins. The barbers rubbed their shining razors up and down on the leather straps hanging from the branches, rubbed and rubbed, until they were sharp as sharp. All the air was flickering with their scissors.

Amos was our friend and he put me onto the high stool and wrapped the big blue and white cloth around my neck and painted my face with soap, quick and smooth like cats' licks. He picked up his razor. 'Shave, sir?'

It was like feathers on my chin. And when he rinsed his razor in the tin basin it made a *ding-ding* sound, like the tram bell. Afterwards, he wiped the soap off my chin and said: 'That's better, Martin.'

Georgie took an acorn cup and held it to his lips and whistled. I could never whistle like that.

At lunchtime the kids and their nannies went home and it was just us in the park. We went to the playground – three swings in a row, hanging on light chains from a big frame. The frame was wobbly. First, Georgie sat on a swing and he got me to push him. Then I sat down and he pushed me. Then he showed me how to stand on the wooden seats and you got even higher and the wooden seats of the swings groaned like bears. It was good. Georgie was very useful.

'Bend your knees, Martin. Shoot that machine right into the sky.'

That's what we were doing when a policeman came. Georgie was high in the sky. When he saw that policeman he jumped right off the swing, while it was still high in the sky. The swing went on swinging without him, as if it were drunk. The policeman was very tall and his khaki uniform was rough. He had a big gun in his belt.

I knew policemen, from the meetings. They took out their truncheons and hit people, who bled sometimes. That didn't worry me. It was all perfectly normal.

Sometimes, at the meetings, the policemen took you away, for your own protection.

This wasn't like that.

My swing stopped. Next to me, Georgie's empty swing went on swinging, making a little creaking sound. I remembered what my mom had said. And what Gordon had said. And what Rosa had said. I watched the policeman and Georgie marching away, over the grass, getting smaller and smaller. There was a brown police van parked in Erin Avenue.

Another policeman stood in front of me. He was also tall. He said: 'No one's going to hurt you. OK, m-a-an?'

Someone was screaming. Georgie was being pulled over the grass, then he was at the police van. The back doors opened, then Georgie was gone.

It was me who was screaming.

My policeman tried to lift me off the swing. I was crying so hard I could hardly see his face. He took my hand. He was saying things but when you cry hard like that you go deaf. I thought he was going to put me in the van. I bit his arm. He let me go and I ran away.

I ran to the bluegums. I was running hard when someone grabbed me. It was Amos and he had the big stool in one hand and a white sheet in the other. He pushed me onto the ground and put the stool over me, and the towel over the stool, and someone must have sat on the stool then because I heard Amos's scissors going *snip, snip, snip* and everyone laughing, like they always did, in the barbershop under the bluegums. I sat there in the dark. I sat there for quite a long time. I didn't mind. I didn't want to go anywhere. Then, all of a sudden, the sun was very bright and I blinked.

Amos lifted me up and said: 'Run home, quick, Martin. Tell your grandpa – Georgie's been grabbed by the Ghost Squad.'

I walked very slowly up Sligo Road, practising what to say.

Dr Verwoerd was in his garden. He wore black shoes with little brown socks and his hair was as white as the shaving cream Amos put on the chins of the men he shaved.

When I got to number 99, my grandpa was planting out some flowers and he said: 'These are called Livingstone daisies.' Then he said: 'Martin, what've you done with Georgie?'

Until then I was fine, I was going to say: 'He was grabbed by the Ghost Squad . . .' But it didn't come out like I'd practised because I was crying.

'They took him.'

'Who took him?'

I cried some more.

He said: 'Damn and blast!' He ran and got the Packard out, and shouted to me to tell my mom what had happened when she came home. I stood at the gate and waited. My mom didn't come and I couldn't see down the road and there was no Georgie to lift me onto the gatepost.

I walked up and down on the lawn, then I tried singing a bit of 'If You're Irish, Come into the Parlour'. It didn't sound too good. I was hungry, I kept yawning, even though I wasn't a bit tired. I didn't know what to tell my mom. I hoped and prayed Gordon wouldn't be with her.

Auntie Fee drove up in her blue Anglia and hooted but Georgie wasn't there so she opened the gate herself.

'All alone, young man? Where's Georgie?'

I told her and she hissed the way she did when she was surprised and blew grey smoke at the sky.

'Well, that's all we need. On the swings? No wonder the cops nabbed him, what did he expect? No wonder he got tossed in the back of the Black Maria.'

'But he's our Georgie.'

Auntie Fee said: 'He also happens to be your nanny and nannies mustn't use the playground. They can watch – that's all. If the cops see a native boy on the kids' swings, he's for the high jump.'

'Will they put him in jail?'

'You bet. He'll be clapped up in the clink by now. And they'll throw away the key.'

I started crying again and that's when my mom got home and Auntie Fee said: 'Keep your hair on, Monica, but Georgie just got nabbed by the Ghost Squad.'

Her eyes got so big it hurt to look at them. 'He *didn't*. Martin, tell me he didn't.' Then she said: 'Thank the Lord Gordon isn't here.'

I thanked the Lord. My mom said to Auntie Fee, over my head: 'If I've told him once, I've told him a hundred times: "If Georgie gets on those swings, we're for the high jump." I did say that, didn't I? But he wouldn't listen, would you, Martin? *Now* look what's happened. Really and truly – I ask you – what'll Gordon say? He's always said Georgie's going to be nabbed by the Ghost Squad. Honestly, Fee, what have I done to deserve a child like this?'

Auntie Fee said: 'You're the one who got pregnant.'

'Don't be common.'

Auntie Fee said: 'You asked. I'm telling you.'

I felt bad. I felt bad in the way I felt bad when I wouldn't take my mother's blood and nearly died instead, and she didn't know where to put her face.

'I'm sorry.'

'Being sorry doesn't help,' my mom said.

My grandpa came in. He had the two policemen with him, the tall one who took Georgie away and the one I bit. Georgie was between them.

'They want to see his room. They say they have their reasons.'

The tall policeman said: 'We got reports this boy sells illicit liquor on the premises.'

My grandpa was very cross. 'You terrify my grandson

in the park, and all because you suspect the gardener's running a shebeen?'

The bitten policemen said: 'The boy was using the swings. That playground's reserved – for children only. It says so on the notice. We get complaints. We get people saying: "How can my kiddie use them if natives are using them?" '

The tall policeman said: 'Unlock the boy's room.'

'We haven't got a key,' my mom said.

The policeman I had bitten got big eyes. 'This is your boy but you don't have a key to this boy's room. Is that what you're saying, hey?'

'It's his room,' my grandpa said. 'We don't have a key.'

'He's your boy. You must have a key to his room.'

The tall policemen said: 'Open the door or we must smash it down.'

'You mustn't,' my mom said.

Georgie took out his key. 'Don't worry,' he said. Like he did when he pulled bricks off me, or fixed my kite. He was so easy, we were the worried ones, he wasn't frightened at all, he was making it better for us.

We went to his room and he opened the door. His room was very white. White walls and white blankets and a picture of King George on the wall. His bed was standing on bricks, and this made it look tall and skinny. There was a brown cupboard with a speckled mirror, and a basin with a glass on it. The tall policemen got on his knees and looked under the bed, and he looked on top of the cupboard and in the basin. They didn't like the room, they didn't like King George, they didn't like Georgie.

'Open the cupboard,' the first cop said.

'You mustn't,' my mom said. Again.

Georgie said: 'It's OK.' He opened the cupboard and his suits were hanging there, like jewels.

'Where did he find those?' the first cop said.

'I gave them to him,' my grandpa said.

'Sheewizz,' the bitten cop said. 'Why did you do that, man?'

The tall policeman said to Georgie, softly, but loud enough for us to hear: 'We know you. You're selling home brew. Isn't it? *Skokiaan.* Beer. *Witblitz.* From your *kaia.* In the backyard. No so? Running a shebeen. You watch it, my boy. Or we're going to have you for breakfast.'

They went away then.

My grandpa put his arm round Georgie. 'I thought they had us there.'

'Where have you put it, Georgie?' my mom said.

Georgie went to the window and looked to see that the Ghost Squad were truly gone. Then he took us into the passage outside my mom's room and opened the cupboard where she kept all her lovely boxes, full of tissue paper from Pickles, the Langham Hotel, the Silver

Fir and Cranford's the drapers. Georgie pulled out one of her silvery hat boxes from Le Chapeau. The box clinked.

'Clink-clink,' Georgie said to the box, as if he were talking to a parrot.

'My godfathers,' my mom said.

Georgie lifted the lid and there were lots of bottles, under the paper, with their noses shining. He kept different bottles in special boxes. Beer was in Bridget Wools, whisky was Warner Girdles.

My grandpa was very pleased. 'What a fellow you are. Burying the booze under Miss Monica's unmentionables.'

'Ex-cuse me,' my mom said. 'Those are plain, empty boxes.'

'Not quite *so* empty.' Auntie Fee laughed, high, like a seal barking. 'Georgie, I'm proud of you.'

My mom said: 'Thanks a million, Fee. What about me? What if they'd looked in my cupboard?'

Auntie Fee said: 'What if they did? It's only Georgie who has to worry about hooch. There wouldn't be a problem – as long as they thought it was yours.'

'Bally cheek. There isn't a problem, isn't there? Can't you just hear the neighbours if it ever got out? "Ooh, d'you know? Monica MacBride's got a cupboard bursting with drink." That's all I need. Know what I mean?'

I held her hand. She looked sad. First, she'd been the

much-married Mrs Donally. Now she was the shebeen queen. She wouldn't know where to put her face.

'I know what you mean.'

'Thank you, darling. At least *someone*'s on my side.'

17. Marching Orders

In the days when we were warm and happy and together, my mom did politicians. She could take them off to a T. She could do Dr Malan. She got fatter and darker and crosser, she wagged her finger, she said: 'No, no, no.' She could do old Hans Strydom, he was 'The Lion of the North' and she roared, just like him.

My grandpa said Mr Snippalipsky should put my mom on the stage.

Mr Snippalipsky said: 'Anywhere but here. Alas, ours is a mining camp. There is no larger assembly of philistines gathered anywhere. What the punters want is custard pies, pratfalls and Gaiety Girls.'

My mom said old Malan wasn't too bad. 'Better the devil you know.'

'Better no devils at all,' my grandpa said. 'Best of all, let's keep Our Djann at the helm.'

My mom could do General Smuts, in his silvery preacher's voice. 'Now listen here, people, this is what I've got to say. I haven't much time . . .'

And it was him, Our Djann, to a T.

My grandpa would listen and smile. 'Monica, you're a born mimic. But a little respect, if you please.'

'I take off Dr Malan too, Daddy. I don't really see the difference.'

'There is all the difference in the world. The Malanites are bullies and bores. They have not a whisper of style. Vote them in and the country goes to pot. Sure as God made little green apples. General Smuts, per contra – Our Djann – now there's a master of style. God grant us a tincture of style, a trace, a smidgeon, a tiny touch. Martin, my dear . . . The Boers had it, even the Brits had it. The New Lot are without a shred of it. If anything sinks this place it will be a lack of style. Please God that Our Djann carries the country. Please God, again, that our Matthew carries Boksburg North. Or we're for the high jump. Look at the New Lot. Ugly men with ugly minds and uglier clothes. Malan only has to appear and style goes out of the window. Nastiness, darkness are their ways. Ways of death. And they're spreading.'

'Oh, Daddy, it's not a fashion show.'

'Fashion goes to the soul of it, dear Monica. To see the way most men wear their shirts, or their shoes, fills me with dread. Once upon a time, it was different. The old Boers had style, De Wet had style, Louis Botha had style. They were well-fleshed, they were full-juiced. Djann Smuts has style. The New Lot, per contra, are oafs. They are desiccated and denuded. Just looking at them scares the bejasus out of me. I feel the shadows creeping, I feel the darkness coming. Do you feel it, Martin?'

I did, I did. Only it was my darkness I felt.

Once upon a time, there was me and my mom, and we had a deal. Then there was Gordon, of the rough moustache, of the cold watery blue eyes. He was worse than the Sheriff of Nottingham. He *did* the most horrible things, like holding my mom's hand. He had the most horrible knees. He laughed, he said things like:

'I wouldn't take Mor-ton to political meetings if I were you. Leave politics to the politicians. Murky business.'

'I've got my eye on that boy George. He's for the high jump. Things are going to change round here, now that boss Gordon's around.'

'I'm going to take you to the cricket, Mor-ton – just you and me.'

'Why d'you wear a sailor suit, Mor-ton? Hey, *boet*? Sailor suits are for nancy boys. You're not a nancy boy, are you, Mor-ton?'

'Why d'you wear your hair in a quiff? Quiffs are for girls. Not so, Mor-ton?'

'He's just teasing. Gordon's really fond of you,' my mom said.

I couldn't say anything, except in my head.

'He's *yours*. Don't give him to me.'

*

The next time the Verwoerds asked me to their house they said please – no nannies, this time. Not even on the pavement. Leaving them outside on the pavement made Sligo Road look like a native location.

My mom said: 'Gordon will take you. Won't you, sweetheart? And you'll hold Gordon's hand, won't you, Martin?'

Gordon said: 'What if people see?'

'See what? You're just walking a child down the road.'

'I meant being seen as someone—'

'Someone what?'

'Someone, well, like a nanny.'

My mom looked flabbergasted. 'How could they see you like that? Nannies are never white.'

Gordon walked me down Sligo Road and we didn't hold hands and we made like we didn't know each other.

He kept talking to himself.

'What is it she wants? Tell me that – hey? I mean, I come along and she's got a kid. I don't make a fuss about that, do I? Don't be daft, she says. Well, who's being daft? This is South Africa. If a chap walks down the road with a kid in tow, what are people going to think? You have nannies for that sort of thing. Proper nannies.'

He saw me looking at him. 'And I don't want any lip from you, savvy?'

I started holding my breath, it felt better. I went a bit deaf that way and I only half heard him.

'I'm the one who took up with her. Right? Good for her. Point is – what do I get out of it? Correct me if I'm wrong, but looks to me as if the rest of you do fine. You do OK – you get a father. She's OK. She gets a husband. But what do I get? I get to be a white nanny – thanks a ton. Let me tell you, one does not go swanning though the leafy suburbs, on foot, with a kid. Not if you're a white man ... Not unless you wish to be mistaken for a domestic factotum. I mean, what does she want, your mother?'

I didn't know what she wanted – except that she wanted Gordon. I was thinking about style and angels and darkness and messengers. Everyone gets messengers. Only you don't know *this* is your messenger. Maybe, it's an old man in a cloak, who turned out to be King Richard the Lionheart, like it was for Robin Hood. Or you met an old lady when you're on the way to market, with your poor old mother's only pig, like Jack and the Beanstalk. Or you got Demiopolous, in his leather cap, like my mom did, when she heard the news that my dad had bought the farm.

Ali Baba got the genie.

Someone – I forgot who – got Rumpelstiltskin.

Adam and Eve got the snake. Only they didn't know it was a snake. They were in the Garden. Things were fine. Just fine. It was home to them, that garden. Next thing, they ate the apple and they were out on their ears, chased away by the cherubim. Lost for ever. Even if they found their way back home to the Garden, the angel would be waiting, with his fiery sword, turning this way and that.

Wendy got Peter Pan.

Peter Rabbit got Mr McGregor.

The Angel of the Lord declared unto Mary, and she got the baby Jesus. But I got Raymond, he came to tell me: if you think I'm bad, look what's round the corner . . .

The Angel Raymond declared unto me, and I got Gordon.

The doctor was in the street, waiting for us, his pink face smiling and a dollop of creamy hair on his forehead.

'Probably making sure no one parks his picannin on the pavement,' Gordon said to himself.

Dr Verwoerd gave Gordon his hand. 'Good afternoon, *meneer*. Thanks for bringing your child yourself. We don't like domestics all over the pavement. It makes a black spot in what is otherwise a very pleasant suburb. Do you follow me?'

Gordon nodded. 'You want to kick the black spots into touch.'

'I see you're a sportsman.'

'I'm from PE. Everyone's a sportsman there. What about yourself?

The doctor shook his head and his dollop of creamy hair shook too. 'I am too busy.'

'I can believe that. You've got a lot of work to do. Every white spot has a bit of black in it.'

The doctor's eyes were wide and blue and dreamy. He spoke very softly, very kindly. 'It's God's work. And God's time.'

Gordon pushed me forward. 'Here's the boy.' He walked off, then he stopped and turned. 'Just one small question: after you've kicked the buggers into touch, and they're all living somewhere over there, how do you get them to work for us over here?'

'I don't want them working for us. I don't want to work for them.' He lifted his hand as if he were blessing Gordon. 'Thank you for bringing your son. Come, Martin.' He opened the gate and pushed me into the garden.

Gordon looked at the doctor as if he was going to say something like 'He's no son of mine,' then he looked at me and went away. I watched him walking away, till he was gone, and then I let out my breath.

The Cruickshank twins came again that day, and a boy called Barrie, and Rosa Snippalipsky and Dora Devine, but they left their nannies at home. We played games that the Boers used to play when they were in their ox-wagons trekking across Africa, fighting savages. We started with *kennetjie*. It was very hard to get right. You had to balance a small bit of broomstick across a longer bit, like a sword, and then you flipped the small bit into the air and hit it across the garden. Then we hooked our fingers together and pulled. This was called finger-wrestling. Then we played 'knifey-knifey'. I had to stand with my feet apart and Barrie threw a knife into the grass, next to my foot. Then it was Rosa's turn but she said she'd only do it standing on her hands, and she did, even though Barrie said she could bleed to death if he hit a vein. But he didn't. Then we played 'Boers and Savages', and I was a savage and Rosa Snippalipsky was a Boer wife and Ted gave her a white bonnet with long white strings that tied under her chin and didn't fall off when she walked on her hands. The Cruickshank twins were also supposed to be savages but they cried every time Ted lifted his broomstick and shot them. Dora Devine climbed into the tree and wouldn't come down and Barrie said she could be the lookout because she was in the tree already, and she sat up there showing her pink pants. Every time he shouted 'Here come the savages' Dora started crying and said: 'Where? I can't see nothing, Hennie.'

He said: 'Hell, man, it's just pretend. Don't you know what pretend is?'

When it was time to go, Gordon was waiting. He didn't even come inside, he put his head over the gate and said: 'Let's get out of here, Martin.' And we went, without saying goodbye or anything, and all the way back up the road he was talking to himself: 'Fetching and carrying, like a bloody nursemaid.'

When we got home he saw Georgie planting out some

daisies and he got really cross. 'It's all very well for you, Mister Georgie, but I'm the one who's been fetching and carrying, while you've been sitting here in the garden doing sweet F— all.'

Georgie said nothing but you could tell by the way his spade went deep into the soil that he was listening.

Gordon went to my grandpa and said he was supporting General Smuts from now on. One hundred per cent. The Malanites were quite mad.

'I had it from Verwoerd, straight. He wants to get rid of blacks, Dan. Stick them away, in their own areas. He wants to wash away what he calls "the black spots" so we can be white by night.'

'He does that. And they say he'll run the show – if the New Lot get in. He'll be Minister of Native Affairs. His idea is racial partition. If they can do it in India, then we can do it here. If they can have Pakistan for Moslems, we can have Bantustan for blacks.'

'That's iniquitous, Dan.'

'I'm glad to hear you say it, very glad.'

'Damn sure. Jim Fish's got it easy – sitting very nicely on his arse, doing bugger all, while the white man works his guts out. Now Verwoerd wants to banish him altogether. What's the point of Johnny Af, if he's not working for us?'

'Why do they have to work for us?'

Georgie had stopped digging and he was leaning towards Gordon.

Gordon shook his head. 'Pardon?'

'You don't have to be a Malanite to ask the question: why should blacks work for us?'

Gordon looked at him hard. 'I'll tell you why, Dan, because if they're not working for us, one day we'll be working for them.'

'Why must it be either way? Why can't we work together?'

'This is war, Dan.'

'Maybe. But it's not Georgie we're fighting, it's Malan.'

Gordon smiled. 'What do you think, Mister George? Do you want to live in the backyard and eat porridge all your life? Or have chicken in the pot? You want to run the show? Better be ready to fight, then.'

My grandpa said: 'That's the mad propaganda of the Brainless Brigade. Separate, segregate, suffocate. No, sir. Why can't we win, together? With Djann Smuts.'

Gordon gave his thin, small PE smile. 'Nice one, Dan – but nonsense. I'll tell you why. Because we're white, that's why. Because this is Africa. Because you only count if you're running the show. Those who don't are dead meat.' He grabbed Georgie's spade and stuck it over his shoulder, opened his mouth really wide and shouted: 'Parade, Par-ade, attenshun!' He lifted his foot really high and banged it down next to the other boot and started marching round the lawn, shouting: 'Can you do this, Mister George?'

'Why do we have to fight – black against white? Why can't we all be free before the law?'

Gordon stopped marching, put the spade down and leaned on it. 'How long does Jim Fish here want to go on doing the garden? How long before he wants to do the government? And what're you going to say then – "Sorry, my boy, back to mowing the grass?"' He laughed his high long nosey laugh and gave the spade back to Georgie. 'Now, get back to work, Mister.'

Georgie and I stayed in the garden after they'd gone.

I said General Smuts was going to win, my uncle Matt was going to win. I said things would be fine, just fine.

Georgie said: 'That's good, Martin.'

But he lifted the spade and put it on his shoulder, like Gordon had done.

I said: 'We're going to eat the Malanites for breakfast.'

Georgie dropped his spade and stuck it into the ground. He put his hand on my head and looked at me for a long time and with his finger he touched my teeth. He didn't say anything.

18. Top-hole

Auntie Fee came now every night, and told me stories and waited when she told me to see what my face said.

'It's just you and me, Martin, and I'm telling. Let's have a look at you.'

Her telling hurt. I was learning how to shut my face up. I didn't mind the hurting so long as she kept telling. My grandpa was staying in Curzon more and more because his spies told him that Uncle Kei was up to something. My mom was away more and more. She didn't even come home to change into her best nylons, which cost the earth.

'Your mom's out on the town. She's gone dancing at the Wanderers. Very swish.' Auntie Fee's eyes were like knives, dancing. 'Lucky old her!'

I just said: 'Why?'

'What d'you mean, why? What sort of a question's that? Your mother deserves someone. And please God, no more soldiers. Someone alive. Not someone dead. Your mother's had death – ' she lifted the edge of her hand to her nose – 'up to here. She's had war in chunks.

Why are you looking at me like that, hmm?' My auntie Fee dug her elbow in me. 'Shame on you. Your mom's only thinking of you – and her. You're getting to be a big boy. You can't stay here for always.'

'Why not?'

My auntie Fee's soft kind voice got softer, kinder, it got a sob in it that was really scary. 'I've told you – you're here through the kindness of your grandpa. Your daddy croaked and Grandpa took you in. But it can't last for ever.'

Why?

'Because nothing's for ever. Now, what are we going to read tonight?'

'Read the war.'

'Crikey Moses, again?'

'Again.'

'Your mom would kill me if she knew. Well, go and get them.'

I went to my room and got them out of Uncle Charlie's kitbag. There was one green logbook and one biscuit logbook, they had writing in gold on their covers and it said SOUTH AFRICAN AIR FORCE, PILOT'S FLYING LOGBOOK, NAME: DONALLY D.H.

Auntie Fee riffled through the pages of the logbooks. 'It's hardly Shakespeare, is it? Know what I mean?'

I didn't know what she meant.

'Read it.'

'You take the cake, Martin. Sometimes I'm sorry I

told you about your dad. On the other hand if I hadn't, who would've?' She riffled through the pages some more. 'Where do we kick off tonight? And please don't say "the letter".'

'The letter, please?'

Auntie Fee sighed out smoke. 'We've had it a dozen times. You know it off pat.'

She gave her muddy little laugh. We sat back in the big green chair. I looked up at Cousin Caítlín's map of Ireland on the ceiling. Auntie Fee picked up the green notebook. Green to begin, biscuit to follow, that was the pattern, you could depend on it. I aimed my nose at Dublin. She sighed, coughed, pulled out the letter that we kept in the green notebook. It was very white and a bit torn and very thin.

'OK – ready? Here goes . . . As requested in your letter dated 25/12/45, the Flying Logbooks belonging to your late husband are forwarded herewith: Kindly sign and return the attached receipt. I have the honour to be, Sir/Madam, Your obedient servant, Major for Brigadier Director-General of Air Force . . .'

It was a good letter, I would sing bits of it later on, you could sing ever so many times '*I-have-the-honour-to-be-sir-madam-your-obedient-servant-major-for-brigadier-director-general* . . .'

Auntie Fee said: ' "Sir/Madam". What's that mean? You'd have thought they could tell the difference. And what a tone to take – "Kindly sign and return the attached receipt . . ." Bloody cheek. What did they think she'd do with these logbooks, flog them on the black market? Ah well, that's water under the bridge.' She picked up the green logbook.

'October 1942 . . . well, fancy that.'

She read slowly, her voice and her cigarette smoke grew together and filled the room. My dad was at 44 Air School, in Pretoria. He had stuck a black and red stamp in the front of his green logbook. It said 'October to November in Pretoria is Jacaranda Time'. My dad wrote everything out in blue ink and drew very nice lines under everything. His writing was very fine.

Auntie Fee said he could have been a bank manager, with writing like that.

'He sang too.' And she started singing: '*I'm dreaming of a white Christmas, just like the ones I used to know* . . .' She stopped and wiped her eyes and hugged me.

In December my dad was doing steep turns, climbing turns, side-slipping and forced landings. Soon he was doing low flying and night flying, which had to be entered in red ink. He could also do restarting the engine in flight (with Instructor Only). Then he went solo, and he could do gliding and stalling. Next thing he could fly Hornets, Oxfords and Tiger Moths.

Auntie Fee said there was no end to his talents.

He moved on to Wellingtons. His instructor was Lieutenant Farebrother and he taught my dad bombing.

He was an Above Average Bomber; he was a Below Average Pilot Navigator.

'You can't have everything,' Auntie Fee said. 'I'm sure this Farebrother fellow tried his best.'

I liked the sound of Lieutenant Farebrother, he was probably very kind. Auntie Fee said you couldn't go on someone's name. Names were tricky. At the end of 1943 my dad had flown 809 hours solo. He could do aircraft emergency exits and the cockpit drill – blindfolded.

Blindfolded.

She picked up the biscuit logbook.

'January 1944 . . . fancy that!'

It was all there. My dad was Posted Up North. He took the Dak. He was in the Western Desert. He transferred to Wellington Xs and started a training course, he was flying flapless and doing circuits and glide landings. There was no end to his talents. And his writing was very fine. On 12 August 1944 he was flying a Wellington with three crew – there was Lieutenant Beswick and Lieutenant Godlington and Sergeant Ballard. Halfway down the page the writing stopped. There were some thick red lines right across the page. And under the lines someone – not my dad – had written 'All killed.' And, under that, it said in big red letters 'COTO'.

'Dear old Bing. Your auntie Fee talked him into bombers. I wanted him to stay alive. Fighter pilots went west first. Did I get it wrong? See these red lines? When you see red lines you know someone's bought the farm.'

'What is COTO?'

Auntie Fee coughed her little cough, high, in the back of her throat. She always waited a bit before she told me. 'That stands for "Carry On Top-hole Officers".' She sniffed again. 'He was only twenty-four, you know. Never touched a drop. Dear Bing. Such a lovely man. I wonder who he's dancing with now.'

'Top-hole?'

'Terrific, titanic, true-blue.'

I thought about my dad and that made me think about Gordon.

'I'll bet *he* was in the war too.'

'Who was, darling?'

I didn't say his name. I never said his name if I could help it.

'Him.'

Auntie Fee laughed. 'Who's him – the cat's father? If you mean Gordon, yes, he was in Italy. In the army. He was the regimental paymaster. He did the books. I'm happy for my sister. She deserves a bit of luck.'

'Why?'

'Shame on you. Doesn't your mom deserve someone, after all she's been through?'

'Why?'

Her eyes were very dark and a bit wet. 'Your mother's in love, silly boy.'

'Why?'

'What a question! Because she just is, that's why.'

Auntie Fee's voice got softer, rounder, kinder and very scary. 'Your poor mom's lost so many people, hasn't she? And she's got you. That makes it difficult.'

Why should I make things difficult, what had I done? I was flabbergasted, I was so mad I wanted to spit.

'Why?'

'Because, my darling, a lot of men don't fancy a girl with a kid. So she saw her chance and grabbed him. You don't understand now, but you will, one day, when you're big. Promise . . .'

'Why?'

She sighed and kissed me. 'You haven't been listening to a word I said, have you?'

When Auntie Fee had switched off the light, I lay in the dark and counted to a hundred, then I sang in my head for a while, first I sang 'Molly Malone' – '*as she wheeled her wheelbarrow, through streets broad and narrow*' – then a bit from Uncle Matt's election manifesto – 'The future of the white man is bright under General Smuts . . .' Then I cried a bit and I wondered what map it made on the sheets but it was too dark to see. Then I went to sleep.

19. Bombs Away

One Sunday morning after Mass the Packard was standing outside the front gate. It was snorting and shaking the way it always did after Georgie had cranked it. Georgie had the crank handle over his shoulders like a gun. He smiled at me with all his teeth. He did that a lot, he had a strong smile. I wanted to have a smile as strong as that when I grew up.

My grandpa and my uncle Matt and my gran were in the front seat, and they were singing 'It's a Long Way to Tipperary' and banging their hands on the sides of the car to keep the beat. My grandpa wore his yellow driving gloves; they were made from a pig's skin. Auntie Fee was in the back with Uncle Jack. He was wearing his lucky white scarf.

'Hop in, Martin,' Auntie Fee said. 'We're all going to Curzon. Only your mom's not coming with us.'

I didn't say 'Why not?' but I must have looked like I said it because Auntie Fee said: 'She's got better things to do, that's why.'

I didn't see how my mom could have anything better to do.

'What things?'

'Your mom's got a friend,' Uncle Jack said.

Auntie Fee spoke over my head to Uncle Jack, using her special voice: 'Let's change the subject, please. It's very sensitive about its M-O-T-H-E-R. Very. It threw a cadenza when she S-L-E-P-T O-U-T the other night. We don't like it. We tend to become very upset. So, no talk of M-E-N, right-ho?'

'Right-ho, Finoonie,' Uncle Jack said.

'Are you hopping in?' Auntie Fee looked down her long sharp nose.

I shook my head.

'No one's forcing you to come. But just think of what you'll miss, if you don't. We're all going to the Big Show. They've got aeroplanes there and, look, Uncle Jack's wearing his lucky white scarf, and you know what that means? It means Uncle Jack's going flying. And if you're very, very good, he'll be taking you up for a flip. You'd like to go for a flip with Uncle Jack, wouldn't you?'

I got in and sat between Uncle Jack and Auntie Fee.

The veldt flashed by, bare, brown, hot and flat. Nothing but veldt for hours. Except now and then a telephone pole jumped out at you. The Packard rode on its springs. You felt like water in a glass.

My grandpa started singing:

'Now Jim O'Shea was cast away,
Upon a desert isle,
The natives there, they liked his hair,
They liked his Irish smile . . .'

My uncle Matt said: 'Make no error, Dick Crossly-White is completely arseholes a lot of the time.'

'He's a thirsty sort of a bugger, all right,' Uncle Jack said.

'Randy too. He'll hotfoot it after anything that moves,'

'And quite a lot who don't,' Uncle Jack said. 'He's not fussy is old Dick.'

Auntie Fee said: 'Please, boys. We have a C-H-I-L-D present – and *its* ears are out on stalks.'

My grandpa's hand on the wheel in a yellow glove tapped the time.

'*. . . So they made him chief Panjandrum, The greatest of them all . . .*'

Uncle Jack said: 'Old Crossly-White's in the bar, at the Grange, most nights. Completely motherless.'

'Paralytic,' Uncle Matt said. 'Kei keeps throwing drinks at him. Doubles, trebles. Until he conks out. Then Kei phones the missus. Missus comes down in the Lagonda and says: "Are you OK? Hey, Dick?" Funny question. The chap's so skew-whiff he doesn't know if his name's Arthur or Martha . . . Takes two blokes to lug him out of the place. Nice car, that.'

'That missus of his is some cookie,' Uncle Jack said.

'Dim as a Toc-H lamp,' Uncle Matt said.

'It's not her brains she trades on.'

'What the hell is Kei up to?' Uncle Matt said.

'Something he oughtn't,' Uncle Jack said.

'That's for sure,' my grandpa said.

Auntie Fee said: 'Will you men please shut up.'

In Curzon we drove down Long Street, and Auntie Fee pointed up to the banner stretched rubbery tight across the whole street.

'D'you know what it says? It says "Curzon Grows 'Em Bigger".'

'It's a coming place, Curzon,' my grandpa said.

'It's been a long time coming,' Auntie Fee said.

'It's been and gone, Mac,' Uncle Jack said.

My grandpa wouldn't hear a word against Curzon. It would be the coming place one day and those who didn't see it kept their brains in the cubbyhole.

He and my gran sang as we drove through town:

'Sure, I've got rings on my fingers, bells on my toes,
Elephants to ride upon, my little Irish Rose,
So come to your Nabob, and next Patrick's Day,
Be Mistress Mumbo Jumbo Jij-ji-boo J. O'Shea.'

Out at Crossly Hall the dust was as high as the car roof, with all the traffic of cars and wagons. The air was hot and fluttering with flags, and smoke from the cooking fires that smelt of fat and ashes. The big front field was full of planes lined up like cars. Mr Crossly-White's mausoleum was painted white and the South African flag flew from the roof. High in the sky were big yellow balloons, painted like Mielies. I could hear the man with the loudspeaker van playing 'Hitler Has Only Got One Ball'.

Mr Crossly-White came over. He didn't look very thirsty for a thirsty bugger. He moved slowly. If he chased anything that moved, how did he catch them?

'What-o, Jack,' he said.

'How's it, Dick?' Uncle Jack said.

They looked at each other. You could hear them breathing.

'Going up for a flip?'

'Bloody sure. Taking my co-pilot.' Uncle Jack patted me on the shoulders.

'Bit young, isn't he?'

'Do you think so? Why's that? He's a bit on the short side, maybe. But he knows what's what. Damn sure he does. His daddy was a pilot. Runs in the bloody family.'

Mrs Crossly-White came over next, and she had on a green turban and there were freckles around her white neck, which felt smooth and powdery when she pressed me there.

'Hello, my friend. So you're going for a flip? You're going to be a pilot. Just like your daddy. He was wild was Dennis.'

'We're on our way,' Uncle Jack said. 'But first we're going to stock up on some ammo.'

He took me over to a stall, and it said BLOW THE NEW LOT TO HELL AND GONE – JUST SIXPENCE A BOMB. On the shelves were bags and bags of meal, fat and bursting, spilling white powder. You bought what you wanted and a black man brought it over in a wheelbarrow.

Uncle Jack bought three bags and said to the black man: 'Follow me, Johnno. We're taking the Valencia.'

There was a grey plane with a ladder up to the cockpit and blue markings on the wings and I could see some rust.

'The Vickers Valencia', Uncle Jack said, 'is a pretty odd bird. I did time on these when I flew in the Empire Air Train. Slow. Bloody slow, in fact. So slow you wonder if you're airborne. Top speed about 80 mph. Hell, man, you could outrun her in the Packard. But it'll give you plenty of time to aim.'

We climbed up the ladder. There was a little seat behind the cockpit.

'That's where you sit, Martin. That's Bomber Command, and you're it.' He showed me the big white cross in the middle of the field. 'That's your target. When I give you the thumbs up, heave that bag over the edge. Aim for the centre of the cross. Do you read me?'

I read him. I read him so well I started shaking.

'Good man. Here we go. Chocks away – give 'em hell.'

Uncle Jack's lucky scarf waved goodbye to the farm, there was a roar, the sky turned on its side, the wind smashed into my face and we were in the sky. Uncle Jack stood up to fly the Vickers Valencia, as if he were driving a tram, and I sat in the little seat behind him. We went round and round over Curzon. I could see the roof of the Grange Hotel and Gandhi's Pink Emporium. I could see the houses of the New Lot in the veldt, across the railway line, and fields of mielies green as grass for miles and miles. The roof of the Grange Hotel was rusty red. The big banner across Long Street – CURZON GROWS 'EM BIGGER – was like a piece of string. The planes on the ground were tiny. Only Crossly Hall was huge, the chapel and the polo field and house were as big as the whole of Curzon. The big white cross in the middle of the field looked quite small.

Uncle Jack laughed in the wind. 'Shufti. Jerry at six o'clock. Hold onto your hat. We're going in.'

We came in low. My heart was booming, I had to put a hand over it to stop the sound, even with the air in my ears, it was like a drum. Uncle Jack laughed again. His white scarf was wide and streaming. The sun was on his moustache. People were looking up at us, with their hands to their eyes. I could see Mrs Crossly-White's green hat. I stood up in my seat and held the bag over the edge.

Uncle Jack lifted his thumb. 'Bombs Away.'

I dropped the bag over the edge. I leaned out to watch it fall – and it burst almost bang on the cross, there was a cloud of white and Uncle Jack lifted his thumb. We went round again and came in even lower but I let go too soon and the next bomb missed by miles. I climbed out of my seat and held onto the wing. The wind was loud. I wanted to be sure. I waited and waited – we were right over the target. Everyone on the ground was looking up. I leaned some more till my nose was on the X and let go my bomb. I hung there, leaning out, looking down. It burst – bullseye. I stayed like that but Uncle Jack pulled me down so hard I fell into the little seat, and he pointed his finger at his ear and turned it round and round.

Back on the ground he said: 'Jesus H. Christ. You palooka.'

He said to Mrs Crossly-White: 'I turned my back for a mo and the little bugger's halfway to paradise. Next thing, he'd have been walking on the wing. Sheez. This boy's bats.'

'Like father like son,' Mrs Crossly-White said. 'Dennis loved to chance his arm. You're just like your dad, aren't you?'

I tried to say 'yes' but it didn't come out. I was too full of something to say anything. My throat was swelling up and I felt like a balloon. It was the best thing anyone had ever said to me. It was a very good day.

There was nothing wrong with that day. I'd been a bomber, I'd been as bats as my dad, I'd chanced my arm, I'd jolly well nearly bought the farm.

Only I hadn't. I was glad about that too. My mom would have been very upset. She'd have had a cadenza. You could depend on it. If I'd gone off to join the Glorious Dead she wouldn't have known where to put her face. Mrs Crossly-White would've come round to tell her what I'd done, and that would have given my mom the screaming heebies. She would've been flabber-gasted.

I could hear her: 'Martin – how *could* you? What have I done to deserve this child?'

We drove back to the Grange and Uncle Jack kept saying: 'Sheez. You little bugger.'

And I kept thinking: 'I've got it all – height, fight, dynamite.'

I needed to go somewhere quiet. So I went to the bar. The bar smelt of cork bottle tops and old beer. I went through into the pantry behind the bar and climbed the ladder and sat there at the top. It was cool and dark. I liked sitting there, my head touching the ceiling, pressing my nose into the crack between the wall and the ceiling.

I looked into the bar through the eye of Aphrodite. Nothing, just coffee-coloured shadows and the soft shine of the long wooden counter and the smell of last night's beer, and totwash, and cork bottletops lifting like a mist to the hole in the thin wall.

I was going to stop looking when Uncle Kei came in. Mrs Crossly-White was with him. Her dress was pink and she had on a big white hat. They were friends, because they were holding hands. They sat at the bar, on the oak stools, and poured a couple of spots, and they clinked glasses and she took off her hat. She said something but I couldn't hear what. And Uncle Kei, as usual, said nothing.

Mrs Crossly-White got up off her stool and wandered round the bar. As she passed the billiard table she stroked the green felt top and she came and stood right under the painting of Aphrodite, and stared straight up at me – staring straight down at her. My legs were shaking, the ladder went all jittery under me.

Then Uncle Kei came and gave her a big hug and they went over to the billiard table and she climbed onto the table. 'No leaning or smoking' said the sign. I'd never seen anyone climb on the table before. Then he did too. They went right in, under the big light with the fringes that hung over the table, and I couldn't see anything, except her shoes. They were pink, like her dress, and the soles were dusty from the street outside. One shoe fell off when she lifted her foot into the air. Sometimes I saw her fingers, sticking out past the fringes of the big light. Her fingers went up and down, and her other shoe came off.

When they got off the table Mrs Crossly-White was holding her shoes. I was sure she had taken them off in case she tore the felt. She put them on again, holding onto Uncle Kei with her one hand and hopping on one foot. Then she went out and Uncle Kei went over to the Gents and closed the door.

I could see why people had trouble with Uncle Kei. You weren't supposed even to lean on the table. My grandpa worried about the Boers tearing the felt with their cues. It cost a fortune to replace. I could see why you had to keep an eye. Uncle Kei had predilections – which is to say, leanings, inclinations, urgings within. I could see that. When he climbed on the billiard table he didn't even take off his shoes.

20. Onions

Rosa came to me and she said: 'How's things with PE, Martin?'

I didn't say anything.

'We're going to the show tonight. To see Daddy on stage. There'll be songs. Do you want to come with us to the show? Do you, hey, Martin?'

I wore my sailor suit that night. Auntie Fee took me next door to the Snippalipskys' and she said: 'This young man's going out on the town.' Rosa had on a white dress with a blue sash and her red hair was pulled tight behind her head and clipped in a brown comb. She wasn't walking on her hands. She was walking on her feet as if she'd been doing it all her life and hands were just for afternoons. Her feet were in white shoes that closed with a button and had round toes, which looked to me – I didn't know why – like the noses of lambs. She gave me her hand.

'Do you know what that smell is?'

I said I did but I didn't.

'That's lavender soap. Do you know what lavender is?'

I said I did but I didn't.

'It's a sort of purpley flower. This clip in my hair is pure tortoiseshell. Have you ever had a tortoise of your own?'

I didn't say anything.

We went to the Coliseum. It was a soft red shining place. We sat right in the front. Mrs Snippalipsky talked to me and I listened. She liked words that sounded the same.

'Giving advice is my vice, Mr Snips says, but it's a nice vice, hey? Keep your eyes open. Mr Snips is on stage tonight. Let's see if he muffs his stuff. Right? He's a whizz at disguise. Don't ever marry an actor. Sometimes even Rosa and I don't recognize him – and we're related.'

There were verandas sticking out of the walls, and on the verandas were lots of men with binoculars to their eyes. Just like the punters at Turffontein, when we went to the racecourse with my grandpa. The music started, very loud, and I saw a whole lot of men sitting under the stage.

Mrs Snippalipsky said: 'That's the pit, Martin. Where the band sit. They make the music,' and she gave me a fig. 'It's a platform and the platform can go up and down. Watch . . .'

And it did, like a lift. Going up and up into the air, with all the men on it, still playing, and a man waving a stick at them.

'That's the conductor, Martin. He's a sort of traffic cop. He sees to it that the band starts and stops at the same time. Anyone out of time the cop bops.'

Mrs Snippalipsky pulled things from her sleeves. Egg sandwiches and Lemos orange in a big bottle and fat slices of her famous Sachertorte, wrapped in greaseproof paper, 'in case we get peckish'. The curtain went up, it was a red wave, it was brilliant. An old man came on, but he wasn't Mr Snippalipsky. He wore a big khaki hat, he had bullets looped around his body, and he said he'd be singing 'The Song of the Boer'. And he did. He kept singing some bits of it, over and over:

> 'Then ride, ride, ride!
> For my loved ones are waiting for mee-hee-hee,
> And tonight I shall bide,
> With my vrouw by my side,
> And my little ones round my knee-eee-eee.'

Everyone clapped and stamped and whistled. Mrs Snippalipsky asked us please not to stamp. 'It's *so* very common. Carthorses stamp. Miners stamp. Jo'burg is still a mining camp.'

I asked her if miners stamped in their camp and Mrs

Snippalipsky said: 'Heaven knows, Martin. I think they should be shot, should they not?'

Another man came on, his face was all black, except for his lips, which were very white, and his eyes, which were very round. It still wasn't Mr Snippalipsky. He sang a sad song about being far from the old folks at home and all the miners stamped hard. Then a whole lot of girls came on. They wore frilly skirts and kicked up their legs almost as high as the top of the curtain and all the miners stamped some more and whistled and shouted: '*Vat hom*, fluffy!'

Mrs Snippalipsky said: 'Gaiety Girls. Fake pearls – fit for earls. Mr Snips brings them over from England. I wish he wouldn't. Mr Snips would do Shakespeare, given half a chance. But the oafs would murder him. This is Jo'burg. Lots of oafs with no loafs.'

We ate more egg sandwiches and Rosa and I passed the Lemos bottle to each other.

Rosa said to me: 'Are you liking it, Martin?'

All I could do was nod my head, even though I knew she couldn't see me in the dark. I didn't understand how she could ask me that. I had never felt so *light* in my life. I nodded very carefully because my head was huge and filled with air and coming to bits like a thistledown, with each bit floating this way and that on the big waves of music from the lighted square when the women kicked their legs to the sky.

Rosa whispered in my ear, her breath was soft and smelt of egg. 'If you look up, you can see stars in the roof.'

It was true, there were stars shining in the dark. I laid my head back and looked up into the curving dark where the tiny lights shone and the more I looked the more I saw. Mrs Snippalipsky pointed to the boxes, which stuck out from the walls, where the men held binoculars to their eyes, like we did at the races.

'Look – up there. Sitting in the boxes. Lah-di-dahs.'

I thought she'd said ha-di-hahs.

'No, dear. Not ha-di-hah birds – bods. Up there, on their perches. Odd bods.'

The bods with the binoculars stared down at the Gaiety Girls. I wondered if they were blind. Mrs Snippalipsky said their eyesight was just fine.

'They come to look at the girls' legs – and their panties – my dad says so,' Rosa said. 'Their behinds.'

Mrs Snippalipsky said: 'Rosa, sweetheart, never mind the behinds, remember our guest.'

The Gaiety Girls turned their backs and flipped up their skirts and bent almost to their toes and showed their behinds just like Rosa said they did, and the noise from the miners was so loud I had to cover my ears.

Mrs Snippalipsky said: 'Imagine – coming all the way from England to show your BTMs to a bunch of *takhaars* from the *bundu*. If I went halfway round the world I'd want more to show for my travels.'

She handed out her famous Sachertorte, dark and sweet, and we licked our sticky fingers in the dark and the seats were very warm and soft and I could have stayed there for ever. Rosa and I ate dried figs next, and she said: 'Martin, do the pips get stuck in your teeth?' The band played some more, the traffic cop bopped, the odd bods stared, the Gaiety Girls showed their BTMs. I felt my teeth with my tongue. I told Rosa I could feel the fig pips sticking in my teeth, and she said: 'I'm glad, Martin.' And I felt happy she was glad.

A very old man came on. He wore a blue dressing gown and he leaned on a walking stick and he held his hip as if it were very sore. On his shiny black shoes were big brass buckles. Leaning on his stick, the old man sang a song about onions and one bit kept coming back again and again:

'He's gone for ever more, at the age of ninety-four
And the memory of him I'll always s-a-v-e . . .
So I'm going to the graveyard, to fulfil his last request,
Just to plant a bunch of onions on his gr-a-v-e.'

Mrs Snippalipsky said: 'It's Pa.'

Rosa said: 'It's Pa, all right – he's a whizz at disguise.'

I looked and looked but I couldn't see Mr Snippalipsky. I saw this old man, leaning on his stick, singing about his onions.

Mrs Snippalipsky said: 'What an old ham that man is,

not so, Martin? Ham as in acting, not ham as in spam.'
She laughed again, sweet and dark, like her Sachertorte.

Afterwards, we drove home in the Snippalipsky Buick,
and Mr Snippalipsky said: 'Men up front.' Rosa and her
mom sat behind us and I could smell lavender soap. Mr
Snippalipsky smelt of paint and Mrs Snippalipsky asked:
'Did you have enough to eat, Martin? Theatre is hungry
work . . .' and Mr Snippalipsky said: 'You're telling me,
Mother.' Then he sang his song again: *'He's gone for
ever more, at the age of ninety-four . . .'*

I thought it was nice to be a ham, nice to be a whizz
at disguise.

Mr Snippalipsky said: 'What's the news on the PE
front, Martin, old chap?'

I tried to speak but I couldn't and Mrs Snippalipsky
said: 'Now, don't upset the child, Joel.'

I didn't know I was upset until I felt the wet on my
cheeks. I was glad to be sitting up front next to Mr
Snippalipsky, because there was more room and you
need room when you cry. Trouble was, the more glad I
felt to be sitting up front, the more I cried. The tears ran
down my cheeks and down my chest and I even felt
them on my legs.

Mr Snippalipsky gave me his handkerchief, very big
and soft, and I pushed it to my face and kept it there
until the tears stopped coming, which took quite a while.
I wanted the car to go on driving.

We stopped and we were outside the Villa Vanilla and they said: 'Thank you for coming, Martin.'

I just jumped out of the car and I heard Rosa shouting after me: 'Didn't you like it, Martin?'

That night, the music went round and round in my head. I could smell Rosa, I could taste Mrs Snippa-lipsky's famous Sachertorte, and all the time I sang: '*So I'm going to the graveyard, to fulfil his last request, just to plant a bunch of onions on his grave . . .*'

I sang till I went to sleep. In my dreams I lost the onion man and I got the man with the *vrouw*, and he went riding, riding, all night.

21. *In Flagrante*

It was the Saturday after the Coliseum. We went to the races, and Auntie Fee won three guineas on a horse called Brown Sugar, who won by a nose from Dolly Grey and Little Caesar. The odds were three to one. We came home to the Villa Vanilla and everything seemed fine. We sat out under the palm tree, like always, and Uncle Jack whistled 'Good Night, Irene'.

My grandpa said, like always: 'Time for a spot. Georgie, bring lots of ice.'

That Saturday looked like every other Saturday. Only it wasn't. That Saturday was the engine pulling along behind it all the other days of my life, days when people sang and the stories were good. It was a long, long train, and it seemed fine, but it was racing on at about 100 miles an hour, straight into a brick wall . . . *Keee-rash.*

And we were all up front in the train that Saturday.

Uncle Jack said: 'Mac, with this bloody election . . . we may lose our shirts.'

My grandpa said: 'It's a dead cert.'

The wooden front gate opened and my mom jumped

up and pressed her hands to her mouth and said: 'It's
Gordon.' As if she was surprised, as if we didn't know
who it was, which we did. As if we were pleased to see
him, which we weren't. His long khaki socks, reaching
up almost to his knees, and his shirt reaching down
almost to his knees, which were round and bald powdery white. He walked across the lawn, giving out these
crumpling waves. They hit you and it hurt.

He shook my grandpa's hand. 'Don't let me interrupt.'

'Sit down, man. Georgie, fetch a clean glass. Will you
take a drink?'

'A beer, if I may, thank you, Dan.'

I felt his eye come to sit on me, like a fly landing on
my arm.

'And how is young Mor-ton today?'

I just gave my goggle-eyed stare.

My mother said: 'He's fine. You are, aren't you,
sweetheart?'

Georgie came back with Gordon's beer.

Gordon poured out the bottle and lifted his glass.
'Cheers, Dan.'

My grandpa smiled. 'It's Georgie's beer.'

No one moved. Gordon was looking at Georgie. The
light was grey around the sharp leaves of the palm tree,
the same colour as the rubber garters my mom made me
wear to keep my socks up.

My grandpa said: 'We had a fine day at the races.
Monica tells me you don't like a flutter, Gordon.'

'Where I come from there wasn't a penny to spare, Dan. Never got the knack, that's all. I've nothing against it. In principle. No, indeed.'

The circle on the lawn got holes in it and the wind blew through the holes. I wrapped my arms round myself.

Georgie was licking foam off his beer glass.

My mom said: 'Georgie, please don't do that.'

'Dan, a word, if you'll permit.'

'Feel free,' my grandpa said.

Gordon looked across at Georgie, he looked across at me.

'We're family,' my grandpa said.

'With respect – it's rather private.'

'Well then, let's go inside.'

Georgie lay on the grass. He had a hard shine in his eyes. He took some beer in his mouth and he rolled it between his cheeks, and got up very slowly and began snipping roses. That's what he always did when he had no place to be. He went off and made somewhere of his own. I built secret places and hid in them. Georgie went inside himself. He did it in church and at political meetings, he did it down at the swings and slides when the Ghost Squad came, he did it when he saw Gordon. But he wanted to know what Gordon said all the same. I saw that when Gordon told him about chicken in the pot, he listened, when Gordon marched he looked, when

Gordon said that if we didn't win we were dead meat, Georgie looked at him all the time. I didn't like it.

Gordon came back, walking in a funny way, with his toecaps pointing out and the ends of his shorts bouncing on his knees.

My mom gave her brilliant dark smile. 'Well, how did that go?'

'You could say it was fairly successful. Yes, indeed. I enjoyed a modicum of success.'

My gran said: 'But where is Dan?'

Gordon said: 'He was on the phone when I left. He was having words.'

I lay on the grass. 'Modicum,' I said. What did it mean? I didn't care. It sounded like lead, it took you down, like being buried – 'mo-di-cum'.

My gran said to me: 'Let's go and find your grandpa.'

He was sitting in his study and his eyes looked sore. My gran put her hand on his arm. 'Did Gordon say something to upset you?'

'Sweet Jesus.' He blinked and shook his head. '*Gordon?* A drink is what I need. Where is that factotum? Martin, tell Georgie to bring me a whisky.'

My gran pressed her fingers hard to her lips, as if she were kissing them.

'Kei's been at it. Hasn't he?'

'According to Leuwenhoff, he's excelled himself this time.'

Georgie came in with the tray, poured him a drink and my grandpa had a big sip.

'God bless you. Georgie, guess what? Boss Kei has been up to no good. And we know what no good he gets up to, don't we?'

'It's some floozy,' my gran said. 'It's some flirty miss passing through town, flogging bar ashtrays or perfume, and Kei's got up to what he ought not to?'

'Worse, much worse.' My grandpa sipped his drink. 'You'll recall Dick Crossly-White spent a lot of time in the bar?'

'Of course I know. Dick Crossly-White drank himself silly.'

'And beside the bar is the billiard table?'

'I know that too, Dan. Why are you telling me this?'

'I am telling you because it was in the bar, upon that very billiard table, that Kei disported himself with Jean Crossly-White.'

'Dan, Dan, tell me it's not true.'

'On the Sabbath, if you want to know the worst. According to reports swirling round Curzon like poison gas, there was adultery on the green baize.'

'What's adultery, Grandpa?'

My grandpa said: 'Adultery, my dear, is an illicit conjunction with someone else's wife or husband. An unlawful getting or joining together of persons who should not be got or joined together.'

'Georgie, please take Martin outside,' my gran said.

My grandpa punched his fist into his palm. 'Mother of God. All I asked Kei to do was run the bar. Instead he's found *in flagrante delicto*, on my billiard table.'

'It's a weakness of the glands, Dan.'

'It's his priapic fits, Mabel.'

'We knew about his predilections.' My gran took his hand and held it.

'Crossly-White's making noises about suing Kei for "alienation of affection".'

He saw my eyes. He put his arms round me and kissed the top of my head. 'That's when someone loves you, and another person comes along and stops that person loving you.'

I remembered the bar but I couldn't think of anything that could have caused trouble. Mrs Crossly-White's shoes had fallen off, and that was fine, because you weren't supposed to put anything on the billiard table.

My grandpa groaned. 'Dick keeps saying he gave us the Hall for the Big Mielie Day and this is how we repay him. He also happens to be chairman of the Liquor Licensing Board. He can close me down tomorrow. If I lose my liquor licence it's tickets.'

After a while, my gran said: 'And Gordon?'

'Gordon?' He looked at her as if he didn't know who that was. 'Gordon? Small beer and no great surprise. He's very brittle is that man. He spoke. I listened. Then the phone went.'

'He wants to marry her?'

'He does.'

'It's not been easy for her. Poor girl.'

'Mabel, it's madness. If she remarries – bang goes her air force pension. And what's she getting in return? A pinched and peaky revenue man. A gamekeeper. A man who never has a flutter . . .'

My gran said: 'He's not much fun, perhaps—'

'A bank clerk. A bog Methodist to boot.'

'Presbyterian, Dan.'

'She may as well marry a policeman.'

'Oh, Dan, would you go so far?'

Georgie came over and put his hand softly on my grandpa's sleeve.

'Shame, Mr Mac. My heart is sore.'

I said: 'What's *flagranto delicto*?

My gran said: 'Georgie, please take Martin into the garden.'

We went outside and under the tree we saw Gordon and my mom sitting together; they were holding hands. It was a sight to chill the blood. I walked up to them and said: 'Uncle Kei's been having adultery.'

'What did you say?' my mom said.

'Uncle Kei's being doing adultery – with Mrs Crossly-White.'

My mom jumped up and she pushed her hand to her mouth and said really loud, in her absolutely flabbergasted voice: 'Martin. What are you saying? Who told you that?'

'It's true, isn't it, Georgie?'

'Boss Mac – he said so,' Georgie said. 'Poor Boss Mac.'

'That Jean Crossly-White. I *told* you she was a one,' my mom said. 'Ooh, I could strangle her.'

Gordon said in his thinnest voice: 'Perhaps we might enquire of your parents? Directly. Instead of holding this somewhat intimate conversation in front of a child – and a goggling garden boy.'

Georgie swung me onto his back. 'Bathtime, Martin.'

We went inside and he was smiling and I felt really light on his back. We were passing my grandpa's study and I didn't have to ask him, Georgie stopped, and we heard my mom saying: 'What's to do, Daddy?'

He said: 'Nic Leeuwenhoff gave it to me straight. "Get yourself down here, quick as you can, Dan – if you want to save your hotel. Or there won't be a hotel to save . . ."'

My gran said: 'It seems the lovers won't be parted.'

'Money talks,' my grandpa said.

'Correct me if I'm wrong,' Gordon said. 'But are you planning to bribe Kei?'

'Damn sure I am,' my grandpa said.

Georgie started walking. 'Hold tight, Martin.'

On we went. I felt his muscles under his shirt and I held very tight.

22. Lake Como

Things looked the same at the Villa Vanilla, only they weren't. At the right time in the afternoon Georgie still lifted me onto the gatepost to wait for my mom. And she still ran when she saw me and kissed the top of my head. 'Hello, darling.' Then she said: 'Heavens above. I must fly. Gordon will be here at seven and just *look* at my hair.'

My grandpa went back to Curzon and left a big hole where he had been, and the wind blew through the hole. The Villa Vanilla kept getting smaller. I checked every day to see that everything was where I'd left it. I wasn't sure what I was checking on. I was the ghost of the garden. I had to watch my back. I didn't have height or light or fight or dynamite.

Georgie was my friend. He went down on his one knee. He swung me up on his back and then we were off, down Sligo Road. Amos the barber was there, and the Café de Move On. He bought me doorstops and apricot jam and tea. One day we found a big pile of green and orange bricks in Wexford Road. Georgie fetched them in his wheelbarrow and I built a good new house. Georgie passed a little bottle of Crème de Menthe to me through the window and I set up my house, with sacks on the windows in case it got hot, and an oven in case I wanted to bake some bread. Then we played being me and my grandpa.

Georgie dressed up in a silver suit and took my grandpa's cane and put on my grandpa's fedora. I wore my hood. We perambulated round the garden, stopping outside all my houses and doing a bit of doffing. Georgie was so good at being my grandpa, sometimes you couldn't tell the difference. Except that my grandpa walked in the street. Georgie and I always stayed in the garden.

'If Georgie went walking down Sligo Road dressed like that there'd be riots,' my mom said.

'If Georgie doffed his hat to a white man he'd probably be shot,' my gran said.

'Why?'

'Why? Because this is South Africa, that's why.'

My mom said: 'What will I tell Gordon if he sees you two, prancing around like this? I'm used to it, he isn't. He's from PE.'

We didn't go racing on Saturdays any more. Gordon came round and we sat, and got hot. Gordon was a great sitter, he'd sit in the chair and whistle something very softly, resting his long thin hands on his small bald knees and he'd half sigh, half talk to himself, letting his breath out in a long 'Huh-jhuh'. Sometimes, I don't know why, he said: 'I'm six one in my socks.'

His socks were grey and short and thick, and my mom told Auntie Fee: 'His mother knits them herself.'

'Hoo, boy,' Auntie Fee said.

One day my mom was sitting with Gordon under the palm tree and she said: 'Gordon's a real softie at heart. Go and call Georgie, he wants to talk to you both.'

I was a bit frightened. 'Why?'

'You'll see,' my mom said.

I fetched Georgie. Gordon had a lot of light in his small blue eyes. He looked down his long nose.

'Sit down, boys.'

We sat down on the grass. It was terrible.

My mom waved her hand at the garden. 'Look at the mess. Shacks, sheds, lean-tos. A whole shanty town in our garden.'

I looked, I saw my houses, I didn't know what she meant.

'I'm sorry, darling, but they've got to go.'

'Go where?'

That's when Gordon got his little smile. The one that made more lights shine in his blue eyes. 'How's about this for an idea, Mor-ton? What you've built yourself is a native location. A shanty town. But you didn't ask anyone if you could build your location – right? Your mom is saying you can't go building shacks just like that.'

'Why?'

'We'll let Georgie answer that. What happens to shanties in the wrong place – will you tell us, Mister Georgie?'

Georgie said: 'They're knocked down.'

'Spot on, Mister George,' Gordon said. 'Flattened with a bulldozer.'

'Who knocks them down?'

Georgie thought and said: 'The government.'

'Why?'

'It's the law,' Gordon said. 'You can only build shacks where they say you can build shacks. Otherwise, you'd have shacks all the bloody way from Cape to Cairo. Nasty slums. Like you've made in the garden.'

'But they're my houses.'

Gordon smiled again, it was terrible. 'And you may go on building – in the backyard. Behind the wash lines. Out of sight. Nothing in front of the house.'

He looked at Georgie. 'You savvy, my boy? Any houses you can see from the street get knocked down. From now on, Georgie's the government, right?'

My mom said: 'That's fair, darling. We're not stopping you building. And you can thank Gordon for that. We're just saying – do it in your own area . . .'

I knew a lot of Georgies. He had been my nanny and a shebeen king and the family bank, he had been my grandpa in his silver suit, perambulating but not doffing. He had been my trusty henchman, Little George. Now he was also the government, he pushed his wheelbarrow all over the garden. 'Beep, beep – here comes the government . . .' The wheel of his barrow had a squeak and he took away all the bricks, back to where I'd found them. It broke my heart when the bricks banged in the bottom of the barrow. Soon there was nothing left where my houses had been.

'Sorry, sorry, sorry,' Georgie said. 'It's the law.'

You could see he liked being the government. Better than he liked doing the garden. Just like Gordon said.

I started wearing my hood all the time. It felt safer. I kept my bow ready. Gordon always said the same thing when he saw me: 'How's the old bahm-teckla, Mor-ton?' Then he said: 'I'm just pulling your leg, aren't I, Mor-ton? We're not at war, are we? I was just joking. You can take a joke. Can't you, boy?'

He wasn't pulling my leg, we were at war and I couldn't take a joke . . .

'Can we please not fight?' my mom said.

Gordon talked about Italy. That's where he'd had his war. It wasn't a war like my dad's war, he didn't go dancing, he didn't take the Dak. He didn't like anyone he'd met in the war. Not the ruddy Limeys, or the damn Yanks, not the bloody gyppos. And he said the filthy Eyeties were one rung below the effing munts. The only thing he liked about his war was the lakes.

'Am I permitted to talk about Como?' Gordon said.

'Como and Majore. Marvellous stretches of water. The Great Caruso – a magnificent voice.'

My mom lifted a stiff hand to her forehead, like a salute. 'No more war. I've had war up to here.'

She was like that. A door opened in her head and she walked through it and she didn't care that you were knocking and calling on the other side. It meant you hadn't done what she asked and she was deaf till you did.

Gordon didn't know that.

'Come on, Monica, Lake Como isn't war. The Great Caruso isn't war.'

My mom had on her tough-as-nails voice. 'Lake Como and the Great Caruso can take care of themselves, thanks very much. This is a big day and I want happy things. I want us to tell Martin our news.'

Gordon lifted his nose high, sighed through it and then spoke down it.

'Your mother feels you should know – your mother and I are getting married. I'm going to be your father, Mor-ton. You'll be my son. What do you think of that?'

I started walking away, quite fast, because my legs felt empty, as if they were full of air and could go bang like balloons before I got to where I was going. I knew Gordon wanted to marry my mom – my grandpa said so. But I never, ever thought my mom would want to marry Gordon. Why would she want to do that?

And even if she did – and I wasn't saying she did – but *if* she did, why would that make me Gordon's son?

I went and sat behind the mulberry tree. I put the tip of the jacaranda exactly *there* and I put the tip of the red roof exactly *here* and I closed my eyes and breathed very slowly. Then I sang a bit of 'Macushla'. I felt nicely sad. My heart was going very fast. I counted to twenty-one. Then I sang in my head some bits of 'Old Man River'. I took my time over *'He don' say nothing – he must know somethin' . . .'* Then I tried out some words. I started with 'a clip round the earhole'. It tasted awful. I spat it out. I tried 'priapic fits', *'in flagrante delicto'* – the taste of biscuits. While I was tasting, I was thinking: 'What am I going to do with Gordon?'

The sun was warm, the peace of my place was soft, the clouds were high. Maybe I would run away and find Lieutenant Farebrother and say to him: 'Excuse me, sir, but you knew my father before he got killed. Please can I come and live with you?'

And he would say: 'Of course you can, Martin, old man.'

'Fare-brother' tasted good – even if names could be tricky.

I thought and thought and I always came back to Gordon. What to do with Gordon? I said: 'I can be his son. As long as he isn't my father. Or . . . he can be my father – if I don't have to be his son.' But not both. I said: 'I don't care if he's six one in his socks. I don't care if he's getting married.'

Then I heard voices in my head. It was so good, it was so right, it was nice. I was happy. The words jumped into my head and I knew what to do with Gordon.

'Kill him,' they said. 'Just kill him.'

How to do it? I went and got my bow and arrow and shot six arrows at the palm tree in the garden but they all bounced off. That wasn't any good. Robin Hood would have sent an arrow winging into Gordon's black heart. Then I heard Georgie being the government and the bricks falling into his barrow, and I knew how to do it.

23. Teepees

I built a house with purple face-bricks, sharp and new. I got them from the corner of Wexford and Tipperary Roads. I built my house in the middle of the lawn, under the palm tree – right across from the white pillars and the red stoop and the yellow shutters. It was big. It had a dining room and a kitchen and a larder and a big front door. I put bricks across the front door so no one could come in till I was ready. It had corrugated iron for a roof and a hole in the iron where the chimney would be. People could talk to me through the chimney. My house was the tallest ever, it shook when I breathed. I kept building the walls higher and saying: 'Oh, please God, please don't let it fall, not yet . . .'

When it was finished, I sat down in the dark and waited.

Georgie stuck his head through the chimney hole. 'What you doing, Martin? This house is in the front garden. The government's going to have to come along – and do you-know-what. Are you up to something, Martin?'

I didn't say anything. He looked at me and he looked at the tall walls and he knew I was up to something. He went away to tell my mom. Everything was going fine. I wanted to give my mom one last chance.

Her face was at the chimney hole then. 'For pity's sake. What are you up to? Gordon is going to have a fit. A shack, right in the middle of the lawn. What are you doing to me?'

I looked up at her. 'Why?

She got her frown, her pretty 'ex-cuse me' frown.

'I don't understand – why what?'

'Why's he here?'

'What kind of a question is that?'

'Why?'

'I wish you'd stop saying that. What was I supposed to do?'

Do? She wasn't supposed to do anything. What was there to do? Except do nothing. We were fine, we had each other, why did she have to go and change it?

'Wasn't I entitled to a life?'

I knew how she felt when she felt flabbergasted. How could she ask me a question like that? A life – until Gordon we'd had a good life. We had a house and a garden and a deal and everything was fine. Now it was broken.

'We were all alone, who was going to look after us?'

Look after us? *We* were going to look after us, that's who. *Alone?* We weren't alone, we had us – until now, until Gordon. It got boiling hot inside my head. I was shouting in my head. It wasn't fair. If she wanted this Gordon then let her take him – but DON'T, DON'T give him to me.

'Gordon wants what's best for you – for us. You'll see.'

I knew what Gordon wanted. A boy needs to watch his back.

'I don't say you have to like him. Not straight away. But please, please promise me you'll try. That's all I ask.'

I heard her going away, she was crying. I wanted to say: 'Please don't cry, I'm sorry, come back, I promise . . .' But I didn't. She wanted a Gordon, any Gordon would do. Maybe it would have been OK if we'd got some other Gordon, only we got this one and I had to do something about him.

I closed the hole in the roof with the corrugated iron, took down the bricks that closed my door and opened it. I was ready.

He came though the doorway, crawling on his knees. 'Time you and I had a little chat.' His voice was quivery in the dark. I could see a bit of his moustache. 'Your mom is very unhappy. "Talk to him, Gordon." She says it all the time. I must tell you that I like you, really. I said it was a waste of breath, you were so dead against me nothing would change you, but she made me try. Here I am.'

He sat back on his heels. In the dark he looked like a

horse. I leaned back against the walls. I felt the bricks move. 'Bricks, be my friends,' I prayed.

'What do you say? War or peace?' Gordon's voice was high in his nose, more quavery, more angry, and if it hadn't been Gordon he would have been crying but I didn't believe Gordon could cry so I didn't believe he was doing it. 'I've done as I promised your mom. I've tried to talk to you, man to man – and what do I get? You sit there, like some sort of bloody spastic. If you want bloody well war, that's what we'll have and I'll break you down to sawdust. Watch me, Mor-ton, watch . . .'

Gordon started to crawl out of my house, backwards on his knees. I leaned back, I pushed and still nothing happened. The walls wobbled but they wouldn't fall. Then he was gone and I was sitting there with my eyes shut and the house fell down.

I lay under the bricks, close to the ground. I had a lot of dust in my mouth and something wet on my face. I didn't care. I was low down, small, close to the earth. I lay there. Maybe I was dead. The dead were short people, that's why you could talk to them. Tall people thought they were so great just because they were walking around. Being tall. Tall walls, tall people. *Teepees.*

My grandpa was right. You looked up and there they were, looking down, like trees with knees. *Tee-pees.* Their faces up there, in the sky. You tried to talk to Them but they didn't talk like you. Their ears were so far off the ground. You said to Them: 'But that isn't what you said – *this* is what you said,' then they looked at you like you were mad. They went deaf, went cold and went away. They didn't remember.

Teepees said: 'That was then. This is now.'

You said: 'But you *promised* . . .'

They said: 'Did I?'

Blotting out the sky, putting out the sun. *Teepees* thought they were the bosses of everything.

They gave me the screaming heebies. Yes, sireee.

Repeat and remember . . .

I heard my mom: 'Glory be, this child will be the death of me. First, he builds the biggest ever shanty where he isn't allowed to, then it collapses round his ears. Martin, what are you doing to me?'

I heard Gordon: 'Planning to bump yourself off, Morton? And your hat too? This is one shack the government won't have to demolish, you've done it yourself.'

I lay very still. Glad the bricks were on top of me. Glad I didn't have to look at any of them. Georgie began to pull the bricks off me. I wished he wouldn't. Better die in the ditch than live with the New Lot, said my grandpa. Better dead in your own house than alive under Gordon, said I.

I heard Georgie: 'Hold tight, Martin, I'll get you out.'

I hated Gordon but it wasn't any good – I hadn't killed him. That was all that mattered. It wasn't Gordon dead under the bricks, it was me, and Gordon was up there, in the sky.

24. The Walk

I got up quite early the next morning and went to the
kitchen. I put on my Robin Hood hat. I got the bread
out of the yellow bin and the black-handled bread knife
from the white drawer. A little grey light was pushing
through the blinds. I didn't like the way it looked. The
handle of the bread knife was very black. It was hard
cutting the loaf. I got a few slices done and wrapped
them in greaseproof paper, like Mrs Snippalipsky did. I
cut some cheese, took three tomatoes, put it all in a tin
lunchbox and went out of the house.

I walked in the garden. I was in 99 Sligo Road all
right, but it was also *some other place*. It felt different,
and a bit cold. I had scratchy spaces behind my eyes.
Things had another look. Like they weren't expecting to
see me this early, like they hadn't had time to get ready
to look the way they were supposed to look. Like I
wasn't supposed to be there.

What if you only *thought* you had a place. What if it
was only pretending to be your place – while you were
around? Then as soon as you turned your back and

went off, it forgot you, because it wasn't truly your place. It was its own place. Everywhere was its own place. You were nowhere, really.

I walked to the gate and climbed very quietly over the cool brown wood. No one heard me, not even Georgie. I walked down Sligo Road under the cool shadows of the trees. I passed Dr Verwoerd's house and it was very quiet, and when I got to Park Road, across from the lake, I could see the grass was all wet. I walked over to the swings and slides. I even swung for a bit, until it got too cold.

I walked along Erin Avenue, towards the zoo.

I started singing, but quietly: '*Never mind the weather, as long as we're together, we're off to see the Wild West Show, the elephant and the kangaroo-oo-oo . . .*'

In the early morning I could smell the zoo, and I thought of all the animals behind the black pointy stakes of the fence, the tiger with his grin, the elephant that my mom took me for rides on and the monkeys cracking monkey nuts and throwing the shells at people. Suddenly I wanted my mom and I wanted to go home. But then I didn't. If I went home Gordon would be there.

I walked the way the tram went, the way we drove in my grandpa's Packard on our way to the races. Climbing the long hill towards Parktown Ridge and the mansions of the abysmally rich, who were worth an absolute mint. The road looked bare and grey and chill, and I didn't like that much – on the other hand I knew no one was

watching so I sang a bit more: '*Ha, ha, ha, hee, hee, hee*
... *Little Brown Jug, I love thee*...' I sang like I was
marching, like I was my own band and my own conductor, banging one foot down in time to the words.

It felt good to get a rhythm going.

Next I did 'The Song of the Boer': '*Then ride, ride,
ride*...'

The road ran up the Ridge and when I got to the top
I sat down on the pavement and ate my sandwich. Then
I was still hungry so I ate another, and soon all my food
was gone. I didn't want to carry the empty lunchbox so
I put it behind a hedge and walked on.

A car came up the hill and went over the brow, where
the road branched for town to one side, and Turffontein
on the other, and I was so pleased to see the car I
stopped and watched. There was a man driving. He
wore a brown suit and glasses and he sat next to his
wife, who wore a brown hat with a green flower on it. I
waved; they slowed right down to a crawl and stared
and stared.

I hoped they'd stop and ask me who I was and where
I was going. But they didn't.

I walked slowly. My feet seemed to know where they
were going. When I got into town, I knew where I was.
The air had got a bit warmer and there were a lot of
cars and no one stared. I followed the tramlines. I knew
the names of the streets, the conductor on the tram used
to call them out – Jeppe and Eloff and Commissioner ...

I knew where I was, I knew where I was going. Only I couldn't find it. I walked some more. I was still fine. Yes, siree. I walked and walked, and the town got more and more busy, the trams came past with their bells ringing, grinding the ground under my feet. I stopped and watched the trams, the driver stood up twisting two handles, and I knew one was to make the tram go faster and the other was to make it stop but which was which?

I passed the Corner Lounge, which was above Cuthbert's Shoe Shop, and Ciro's, where my mom used to dance with my dad to the Palm Court Orchestra, before he took the Dak Up North. I passed the Coliseum, where I'd been with the Snippalipskys just one night ago. In the street outside the Coliseum there were lots of snake charmers sitting in front of their baskets, playing penny whistles, and one man with a thin nose said: 'You want to see my cobra, sonny? Only a penny.' But I didn't have a penny and I didn't want to see his cobra.

I walked a lot but I didn't get any nearer to finding it. I sat down then, on the pavement. A man came and sat next to me. His black shoes were very shiny and his grey socks were amazingly smooth. He wore a hat with a green ribbon, and his moustache was cut very sharp. He did look at me when he sat down, but he didn't look at me when he spoke, and it made it easier to speak to him.

'Where's your mommy?'

'At home.'

'Where's your daddy?'

'He's dead.'

'Shame, little boss.'

'He bought it, Up North.'

'My heart is sore.'

'I'm half an orphan.'

'Shame, my little boss.'

'I don't mind.'

'Where you going, little boss?'

'To Anstey's.'

He stood up and held out his hand. I didn't have to ask him where we were going, I just knew. People stared at us, but I was used to having a man nanny and holding his hand and having everyone stare at us.

Anstey's was the same as always. We walked through the revolving doors and over our heads the brass canisters whizzed, and the elevators climbed like snakes right through the air. They were better than cobras any day. The floorwalker saw us. He wore his black jacket and black tie and pointy collar. This time he said: 'Well, my boy, what do you want?'

I thought he was speaking to me and I said: 'I've come for tea and rabbit scoff.'

He wasn't talking to me, he was talking to the black man, who said: 'This boy wanted to come to Anstey's, so I brought him.' He patted me on the shoulder: 'Go well, little boss.' He walked away. I was sorry to see him go. I watched the green ribbon in his hat until I couldn't see him any more.

The floorwalker said: 'Well, I'm blowed.' He called someone. 'Come look what the wind's blown in.'

It was Maisie the manageress who came to look. I was sure she'd know who I was but she said: 'What's your name?'

'My name is Martin Donally. I live at 99 Sligo Road, Parkside.'

They seemed to stop worrying then, they asked me what I'd like to eat and I said cheese sandwiches and rabbit scoff, and they brought me a big plate of sandwiches, with lettuce cut so fine it was like shoelaces, and a glass of orange juice. I ate it all. Then the floor manager let me send a brass canister whizzing across the roof of the shop. All the counters had curtains across them and you could hide right inside the counter.

I really liked being there, it was a good place, Anstey's.

I was riding up and down on the escalator when my mom walked in. She had Gordon with her and they didn't look at me, not at first. I was sorry I wasn't under a counter then, or behind a curtain. I was sorry I hadn't watched my back. A boy needs height.

My mom said: 'I've been worried sick. How on earth did he get here?'

Maisie said: 'A native man brought him.'

Gordon said: 'Christ Almighty.'

My mom looked like she must have looked when I nearly died and the doctors and nurses had worked their fingers to the bone to save me, when I wouldn't take her blood and she didn't know where to put her face.

'A native. My godfathers. What next?'

'He seemed to know this native,' Maisie said.

My mom put her hand to her heart. 'He walked into Anstey's, with a native. He's only five. I've been half out of my mind. Honestly, Martin, who was this native?'

I didn't say anything.

'Your son—' Gordon said to my mom. 'Correct me if I'm wrong, but it would seem that your *son* – ' he said it like my grandpa said 'sportsmen', using a lot of hiss – 'your s-s-s-on waltzed in here, on the arm of some Af.'

'I know that. I heard that myself. You don't have to tell me that,' my mom said.

'He was no trouble,' Maisie said.

Gordon said: 'Makes a change.'

My mother looked at me, her eyes big and dark and sad. 'What are we going to do with you, Martin?'

'Really, no trouble at all,' Maisie said again. 'We gave him something to eat. No harm's done, hey?'

I liked Maisie. She was on my side. She was beginning to be sorry she'd called my mom. But it was too late. I was caught, I was surrounded.

Gordon said: 'I see we're still wearing our bahm-teckla.'

I reached up and touched my green feather.

'Ach, shame,' Maisie said. 'It's his Robin Hood hat. He's kept it on all the time. That's your Robin Hood hat, isn't it, hey, *boykie?*'

'He's lucky he didn't get carried off by this boy, back to the location. Who knows?' Gordon said. 'He could have been stolen away. Vanished for ever.'

'My godfathers,' my mom said. 'Don't even *say* that, you'll give me a heart attack. I don't know where to put my face. Martin, what do you say to the manager lady for all the trouble you've caused?'

I said: 'I'm sorry.'

'Louder,' Gordon said.

Maisie said: 'It's nothing.'

She was really sorry now, she knew she'd handed me over to the enemy.

My mom said: 'What have I done to deserve a child like this?'

'He's not a bad little chap,' Maisie said.

We took the tram home to Sligo Road. I sat next to the window and my mom sat next to me, and Gordon sat behind us, saying in his very, very serious way: 'I hope you appreciate the pain you've caused your mother.'

My mom said: 'I simply don't understand. Why, Martin, why? Can you tell me why? How do you think I felt? Out of the blue I got the call, and this woman says; "It's Anstey's here. We've got your son. Come to haberdashery . . ."'

I looked at my face in the window of the bus. I saw the feather in my Robin Hood hat.

'With a flash of steel Robin Hood ran the varlet through . . .'

'. . . "Come to haberdashery" – those were her exact words. I very nearly had a cadenza.'

Every word hurt. Not because she was sad but because I was sad. Sad because I'd been found. Through the bus window I saw lots of black men sitting on the side of the road, and I thought maybe what Gordon said was true and black men took you back to the native location with them. We passed the Coliseum and I remembered how I'd cried until Mr Snippalipsky gave me his handkerchief. I nearly started all over again. I remembered back to the stars in the roof, and the men with their binoculars staring at the girls who lifted their skirts and showed their BTMs. And Mr Snippalipsky as the old Onion singer: he really was a master of disguise. I wished I'd been a master of disguise.

'He's gone for ever more . . .'

'I can see your lips moving, Martin.' My mom turned back to Gordon.

'This child talks to himself, and he thinks I don't know but I always know because he moves his lips.'

'Only mad people talk to themselves,' Gordon said.

'What were you saying, Martin?' my mother said.

'Spit it out,' Gordon said. His voice was very PE again. '*Sput Et Ut, Mor-ton.*'

I started singing:

'*He's gone for ever more, at the age of ninety-four,*
And the memory of him I'll always save.
So I'm going to the graveyard, to fulfil his last request,
Just to plant a bunch of onions on his grave.'

'My godfathers,' my mom said, ' "to plant a bunch of onions"? Where on earth did you get that from?'

'From Rosa's dad.'

'And who might Rosa's dad be – when he's at home?' Gordon asked.

'He means the Snippalipskys, the neighbours. They're Jewish.'

'That comes as no great surprise,' Gordon said. 'Bloody Jews.'

He lifted his hand and I thought: 'Here it comes. The good biff, the clip round the earhole.' Then my head went cold and I wondered why. Gordon opened the window and said: 'I'm sick of that.'

My mom said to me: 'Now, look what you've done.'

I reached up to see if my hat was there. It wasn't.

Look what I'd done . . .

My mom said to Gordon: 'You shouldn't have done that. He loved that hat.'

'I beg to differ, Monica. Sometimes one needs to be

cruel to be kind. You do the boy no favours. He's got to learn to cope, and the sooner he's got into a normal environment, the bloody better. No more kiss curls, no more building those funny little shacks. No more politics.'

I shouted then: 'Stop the bus.'

'We can't stop the bus, darling.'

'We *won't* stop the bus,' Gordon said. 'Who the hell do you think you are? It's about time you woke up.'

I sat very still. I was hot, but my head was cold. The bus went on, my hat was somewhere behind me. I opened my mouth a few times but nothing came out.

When we got home I went to find Georgie in the garden. I told him. I kept waiting to cry, but I didn't. Georgie hugged me close.

'Did you see it fall?'

'We were just passing Mrs Minniver's.'

All I knew was that it had gone. I went to my place and sat down. I thought and thought. I started to see something and it was my hat that showed me. The way it went showed me how to go. I would get lost, again. I'd go anywhere they said I shouldn't. If Mr Snips, leaning back in the Snippalipsky Buick, had said: 'We're off to Cape Town, New York, Jupiter – want to ride along, Martin?' I'd have gone. If the black man had said: 'Come back to the location,' I'd have gone. Anywhere would be fine – under Amos's big barber stool, behind the counters at Anstey's.

To anywhere that wasn't home.

With anyone who wasn't Gordon.

I'd go with blasted Limeys and effing munts, nancy boys, blooming Eyeties and damn yanks. Devious little buggers were my friends, and bladdy Jews. I liked hats, stories, silver suits, racehorses, songs, pilots. Whatever he hated, I liked. I liked nancy boys and Georgie and Robin Hood and the Glorious Dead. Once upon a time, I'd been scared of being lost. I wasn't scared any more, I had a plan – I would spend the rest of my life being lost. And if they came along and leaned over me and said: 'That's OK, talking like that, but where exactly do you think you're going to get lost in? Hey? Tell us that!' I had my answer ready and it was a good answer.

'Anywhere that ISN'T *here*.'

I closed my eyes to stop the tears and kept them tight shut, and swayed very carefully and sang in my head: *'She'll be comin' round the mountain when she comes. She'll be wearing pink pyjamas when she comes . . .'*

In the beginning I used to think I never would get lost, as long as I stayed where I was. So I stayed where I was – and it was my mom who got lost. But I didn't miss her like I thought I would.

I really missed my hat.

25. Little Green Apples

I remember election day because nothing happened, and everyone went out and left just Georgie and me. There were bits of paper all over the street. There was an eye on this bit, and a tooth on that bit, and sometimes a bit of beard. It was all perfectly normal. The Brainless Brigade tore down the posters of General Smuts. The Brainless Brigade hated Our Djann, so they came in the night and ripped him to shreds. It was all fine.

Uncle Matt said: 'Morons is what they are. We'll give them a bloody good hiding.'

I remember election day because Uncle Matt wore his yellow flower. He was getting ready to walk the seat in Boksburg North. I remember election day because Mr and Mrs Snippalipsky came by in their car and said they were going to vote early, in case the All-White Wonders made trouble.

'I went to hear Smuts last night, and their foot soldiers climbed into our people with their fists.'

I said: 'The Brainless Brigade always fight at meetings. It's perfectly normal.'

He smiled his Onion man's smile. 'Well, I'm blowed. Maybe they feel about the ballot a bit like PE feels about balls. Show them a ball and they hit it.'

Mrs Snips said: 'I hear you've been travelling, Martin? All the way from here to Anstey's is quite a trip. Just promise me you won't run off to PE?'

I promised.

I remember election day because my grandpa came up from Curzon. His eyes were bruised, but his silver suit was wonderful, and we did a bit of perambulating in Sligo Road, and doffing of his Homburg. It was just like old times.

'Your grandpa is very gay, all things considered,' my gran said.

I heard him singing in his bath: '*I kiss the dear fingers so toil-worn for me. Ohhh, God bless you and keep you, Mother machree.*' He got just the right amount of wobble in his voice. It brought a sob to the heart. John McCormack would have been proud of him. He also sang about the girl he left behind him, where the River Shannon flows – '*and I'll bless the ship that takes me to my dear old Erin Isle . . .*'

I wanted to ask him when he was going home to old Erin to his old mam but I remembered what Auntie Fee said and so I asked him instead: 'Do you want to play the Swiftly Flowing Stream? You can be you and I'll be your old mam.'

'Not today, dear heart. Perhaps tomorrow. We're off

uto see Our Djann, in his glory. You'll tell your grand-children about this day, Martin.'

As Georgie and I went down to the park we passed Dr Verwoerd's house. It was empty, I thought maybe he was still voting. Everyone in the world was voting, except me and Georgie. I remember election day because we were going to eat them for breakfast and I was hungry all day.

We stopped at the Café de Move On and Miriam said: 'What you having, boys?'

We had tea and doorstops, like always.

Rosa Snippalipsky was at the park but she wasn't walking on her hands any more. 'I grew out of it,' she said. I was sad about that. She looked ordinary when she walked on her legs like everyone else. I wanted to say: 'You shouldn't grow out of things.' But I asked her if she wanted me to push her on the swing, and she did.

Rosa said: 'My dad says we're getting walloped.'

'Walloped?'

'In the election. He heard it on the wireless.'

'We can't.'

'Why can't we?'

'Because my uncle Matt's going to walk his seat.'

Georgie said we had to go then, and he carried me back and I held tight to his neck and breathed him in. Leather and coffee and peppermints. We waved to Amos the barber, and he said to Georgie: '*Hau*, it's bad.'

Amos said: 'What we going to do now, Martin?'

I thought he meant about putting on soap and shaving me but he didn't. He put his hand on my shoulder and looked into my eyes. Georgie and I walked home up Sligo Road. Dr Verwoerd still wasn't in his garden.

'What's bad, Georgie?'

'The world's bad, Martin.'

That night there was music and I heard lots of people. Auntie Fee came to my bedroom and she smelt of whisky and Goldflake cigarettes.

'We're celebrating. We've rolled back the carpet. And we're dancing. I can't read to you tonight, darling.'

'Mr Snips says we're being walloped.'

'Nonsense, we're going to walk it.' Then she kissed me. 'When did he hear that?'

'This morning, on the wireless.'

'Well, let no one say I didn't say so,' Auntie Fee said.

I lay and listened to the music, and stored some good bits in my head. *'If you knew Suzie, like I knew Suzie, oh, oh, oh what a gal . . .'* Then a glass broke, then someone laughed and someone else said out loud: 'Here's to Matthew. Hip, Hip, Hooray!' And everyone shouted: 'Hooray!'

Then I went to sleep.

Next morning early I got up and Uncle Matt was in the garden. He wasn't wearing his yellow rosette on his coat and when I asked him why not, he didn't answer but I got a fright because he looked at me. His eyes were wet. For the rest of the day it was very quiet. No one talked to me. My mom came home in the middle of the day and she kept saying: 'My golly, oh golly me. Daddy's taking it very badly. He's in bed. Martin, go and play in the garden.'

Georgie was in the garden but he wouldn't tell me what the matter was, he just shook his head and said: 'Hah.'

Mr Snippalipsky was at the fence and he said: 'The Bone-Headed Brigade won the day. Where's your grandpa?'

'Don't know.'

'I just hope he's right about who they'll come for first – Holy Romans, then the Jews. Tell him I said so.'

Uncle Matt was sitting under the palm tree. The big yellow rosette on his jacket looked like a dead rose. You thought Georgie would come along any moment and snip it off.

He said: 'We've had it, Martin boy. It's a calamity. The New Lot are in. We're out.'

'Didn't we walk it?'

'We did not. Even Our Djann – in Standerton – lost his seat. The Prime Minister. The Walking Disasters walked it.'

He took his yellow rosette off his jacket and threw it into the dahlias.

Everyone was strange, even Gordon, who sat by

himself, shaking his head and saying: 'Well, I'm buggered.'

Only Auntie Fee was herself. 'I told them. Didn't I tell them, Jack?'

And he said: 'You did, Finoonie, I have to say you did.'

Georgie watered the garden from top to bottom, he watered it until everything was streaming. His back was pouring with sweat.

I said to him: 'I'll tell you the story of "The Swiftly Flowing Stream". My grandpa sees a man drowning in the river and pulls him out, and he gets beaten by his da, and then he runs away, to South Africa, to fight for the Boers. You can play my grandpa, and I'll play the man you save from drowning. Shall we play?'

'I don't want to play your grandpa.'

'Why not?'

He shook his head and went back to watering the garden. It was the first time ever Georgie hadn't done what I asked.

I met my gran and she said: 'Martin, won't you go in and see your grandpa? He's in bed. He's not feeling very well, but I'm sure he'd love to see you.'

I wandered into my grandpa's room. He had the blanket rolled round him and he was staring at the wall. I asked him if he wanted to play a story. He didn't say anything. He just lay there with his back to me staring at the wall, without moving. I spoke to him but he didn't speak to me. He was turned away from me, looking at the wall. I wondered if he was crying, like Cousin Caítlín when she took to her bed. I looked at the floor but there was no map.

I went out again and my gran said: 'Did he speak?'

I shook my head.

And she cried and that was terrible. I didn't know what to do, so I went outside. In the garden by the roses I found Uncle Matt's yellow flower. I didn't like to leave it there getting muddy but I didn't want to pick it up so I just looked at it for a bit. Then Georgie came along with the garden fork and he stabbed the rosette right though the middle and carried it on his fork and threw it onto the compost heap.

26. Gordon the Good

My grandpa went on staying at the Grange, because he was saving it. I wished he wouldn't. He should have been on his way home to Ireland, to his old mam, who was waiting and worrying and saying to herself: 'Where on earth has that boy got to?' But he just stayed at the Grange, saving it. Except, sometimes, when he came back to Sligo Road, very white and very tired, and he wouldn't tell me when he was going to Ireland and we didn't go perambulating.

'Daddy is the worse for wear,' Auntie Fee said and she opened her lips wide and spoke the words without saying them, in case my grandpa heard her. 'The iron has entered the soul.'

The iron wasn't any of the things I had thought it was, not a nail in the hoof or a thorn in the lion's paw. It wasn't hot or sharp; iron was cold. The iron pricked your soul and made little holes and the wind blew through the holes . . . and you shivered, the way my mom did when someone walked over her grave.

My mom said: 'Honestly, just to think of Kei and that

Jean Crossly-White, and the grief it caused Daddy, I could wring her neck.'

Auntie Fee came to read to me and I said: 'When's Grandpa going home to Ireland?'

Auntie Fee got her soft and melting look and kissed me and looked at me.

'He's not going.'

'But he must. What about the *Pendennis Castle*? And the captain's table?'

'What about them?'

'What about the string orchestra? And the white linen?'

She hugged me close. 'Sweetheart, if Auntie Fee doesn't tell you, who will? Believe me, he isn't going. Saving the Grange is taking every bean. Ireland's gone the way of all good things. Poor Daddy. He'll never see home again.'

'What about his poor old mam?'

My grandpa promised her, he said he was coming. She'd be waiting. I saw her at the window of the MacBride hovel, waiting and worrying and missing her boy who ran off to Africa to fight for Kroojer.

Auntie Fee laughed and coughed and smoke came out of her nose and hung on her eyelashes.

'No dosh, darling.'

'I'll go to Ireland and see my grandpa's old mam and give her some presents – but first I'm going to Palestine, to see my father's grave and fix the spelling.'

'When?'

'When I'm big.'

'Hoo, boy, how will you do that? It costs the earth.'

'I will. You'll see.'

'Fat chance. It took all your grandpa's money just buying two tickets for Ireland, and you're going to visit Palestine and Ireland?'

'When I'm big. Just you wait.'

'Better hurry, dear,' she said in her ogre's voice. 'Time's running out.'

One day we all went to Curzon. We walked into the bar. Aphrodite watched us, my grandpa was polishing glasses.

My mom said: 'Daddy, can't you find someone to help out?'

My grandpa was warm and big and he smiled, like always, but his eyes were tired. 'No one else but me can save it. Kei keeps talking of coming back.'

'It'll be the death of you, Daddy,' my mom said.

'Then be sure to lay me beside my brother Michael. Believe me, I'll be coming back to haunt the dominee – a good Catholic ghost to put the fear of God into him.'

'Daddy – don't,' my mom said.

'May I make a suggestion?' Gordon said. He was standing right under Aphrodite, his ear was under her breast and she seemed to be smiling at him.

'Fire away,' my grandpa said.

'I'd like to help, if I can?'

My grandpa said: 'That's decent, Gordon, but I fear the damage is done.'

'When you had to bail out Kei, it wrecked you.'

'It's only money,' my grandpa said.

'Those funds were for your trip home to Ireland? You were going home to see your mother, whom I believe is elderly. And ailing, if I hear correctly.'

'What are you driving at, Gordon?' my mom asked.

Gordon held up a hand. 'Allow me to finish, Monica.'

My grandpa was listening and my mom was lifting her eyebrows in that way that said she was feeling flabbergasted.

They were listening really hard.

'What I'm saying is – I've got a bit put away, a legacy my father left me. It isn't huge but it is enough to see you home to Ireland. Say the word, Mac, and it's yours.'

My grandpa was pulling off his yellow driving glove and putting it on again.

'That's nothing short of noble. Isn't it, Mabel?'

My gran reached out and patted Gordon's cheek. 'That is so kind.'

'But we couldn't possibly take it,' my grandpa said.

'Kei needs some help,' Gordon said. 'Perhaps he'd take it?'

'He would,' my gran said. 'Oh, Gordon . . .' She patted his cheek again.

'Excuse me,' my mom said, 'Uncle Kei's gone and

ruined Daddy, he's gone and . . . well, you know what he does with that Jean Crossly-White, and you want to give him money?'

'The garage isn't going well. He talks about coming back and if he comes back to Curzon, he'll have one of his fits, sure as shooting,' my gran said.

'Daddy, you've just bought him a garage. Isn't that enough?'

'He has to live,' my grandpa said.

'It would ease him into a new life,' my gran said. 'He needs easing does my brother. D'you mean that, Gordon? You'd advance some cash to Kei?'

'Certainly.'

'We cannot accept it,' my grandpa said.

'Even if it were a way of making sure Kei never came back?' my gran said.

My grandpa sighed. 'Let's go and tell him.'

We got back in the car and drove over to Heidelberg. Kei had on white overalls, with grease all over his chest, and in yellow letters on his chest it said HEIDELBERG MOTORS – PETROL, PLEASURE, PADKOS. When he saw us he thought we had come to keep an eye on him, until my grandpa said: 'Wipe that frown off your forehead, man. Gordon's got some good news for you.'

Kei and Gordon went inside and when they came out Kei was smiling with all the yellow teeth in his mouth, and he had his arm round Gordon's shoulders and Gordon's white teeth kept jumping up under his moustache like rabbits in the veldt. Kei pointed his finger at Gordon's chest.

'This is the best, the most decent man I've had the privilege to meet. A white man, through and through. D'you hear, young Martin? If I were you I'd consider myself lucky to be his son. Honoured.'

I didn't know what to say. My mom said she didn't see why Jean Crossly-White should always get off scot-free. My gran hugged Gordon again. My mom put her arm round Gordon. It was terrible. My grandpa said: 'Yours was a gift of rare generosity.'

He said to me: 'Generosity – an open hand and heart, giving without counting the cost, spending treasure out of kindness and concern.'

I didn't like the word, I didn't want it. I couldn't use it.

We drove back to Jo'burg and we sang:

> 'And when I die, don't bury me at all,
> Just pickle my bones in alcohol,
> And at my feet lay a turtle dove,
> To show the world I died of love . . .'

I sat in the back of the car. I was dying of something . . . but I didn't know what.

27. The Troll

I was sitting under the palm tree. Gordon came up to me, his chin was high and the edge of a palm tip was touching it, his eyes were smoky, a small grey cloud was next to his ear and I could see the hairs in his nose. I didn't hear what he said till he'd said it a few times.

'We're going somewhere. For once in your life don't ask "why?" OK?'

My mother and Auntie Fee came out of the house and they were crying. They didn't say anything. Gordon backed the Packard down the drive. We all got in. I'd never been driving in the Packard with people who didn't smile. No one sang either.

I started humming: '*If you knew Suzie, like I knew Suzie . . .*'

Gordon said: 'No time for that now, sonny Jim.'

His very black hair was peppery at his neck, and shaven so short it made my teeth hurt. It climbed the bone of the back of his head like the grass Georgie tried and tried to grow in the bare soil around the trunk of our palm tree. Higher up, Gordon's hair got thicker, blacker, shinier, because he wore something on it, something sticky. His ears branched out from the sides of his head and I could see the blue veins that ran from the top edges to the full fat lobes. Gordon's white shirt collar had pointy ends. It was turned down over his grey sportscoat and ran around his neck like a priest's collar. Gordon's shoulders were very straight and the hairs of his grey sportscoat stood straight up.

I sat as far behind him as I could get. When he moved, I moved. He couldn't stare at me, except in the driving mirror. Gordon was a big starer. Gordon's stare crept up on you. You didn't know till you felt something cold and clammy hit you, like a frog jumping onto your wrist, and there it was, Gordon's stare. Looking at you.

My mom always said never to stand out in a storm. Lightning loves a tree, she said. Gordon was a storm, he was what happened when the sky went jagged. Hot. Empty. Angry. The clouds got dark and heavy, the thunder bounced over our heads and the lightning sizzled. Gordon was flash and crash. But no rain. He was parched, desiccated. I was the tree that lightning loved. I never knew where he would strike. His moustache reminded me of veldt grass after a fire, it was short, black, sharp, dry, dead.

Auntie Fee's handbag was red, with big gold lips. It was in her lap. She was snapping the catch. It looked like an angry fish, lying in her lap, opening and closing its shining lips.

I went on singing in my head: '*There's none so classy, as that fair lassie, oh, oh, oh what a gal . . .*'

Gordon was crashing the gears.

My mom coughed the way she coughed when she was edgy.

'Heavens above, Gordon, don't wreck the car. We all want to get there in one piece.'

'If you'd rather drive, please say so.'

My mom didn't say anything, she just raised her eyebrows in her 'ex-cuse me' way. She didn't say anything and the more she didn't say anything, the crosser Gordon got.

'Keep to your bladdy side of the road, man,' he shouted at some other driver. 'Bladdy abbo.'

My mom coughed again and jangled the charm bracelet on her arm. I always knew I'd find my mother in a thicket, in a swamp, in the darkest jungle because of that cough and the golden jangle of the three charms, the boot, the ship, the star.

The golden fish lips flashed in Auntie Fee's lap.

Gordon hissed hotly: 'I ask you – Jesus Christ Almighty – what kind of car's this?'

My mom said: 'Gordon, you know what it is. I told you – it's a Packard.'

'Damn bloody useless American junk. In the war the damn Yanks turned up in Italy, and they had to have ice cream – or they wouldn't damn well march. Coke, or they wouldn't fight.'

He spoke into the empty space in front of him, and I was glad of that. I was spending a lot of time not getting to know Gordon from the front. I couldn't look into his blue-grey eyes without blinking. They were watery and glassy at the same time.

'Give me an English car, any day.'

'Don't blame me. I didn't *ask* Daddy to buy a Packard,' my mom said.

Auntie Fee said: 'The hotel was too much for Daddy. He just couldn't any more. Then Smuts going . . .'

My mom said: 'First Kei, then the election . . .'

We turned into a big garden and went on up a long drive, with stones crunching under the wheels.

Gordon stopped and revved the engine. 'Everyone out. I'll park and see you inside. Hop.'

The car began moving and my mom said: 'You might at least wait until we're out, Gordon.'

'The damn thing will stall on me if I do. American junk.' He raced off, spitting stones from the tyres.

We stood there a bit. Auntie Fee lit a cigarette.

My mom said: 'My golly, now what?' smoothing down her cream frock and coughing and jangling the way she did when we were in church together. For a moment she was more herself. She was more the person I knew and loved.

Auntie Fee took a big draw on her Goldflake, blew

smoke into the air, threw her butt into the grass and stamped hard on it. 'Let's get it over with. Martin, hold your mom's hand.'

We walked down a long hall. It smelt of Dettol and all the doors to all the rooms were open and I could see beds, and people lying in the beds. I didn't know where we were and my mother said nothing. I hadn't been anywhere like this before. Auntie Fee's heels made a chuckling sound the faster she walked, and I wanted to smile. But no one was smiling.

Auntie Fee was counting '. . . twenty-seven, twenty-eight, twenty-nine, thirty – this is it . . .'

We went into a room with a tall white bed. I looked up at the bed. It was white and square and neat and I saw the tip of my grandpa's nose. That was all. I sat down on the floor and the legs of the bed climbed high above my head. There were springs under the bed, they looked like ice-cream cones, only they were made of wire. The bed went sailing over my head. It was like sitting under a bridge. The sort of bridge the three Billy Goats Gruff walked over to get to the greener, sweeter grass on the other side of the river. I was kneeling under the bridge, like the hungry troll – 'Who's that walking over my bridge?' The shining brown floor ran between the legs of the bed like a river. I was on this bank of the river. On the other bank were four ankles and four pointed shoes all in a row. I could see my face in the wooden blocks of the floor. The window was on the other side of the bed, it was also a bright smear on the floor. I licked my finger and traced all round the window. Something sounded like the sea. Long sighing waves. It was my grandpa, breathing, long deep breaths.

I looked at the polished floor. I looked down on my own face – like Raymond had looked down on me, from the wall in my backyard. I saw my round face looking back at me. I didn't like it, so I pulled other faces, but they were worse. I leaned over, I got right down until my nose touched the nose of the boy in the floor, and the floor smelt of pepper and polish.

There were wheels on the legs of the bed. I'd never seen a bed on wheels before. I was feeling at home. In my first days as a home builder, I'd started under beds, they had been my first best secret places, squeezed in the farthest corner, pulling my legs in after me like a snake, pressing my nose into the crack where one wall hit another.

Sitting under my grandpa's bed I got that funny feeling you get when you've gone away from something inside yourself, you've forgotten who you are and you want to give your brain a good poke. To make it remember the person you've forgotten. I had been very happy under beds. I was sorry I hadn't been nicer to beds. But I'd moved out of beds. I'd gone under tables covered with blankets, then into shacks, made with wood and bits of iron, then into houses of brick. I'd been forgetful. And just look how good beds had been to me. I was sorry, but it was too late.

Sitting under my grandpa's bed, I thought about his deep voice, 'dis-com-bob-u-late'. When he read to me, I leaned back and felt the three buttons on his waistcoat climbing up my back. Over my head, I heard my grandpa breathing so hard you couldn't tell if the air was going in or out, a long, long breath, like the sound you hear in a shell when you hold it to your ear.

Gordon's black shoes came into the room. 'I can't stay. How is he? I'm double-parked. I'd better get back to the car – if some effing munt hasn't whipped it by now,' and then his grey flannels, bunching on his black shoes, marched out of the door.

My mom's feet were in her black patent leather shoes and Auntie Fee's feet were in white shoes. All their ankles were crossed. It was funny how they did it together, even though they weren't looking. Ankles were good to look at, the way they bulged nicely on each side of the leg. My mom had a ladder in her best nylons.

My mom's ankles uncrossed themselves and her legs stood up.

'Gordon will be having a cadenza.'

Auntie Fee's ankles stayed crossed. 'Let him. Too bad.'

'We can't do much more here.'

I heard my auntie Fee crying.

My mom said: 'Here, use mine.'

'You're a tough one.'

'I've had to be.'

They went on blowing their noses for a while. Auntie Fee uncrossed her ankles and her legs stood up. They were thinner than my mom's.

My mom reached down and pulled me to my feet. I got out from under the bed, a bit shaky, feeling I'd been down deep. My grandpa hadn't moved. He was still too high for me to see, except for his nose. It was much thinner than I remembered. Auntie Fee put her hands under my arms and lifted me up. I saw his eyes fast shut, he looked very tired, the corners of his mouth were turned down, his moustache was very black, his pyjama top was blue and open and he had some grey hairs on his chest, which I'd never seen before.

Auntie Fee said: 'Say goodbye to your grandpa.'

I didn't know what she meant. How could I? He was sleeping. He wouldn't know I was saying goodbye, so I just looked at him.

Auntie Fee's hands were tight under my arms. 'Shame, poor little boy.'

Me? Poor? I was happy, there in the room with the high bed and the bright floor and the smell of Dettol. It was OK, it was better than going back to the car, and Gordon, who would be having a cadenza. I was sorry to go. If they'd said to me: 'Oh, Martin, you just stay there under that bed, OK?' I would have been very, very happy, I would've stayed there with my grandpa.

28. The Mirror

It was morning, the house was empty so I went into the garden. Georgie was coming out of the sweet-pea patch. He was so wet, so dark, he looked like my Eskimo pie when the sun melted it down. He was streaming. He truly was the least desiccated man I ever knew. He rocked this way and that and his tears were big as raindrops, and they went dripping into the hot red dust with tiny little muddy bumps.

'Poor, poor, poor boss Mac.'

I just stared at him. I didn't think anyone could hold that much water. He was like the fountain down at the lake, which only worked on Sundays. Except that Georgie didn't change colour like the fountain in the lake.

'My heart is hurting.'

I was sorry his heart was hurting but I loved to see his water running, even if he stayed the same colour.

I patted him on the shoulder. 'It's all right.'

He didn't stop dripping water but he smiled a bit, that big smile, and he said: 'I've got something for you.'

He took me to his pale white room. There was the

picture of King George on the wall. There was his skinny bed with each leg on two bricks. I wondered where he was hiding his bottles now that he wasn't hiding them in my mom's cupboard. He got on his hands and knees, reached under his bed and pulled out my Robin Hood hat. It was just the same, only the feather was broken.

'I went and found it for you, Martin. In the street.'

I put it on and he looked at me like my grandpa looked at him when we went to Mass, like I was a study in elegance.

'Let's walk, Martin.'

We went down Sligo Road, and there was the Café de Move On. Miriam said: 'What're you having, boys?'

She gave us doorstops and apricot and tea but Georgie didn't eat anything.

'My heart cries for Mr Mac, he was good. Now what am I going to do?'

Miriam said: 'I am sad, sad. Shame, poor Mr Mac.'

I was hungry.

Georgie got me more doorstops and apricot jam and tea.

'This is your lunch, today. Today's a bad day. They'll all be back later.'

Today, today, today.

Why did he say it so much?

Miriam wiped her eyes, which were wet, and the steam from her kettle moved this way and that like white butterflies. I remembered my grandpa on the high bed, his eyes closed, breathing like the sea. I was sorry Georgie felt sad for my grandpa but I wasn't sad for my grandpa. I didn't know how to feel sad for him. He had never made me sad, not once.

We went to the park, there was no one on the swings and slides, and we could have played outlaws, but Georgie didn't want to play. I lifted my great yew bow and loosed a feathered shaft at his heart, but he didn't fall over, like he always did. He wouldn't even die, not once.

'Not today. Come, Martin, it's time. Now we go home.'

We walked past Dr Verwoerd's house. He wasn't in the garden and Georgie said again: 'He's not here. Now, what we going to do?'

He was strange. Georgie hated it when Dr Verwoerd was there. Now he hated it that he wasn't there.

'Where's he gone?'

'Gone to be the government. And when he is the government, we are going to cry.'

Georgie cried, again. I didn't know if it was for my grandpa or for the government. Having Dr Verwoerd for a government was not too bad. He didn't want black nannies in his garden, and everyone had to do their own washing-up. He might come looking for Mr Snips, if he was after Jews, or he might come looking for my grandpa, if he wanted Catholics. But my grandpa was very brave and Mr Snips was a master of disguise.

Having a Verwoerd government was all right.

What if we had a government of Gordons? That would be bad. There wouldn't be any singing, or building houses where you wanted, or having a flutter on the gees-gees, or riding in the Packard, or tea and rabbit scoff at Anstey's, or sailor suits, or riding on Georgie's back, or Robin Hood hoods. Everyone would be discombobulated, denuded, desiccated. It would be like being caught by the Ghost Squad, for ever and ever.

Heaven forbid . . .

When Georgie and I got home there were lots of cars outside the Villa Vanilla. There were lots of people. There were big black cars in the drive. My uncles wore black ties which lay like shadows against their white shirts. My mom wore the black hat with the veil that made little diamonds on her cheeks. Auntie Fee wore a small black hat without a veil. My gran was between them and she looked very small and very white.

My mom kissed me. 'Go to your gran and say you're sorry.'

I went to my gran and kissed her and said I was sorry.

My gran kissed me back and said: 'Thank you, Martin. He loved you very much.' Then she cried again, and then she said: 'Now I must stop crying.'

Auntie Fee said: 'Georgie, doll yourself up a bit and give me a hand. I never knew there'd be such a crowd. I need help with the drinks.'

My gran said: 'I have just the thing for dolling up Georgie. Come, Georgie.'

More and more people were hugging each other and shaking hands. Inside the house were big tables spread with sandwiches and cakes and bottles. It was like a party, except everyone was sniffing and wiping their eyes. Everyone was pale. The food seemed to have got there by magic. A great feast lay spread on the greensward where Robin and his merry men would sup till midnight . . . Soon the room was full. I had never seen so many legs.

Auntie Fee said: 'What I need is a good stiff snort.'

Uncle Jack brought her a drink. He punched me very softly on the nose. He gave me a shilling and said: 'Sorry, Martin.'

I was really pleased with the shilling.

Auntie Fee took me on her lap and stuck her cigarette into the corner of her mouth. She smoothed my cheek and her eyes got that misty soft sad look that meant she had something very, very scary to say.

'Martin, your grandpa was buried today. He's gone to heaven.'

I just looked at her and she said: 'He's with Jesus.' She kept blinking because the smoke got in her eyes.

'We've had the funeral. We didn't think you needed to come.'

'Why?'

'Because you're too small. We didn't want you to be frightened. Are you frightened, sweetheart?'

I said I wasn't. But I was. I shivered, as if someone had walked over my grave.

She was pleased, she hugged me. 'Grandpa's dead. Try not to be sad.'

I wasn't sad because my grandpa was dead. I'd seen my grandpa, and he was tired, he was sleeping. And even if he *was* dead, then he knew what he was doing. He'd gone to join the Glorious Dead, that was OK. He'd bought the farm, like my dad. A lot of my favourite people were dead. I'd jolly well nearly died myself, once. I wasn't sad – I was frightened. Auntie Fee was so loving. She gave her little cough. She was going to say something, she was so soft and kind. She hugged me again. It was scary.

'Remember Auntie Fee telling you that you can't stay here, in Sligo Road, for ever. D'you remember? I told you, didn't I? Well, you're not staying here. Your mommy's getting married. To Gordon. And so she'll have someone to look after her. And take care of you too. You won't be staying here much longer. You'll be leaving the Villa Vanilla soon, and going away to a new place. Your own place.'

When I thought about Gordon taking care of me, in my very own place, my skin got very cold.

I said: 'Who's Grandpa dancing with now?'

Auntie Fee laughed. 'Any good-looking angel will do for your grandpa.'

I climbed off her lap and got lost in all the legs. There were lots of people I didn't know. I walked onto the stoop and there was Uncle Matt. I asked him why he was wearing a black tie.

'I'm in mourning. Mourning's when someone's dead. Someone you love, and so you wear a black tie, as a sign of respect.'

'For who?'

'For us. For you and me, and your grandpa. And Grandpa's people. Our people. Djann's people. We got done in. The New Lot scooped the pot. The sun's going down, Martin. We won't see it up for a long, long time.'

Mr Snippalipsky came and shook Uncle Matt's hand. 'Mr Mac was a fine man. He should never have gone back to Curzon.'

Uncle Matt nodded very slowly. 'No option. Someone had to patch up the mess Kei left behind. But it was Smuts going that really finished him. It was fatal. Daddy turned his face to the wall, never got up.'

'He's gone on to better things,' Mr Snippalipsky said. 'For the rest of us, it's a walking disaster and we have to live with it.'

He put his arm round my shoulders, his hand near my ear.

'I hear you went walkabout? And got right into town, all on your lonesome. I'm very impressed. A great explorer in the making. Martin the Navigator. You could be the next Dr Livingstone.'

I wanted to take his hand that was near my ear and hold it tight. I wanted to say: 'Please, Mr Snippalipsky, can I come and live with you and Rosa and Mrs Snippalipsky? I won't take up any room. I can live under a bed, or in the garden. I won't be any trouble . . .'

Before I could say anything I saw Gordon, taller than the others, wearing a brown suit with a grey tie. He didn't see me. I went away and hid among a forest of legs.

'Fleet Robin easily outran his panting pursuers . . .'

Then Auntie Fee grabbed me. A round lady with brown hair was with her. The lady wore a black coat and a black hat with black flowers in it.

'Martin, this is your granny Donally. This is your dad's mother.'

With my eyes, I went right up the lady's face, grabbed hold of it and climbed up it, holding on tight. And when the lady shook her head as if she wanted to shake me loose, I stuck there, I swung there, staring. My heart was very fluttery. My head was fizzing like lemonade.

'Martin, where are our manners? Don't we know it's

rude to stare? Don't we say something? Like "How do you do, Granny Donally?"'

In my picture of my father in its wooden frame, with the cracked glass, he had on this big cap, tilted over one eye, and so all you saw was one eye and his nose and his chin. You couldn't get hold of him the way I got hold of Granny Donally's face. Nothing about her, not her eyes, or the little hairs on her upper lip, looked like him. She had a pinched chin (his was round) and a big forehead (his was hidden). But it didn't matter. This lady, more than anyone else, more than my mom, more than Auntie Fee, more even than Uncle Jack, had known my dad.

I stared and stared until my eyes were full of her.

'Goodness me. What a fierce little boy. He's very quiet, isn't he?'

'He talks all right,' Auntie Fee said. 'When he's in the mood he'll talk the hind leg off a donkey. Martin, say something to your granny Donally.'

The lady in the black hat smiled. 'He looks just like his father.'

'Martin, say something,' Auntie Fee said.

But I didn't. I turned round and ran away. I was crossing the lawn when I nearly ran into Gordon, and I had to stop and freeze. Gordon didn't see me, he was walking after Georgie, who was walking faster, holding the tray high over his head and his buttons were bright. Gordon caught up to Georgie and grabbed the buttons of his waistcoat and said in that high voice, straight from his nose: 'Just what do you think you're playing at, my boy?'

Georgie kept holding the tray over his head, looking at Gordon's fingers on his buttons, but he didn't say anything.

'Don't play the dumb waiter with me. I'm talking to you, my boy.'

Georgie still said nothing. The ice was melting in the glasses.

My uncle Matt came and took Gordon's hand off Georgie. 'What's your problem, Gordon?'

'I haven't, as you choose to put it, a problem.'

Uncle Charlie came over. He was round and hard like a torpedo and his face was red.

'Why're you pulling Georgie about?'

'I am not, as you put it, pulling him about.'

'My arse,' Uncle Charlie said.

My gran was there now, and granny Donally, and Auntie Fee who had on her 'I-want-a-word-with-you-young-man' look, but I pretended I didn't see her. My gran was saying to Uncle Charlie: 'Let's remember where we are. We don't want anything today but light. That's the way *he* would have wanted it.'

'That's right. Let's just forget the whole thing – unless Gordon's got objections,' Uncle Jack said. 'You don't have any objections, do you, Gordon?'

Gordon lifted his nose. 'None whatever. When I got

here today, the boy was dressed for the garden. Next thing, he's waltzing about in one of your dad's good suits. It is one of Dan's good suits, isn't it? Correct me if I'm wrong.'

My mom came over. 'I hope we're not having a little scene? Not on a day like this.'

'We're *not* having a scene,' Gordon said through his nose: 'I was merely enquiring—'

'Gordon's never seen a black chap in a suit,' Uncle Matt said.

'Probably never seen a suit at all.' Uncle Charlie swallowed all the drink in his glass, put it down on Georgie's tray and took another.

'Maybe we should have given Daddy's suit to Gordon?'

'Now don't talk rubbish,' my mom said. 'Gordon works in a bank. They all wear suits there. Every day. Even the tellers. Isn't that so, Gordon?'

Gordon said: 'I was merely enquiring where he got it.'

My gran said: 'I gave it to him. Doesn't he look beautiful? Dan would've loved it. He loved the way Georgie wore his clothes.' She went and touched Georgie's arm. And Georgie doffed his hat, even though he wasn't wearing a hat. And I knew what he was doing. He was saying: 'Let's play that I am Mr Mac, going perambulating down Sligo Road, and you'll be Mrs Mac, in the days when we were all together and happy.'

'It was his very *best* suit,' my gran said. She started crying again.

'Happy now, Gordon?' Uncle Matt said.

'What a prize pawpaw,' Uncle Charlie said. 'If you don't like it, why don't you go back to PE?'

Georgie looked from Uncle Matt to Gordon. The ice went on melting.

Auntie Fee came up and put her arms round the shoulders of Uncle Matt and Uncle Charlie. 'Boys, boys, boys. Enough . . . please. Georgie, fetch drinks – chop, chop. There are people here with their tongues hanging out. And for Pete's sake, get some fresh ice. Then make yourself scarce. And you, Martin, come and help me roll back the carpet, and you, Jack, wind the gramophone. This is Daddy's wake and he's going to be sent off as he would've wished. And I'm darned – ' she started crying and shouting all at once – 'I'm blooming well darned if anyone's going to turn it into a fight.'

Gordon hadn't been looking at me till now, but now he did. I hadn't remembered my hat till then but now I did. Gordon drew breath in through his lips, like he was whistling backwards, an empty faint windy sound, with just a tiny rustle around the edges of his lips.

My mom said: 'Martin, darling, you've got your hat back. Where did you get your hat back from?'

Auntie Fee said: 'He's been wearing it all the time. Have you only seen it now?'

'Has he? I didn't notice.'

What she meant was that she'd forgotten. She didn't care to notice, just like she didn't care that Gordon had thrown it off the bus, and she didn't care how much Gordon hated it. She didn't care I had it back again. My mom cared about where she was and what she was feeling, and if you got on the wrong side of that, then you felt her beady eye, you gave her the heebies, she'd had you in chunks. She was as tough as nails. Only Gordon didn't know that. Gordon looked at her, he worried about her. He lifted his forehead and the skin lifted into a lot of sausage lines, it was like a venetian blind going up. He shook his head.

I felt something then – I felt what I was supposed to feel for my grandpa, but I felt it for Gordon. I felt sorry. I felt sad. Then I got angry for feeling sorry.

Georgie got fresh ice and more drinks, and the gramophone was singing: '*Drove she ducklings to the water, every morning, just at nine, hit her foot against a splinter, fell into the foaming brine . . .*' Soon people were dancing.

I went into the bathroom and locked the door.

The voice on the gramophone sang: '*O my darling, O my darling, O my darling, Clementine, Thou are lost and gone for ever, dreadful sorry, Clementine.*'

I climbed onto the stool and took off my hat and looked at myself in the mirror for a long time. I pushed my nose close to the glass and it all frosted up when I breathed. I got a shiver all over me, someone was walking over my grave. That's how he looked. His hair was blond, his nose was thin and straight, his eyes were brown with green flecks. I was staring right into the eyes of my dad.

29. Balls

It was Saturday morning. I was still waking up. Suddenly Auntie Fee was there. She hugged me, she kissed me and told me she loved me to bits.

'You'll never guess what Auntie Fee has to tell you.'

I was scared.

'This very afternoon, in Rosewood church, your mom's getting married.'

'She can't.'

'What do you mean, she can't?'

'She's my mom.' I said it a lot. I couldn't think of anything else to say. 'She's my mom, she can't.' I said it again and again and louder and louder, then I started crying. 'Isn't she?'

Auntie Fee said: 'Of course she is. Silly boy. You don't have to tell me she's your mom. I know that. Have I ever said she isn't your mom? Hmm? Have I? Has *anyone* said she's not your mom? Hey? So let's be straight about that. Your mom'll always be your mom. But today's special. Today she's also a bride.'

'Where is she?'

'Where is she? Very busy, getting ready to be married. That's where she is. What a question.'

'Can I see her?'

'Later. You can't see her now.'

'Why?'

'It's very bad luck to see the bride before the wedding. You'll see her in church. Promise.'

'Are you going to church?'

'Of *course* I'm going. Why wouldn't I be going? I'm matron of honour. Wild horses wouldn't keep me away.'

'But aren't you—?'

'Excommunicated? Yes, siree. But I'm still going, and if that Father O'Keefe says one word, I'll spit in his eye.'

She dressed me in my sailor suit.

'He doesn't like it.'

'Humph. He can take a running jump at himself.'

She combed my hair and tied my tie, she hugged me and kissed me and watched me. 'You're a very lucky boy. Fancy having three grannies. You'll have your own Granny Number One, and Granny Two who's Daddy Dennis's mom, whom you have met, remember? Today, you'll get Granny Three, who is Gordon's mom.'

'I don't want her.'

'Why not? If it were me, I'd be jolly glad having three grannies.'

'You have her, then.'

She looked at me and her eyes got all soft and smudgy.

She put her hand on her heart, to show how much it hurt.

'Is that any way to talk to your auntie Fee? Shame on you. Say you're sorry.'

'I'm sorry.'

'That's better. Three grannies – Granny MacBride, Granny Donally, Granny Stock . . .'

'Stock?'

Blink, blink, went Auntie Fee's razor eyes. 'Yes, darling. Stock – that's Gordon's name. He's Gordon Stock. When a girl gets married she changes her name to the bloke's name. Your mom was Monica MacBride. But today she'll be Monica Stock.'

Monica Stock.

I never thought Gordon had another name, he was just Gordon – Gordon-I-Beg-To-Differ, or Gordon-If-You-Insist, or Gordon-I-Stand-Corrected. Stock. It tasted terrible. A flat plain bad name. A dead name, a sticking-in-the-throat name, a name to choke on, like a fishbone, like a poisoned apple . . .

I could feel Auntie Fee's eyes looking. I tried to make my face a mask. I tried to throw them off, but they stuck to me and my face was doing all sorts of things I wished it wouldn't.

'Your name's going to change. Just like your mom's. From this afternoon, you'll stop being Martin Donally – you'll be Martin Stock.'

'I won't.'

'What do mean, I won't?'

'I won't!'

'Well, excuse me. There is no need to scream. I'm trying to help you and all you do is bite off my head. Shame on you. What's in a little name change? It won't hurt. I changed my name when I married your uncle Jack. I didn't feel a thing. It'll be fun having three grannies, won't it?'

'You have them, I don't want them. Don't give them to me.'

'Nobody's giving them to you, darling, you get them whether you like it or not. And d'you know what? In church today you'll be seeing your new family. We must be very kind to them because d'you know what? They're all Presbyterians. Fancy that. They may stare a bit because they don't know what Catholics do, and we're not to stare back at them, because that would be rude. And Auntie Fee will be there, watching to see you're not rude. This is your mom's big day. We don't want anything to spoil it, do we? By Jiminy, am I looking forward to it.'

Auntie Fee tied my laces and brushed my hair and laughed her nice soft loving terrible way.

'Martin Stock – it's not such a bad name, is it?'

'I don't *want* it. Please, I don't.'

'Don't worry, darling, you'll get used to it in two ticks – promise.'

I had a last try.

'My name is Martin Donally, I live at 99 Sligo Road . . .'

'Not for much longer, sweetie-pie,' Auntie Fee said.

I was sitting in the front pew in Rosewood church, all blue-green and cool and high, thinking about having to change my name.

My gran came in then and she sat next to me and kissed me. 'I miss your grandpa so much.' Then we both cried and she said: 'Hush, boy, dry your eyes, we can't be seen weeping on your mother's wedding day.'

I didn't know why – if they all cried when my grandpa died why couldn't we cry now? This was much, much worse.

Uncle Charlie was on my one side and Uncle Jack was on my other side. Uncle Charlie wore a suit. Everyone had suits on, dark suits, like they did when my grandpa died, only they weren't wearing black ties. My uncles were pink and shining and their hair smelt very good.

Gordon was there in front of me, standing right by the altar rails where you're not supposed to be unless you're taking Holy Communion. Gordon had his back to me, so that was all right.

On the other side of the aisle were people I didn't know. There was a woman with a face like a collie, a long nose and a pointed chin, and there were a few boys in suits. They stared a lot, they stared at the Statue of Our Lady. And the Sacred Heart of Jesus, and the

Stations of the Cross, and especially at the big cross that hung over the altar with Jesus nailed to it, and dripping blood which I always liked because it looked like a rose, pink and cream. They pointed. They whispered.

Uncle Charlie said: 'Those are Gordon's folk. Up from the coast. And what must they think of this? Crucifixes and the Virgin Mary. And Gordon marrying a holy Roman.'

Another man, a bit thinner than Gordon, stood next to Gordon. His hair was even shorter.

I pulled Uncle Charlie's sleeve. 'Who's that?'

'That's Duggie. Gordon's brother. He's best man.'

'He's Presbyterian.'

Uncle Charlie looked at me. 'Well, bugger me. How d'you know?' Then he reached over and pinched my cheek. 'He is too. A bloody Prod.'

I was trying to work out if Best Man and Presbyterian were the same, so I didn't say anything but my cheek stung in a nice way, where Uncle Charlie had pinched me.

Gordon and his brother Duggie kept turning round and looking back. I kept my head down, in case Gordon was looking for me.

Father O'Keefe came in and stood in front of Gordon and he wore a green and gold cloak. The organ started playing then. Everyone stood up and turned round and stared. My mom came in the door, dressed in white. She was holding onto the arm of Uncle Matt, and he was in a blue suit. They walked all the way up to the top of the church. My auntie Fee was behind my mom and I saw why she had looked shiny and yellow. It was her yellow dress with a white sash and a big hat with grapes around the edge of it, and her job was to walk behind my mom. Father O'Keefe looked at her and I wondered if she would spit in his eye, but she didn't.

When my mom got up to Gordon, she stopped and then they knelt down.

When Gordon knelt down the soles of his shoes were bare and shiny, like the back of his head where it had been shaved. Behind him stood Duggie, close to his shoulder. Gordon kept shifting his shoulders under his grey suit, and my mom coughed every now and then, her own cough. Father O'Keefe was not singing or smiling now and his white hair was combed forward over his pink forehead and he was reading from a book.

'Do you, Monica Mary Donally, take this man, Gordon Wesley Stock . . .'

That's when my mom said: 'I do.'

I said in my head: 'I don't.'

Father O'Keefe said the same to Gordon, and Gordon said: 'I do.'

I said in my head: 'I don't.' I said it with all of me. Especially with my tummy.

There was more music. My mom and Gordon and Duggie and Auntie Fee all turned round. I was staring at Gordon's front. He was smiling and blinking, and my mom was holding his arm. They were walking straight towards us. I got right under Uncle Jack's arm and right close to Uncle Charlie. I tried to turn myself into a knife, or a shadow, and I sort of crouched in the pew as Gordon came past and I thought he'd stop and say something, but they didn't stop.

Afterwards we all came out into the sunshine and someone took pictures of my mom and Gordon on the church steps. And then they did Auntie Fee and Duggie. The sunshine was huge and spiky and made me blink. They wanted to have my picture taken with my mom and Gordon but I went and hid behind the church. I found a corner, with a shed. I pushed open the door, inside it smelt of paint. I heard them calling me. I sat on the ground and waited. When I heard all the cars starting up I went out again into the spiky sunshine and my mom and Gordon were getting into the Packard, and Duggie said: 'That's some bus, hey, *boet*.'

Gordon said: 'It's just bloody American junk.'

Auntie Fee saw me. 'Where d'you disappear to? We wanted you for the photos, Martin, but you'd vanished.'

I was pleased, I was Martin, the Ghost of the Garden . . .

Auntie Fee smiled her happy smile. 'Crikey Moses, I can't wait for you to grow up.'

'Why?'

'Because are you going to be big trouble.'

*

There was a tent on the lawn at the Villa Vanilla. It was striped blue and white, and big ropes were pegged into the ground near the dahlias, and there were tables outside the tent on the grass and on the front stoop and under the hairy palm tree. Inside the tent the air was yellow and it felt wet. The band on the stage was playing 'Mona Lisa', which was good because I could sing along: '*Are you warm, are you real, Mona Lisa? Or just another cold and lonely lovely work of art?*'

My uncles were walking about outside the tent drinking beer, and their words came to me in bits:

'Bloody crying shame about Boksburg, hey, Mattie? Took a bit of flak, hey?'

That was Uncle Jack.

'More than a bit, Jacko. Shot down in flames.'

'Credit where it's due. You hit those bastards.'

'No, Jacko, not true. Complete cock-up. The Malanites walked it.'

'There's always a next time.'

'It's finished and *klaar*. There isn't going to be a next time. Sun's going down, Jacko.'

Inside the tent my mom and Gordon and Auntie Fee and Duggie all went and sat at a table and Uncle Matt banged a glass with his fork and said: 'Pray silence for the best man.' Then Duggie stood up and talked about a lot of stuff I didn't understand and everyone laughed all the time and my mother went pink in the face and even Gordon laughed, which was very worrying.

I went outside again and there I found Georgie. He was sitting in the grass with his back to the palm tree. He was a study in elegance. He was wearing my grandpa's best silver suit and on his head he had a funny little hat I hadn't seen before.

'What's that?'

'That's a pork pie hat. From America,' Georgie said.

'Can I touch it?'

'Try it on.'

I gave him my hood and I wore his hat.

'Can we go to the park?'

'Not today, Martin. Today we got to stay here.'

'Why?'

'Because your mother's getting married. But tomorrow we go, like always.'

'Like always?'

I didn't believe him. There was a lot we wouldn't be doing – because my mother was getting married. We sat on the grass not saying much, and not playing because Georgie said it would spoil our best clothes. We were both sad and we didn't know what to say.

Everyone was coming out of the tent. Georgie lifted me up onto the gatepost. The Packard was parked outside the big wooden gates, like it was when we went to the horse races, like when we went to Curzon, like when we went to hear Djann Smuts, or Dr Malan. Only it wasn't going to any of those places.

Uncle Charlie was in the car, tooting the horn. White

ribbons had been tied from the silver bird on the front of the bonnet to the tops of the windows. All the doors, and the back window, had drawings on them. The drawings were done with soap, just like the soap Amos the barber had put on my chin under the trees by the lake. The boot of the Packard was piled with suitcases.

Uncle Charlie tooted again, and my mom and Gordon came running out of the gate. My mom was wearing a grey dress with a white hat and veil and blue flowers in her hat. She had a little bunch of flowers. Gordon was wearing a brown suit that looked like it was made out of carpet or something, hot and woolly with thin stripes.

When my mom saw me, she came to me and reached up to me and squeezed me and lifted me down from the gatepost. I smelt her, warm and very, very deep and full of flowers. She said: 'There you are, darling. I've been looking everywhere for you. What on earth are you wearing? Be good. Mommy has to fly.'

Gordon took my hand and he shook it, which was terrible. 'See you soon, son.'

Then his brother Duggie came and clapped me on the shoulder. 'So this is young Mor-ton. Who lives in Sherwood Forest. I see from his pretty suit that, today, young Mor-ton is also a jolly Jack tar. Hullo, sailor. That's a fine pair of liggs you got sticking out of those shorts.'

His voice was like Gordon's, only higher and thinner.

'And what's this you've got on your head? It's not the famous Robin Hood hat?'

I said: 'It's not a hood; it's a Pork Pie hat, from America.'

'It's a – what? A pawk-pah?'

Duggie leaned back and patted his behind, he did that a lot, the sunshine was in his moustache. I waited for him to say 'bahm-teckla' but he didn't. I thought about his voice, it was very PE. It must be very terrible to live in some place where they went round saying 'liggs' and 'pawk-pah'.

Duggie tried to grab the hat off my head but I was too quick. Ever since Gordon got my hood, I had been very quick. I ran to Georgie and gave it to him, and he put it on and lifted me back onto the gatepost.

Duggie laughed. 'Bugger me, now I've seen it all – a pawk-pah on a picannin.'

A lot of people came and stood around the car. The men were carrying bottles of beer. The women were carrying little shiny packets.

'Step on it, folks,' Uncle Charlie said. 'That train leaves Park Station at seven. And we don't want it going without you.'

My mom bent down and lifted her skirt and took off something and threw it. It turned like a circle in the air and someone I didn't know caught it. Everyone cheered. It was terrible. My mom and Gordon got into the car and waved. The men got hold of the back of the car and bounced it up and down. The women pulled stuff out of the paper bags and threw it into the air and it floated down like paper rain, all different colours, and Charlie waved and hooted and all the men lifted their beer bottles, and the air was still raining bits of paper and behind the car was a long tail of string with cans tied on, and more writing on the back, where the spare tyre was. The Packard went away then. It clanked a lot when it went away, because of the tail of cans, and everyone laughed again.

Afterwards, they went inside. I stayed on the gatepost.

Inside the tent they were singing: '*You put you left ligg in, you pull your left ligg out . . . you duh di-duh di-duh di-duh – and you shake it all about . . .*'

Rosa Snippalipsky came outside; she looked up at me on the gatepost and she said: 'Aren't you coming down, Martin?' She was wearing a blue dress with a white bow in the front and white shoes.

I said 'no'. I sat on top of the gate, looking down on Rosa the way the caterpillar looks down on Alice, really high and mighty, and Rosa very little. I don't know why I said 'no'. It just came out that way. So she went inside.

Where the Packard had been, there was a shape on the ground. The shape was made by the tiny bits of coloured paper and a bit of black oil on the grey road. I hadn't seen so many bits of paper since the elections, when everyone tore up the posters of General Smuts.

It was all perfectly normal . . . except it wasn't.

Mr Snippalipsky came up to me. 'Planning to stay

long, Martin? Up there on your tower, like Simon Stylites? Now *there* was a bloke. He was a saint and he reckoned humans were so awful he didn't want anything to do with them, so he climbed a tower, just like yours, and wouldn't come down. Sat there in the sky – for donkey's years. Pouring scorn on folks from a dizzy height. He told everyone what he thought of them, which wasn't much. Is that how you feel, Martin?'

'I feel sad, Mr Snips.'

'Never mind, it can't be helped.'

He didn't say what couldn't be helped. And I *did* mind. Why couldn't it be helped? I went on looking at the shape of the car on the road.

'Mr Snippalipsky, please sing me the song about the onions again.'

And he did. He really was a master of disguise. He just changed from being himself to being the old man leaning on his stick in a flash – even though he didn't have a stick, even though there was no band in the pit: he made it all happen again, and the roof was full of stars.

'*He's gone for ever more, at the age of ninety-four*
And the memory of him I'll always s-a-v-e . . .
So I'm going to the graveyard, to fulfil his last request,
Just to plant a bunch of onions on his gr-a-v-e.'

Then I clapped and he bowed, then I cried and he gave me his hanky.

'Looks like you could use a drink. Shall we adjourn to the bar?'

I said 'yes'. It was hard to say anything else to Mr Snippalipsky. Anyway, I didn't want to be like Simon Stylites and sit on a tower; you were too much in the open on a tower.

'Weddings are sometimes less fun than funerals,' Mr Snippalipsky said.

We pushed into the tent, it was like walking into warm milk, with Mr Snippalipsky calling out: 'Make way for two thirsty men.' He got me a cold green drink. 'Cheers, Martin, here's to us.'

Auntie Fee caught me then. 'There you are. Here's someone I know you want to say hello to.' She had the tall woman with her. The one from church, with the face a bit like a collie dog's. With white hair on her long chin, and a sharp nose.

'This is your new daddy's mommy,' Auntie Fee said.

I was surrounded, I was trapped, they were everywhere. I was sorry I'd come down off the gatepost, a boy needs height. A cold wind started blowing in my head. I looked around for Mr Snippalipsky. He was gone.

'Aren't you going to give me a kiss, young man?'

'Martin, what's happened to our manners?' Auntie Fee said. 'Someone's talking to you.'

The lady said: 'Shame. It's a big day for a little chap. Did you like the wedding? Did you like your mommy's wedding dress?'

I said: 'Weddings can be less fun than funerals.'

'Gracious me,' Granny Stock said.

'Between you, me and the gatepost, I think we're a teeny bit overwrought,' Auntie Fee said.

I looked at Granny Stock. I said very, very slowly: 'Desiccated.'

'Martin Donally,' Auntie Fee said.

'De-nu-ded.'

'Martin, you promised,' Auntie Fee said.

'Dis-com-bob-u-lat-ed.'

'What a queer little fellow,' Granny Stock said. 'Shame, poor little man.'

Auntie Fee sighed. 'It's just words. Pay no attention. He doesn't know what they mean. He hears and repeats. Like a bally parrot. It was his grandpa who started it. And his uncles. If Martin wants to know something, they tell him. No matter what. He spouts words like you wouldn't believe.'

I looked at the collie woman.

'Consummate, carefree, constant . . .'

Auntie Fee said: 'He gets them from books. He's mad for books, this boy. Anything will do. Scraps of this and that. He's not fussy. He's always at it.'

'He'll get stick when he goes to school,' Granny Stock said.

'I said so. I told his grandpa.'

'. . . peripatetic, perambulate, priapic . . .'

'Martin, that's enough.' Auntie Fee looked up at the heavens, like she did when she was going to say something which was not for certain ears.

'... tremendous, titanic, top-hole ... *in flagrante delicto*, adultery ...'

'Ignore him, he's showing off. We've been quite upset. Know what I mean? Of late about our M-O-T-H-E-R. And about the W-E-D-D-I-N-G. There have been a lot of changes in our young life. It's taking us some time to adjust.'

'Shame,' Granny Stock said.

Auntie Fee pushed me out of the tent. 'That's enough. Go and play in the garden. You've got half an hour, Martin, and then b-e-d.'

I walked out onto the lawn. Georgie was sitting on the steps of the stoop, he was still the very picture of elegance. Then a whole of lot of Gordon's people came out onto the lawn under the palm tree. I went and sat down next to Georgie.

'You going away, Martin?'

I felt cold, like I did when Gordon took my hat.

'No, no.'

'You are. I know. You and your mom. Going away. And leaving Georgie behind.'

I couldn't think what to say so I just said again that we weren't going away. Ever. We went on sitting there, Georgie and me, and then one of Gordon's people came over and took Georgie's hat right off his head. Georgie jumped up and chased it. The man threw it over his head and the Duggie man caught it. Georgie ran this way and that, trying to catch his hat, but he couldn't and everyone laughed.

Someone shouted: 'Hey, what's this thing, man?'

And Duggie said: 'Man, it's a pawk-pah.'

The men ran around shouting: 'It's a pawk-pah,' like they couldn't believe it. And threw the hat high, right over Georgie's head, laughing a lot and falling over.

Georgie came back and sat down.

'What're they doing with your hat, Georgie?'

'They're playing. They think it's a ball.'

I knew this was how it must be in PE all the time.

'Will they give it back?'

'Maybe. Maybe not. That's the game.'

My auntie Fee came out. 'I'm very sad, Martin. What happened to our deal? You were going to put those words right out of your head. What d'you think your granny Stock thought, huh? Hoo, boy.'

'Those men have taken Georgie's hat.'

Auntie Fee looked at Duggie and his friends running and throwing and laughing and falling. 'They think it's a ball.'

'It isn't. It's Georgie's hat.'

She said: 'They're just playing. Isn't that so, Georgie?'

He didn't say anything.

'You've had quite enough for one day. Come along, young man.'

I said: 'Good night, Georgie.'

Georgie still didn't say anything. He sat in his silver suit watching his hat flying.

Inside the house, Auntie Fee said: 'Poor Martin, you must be finished.' She had on her very sweet voice and I started to worry, especially as we didn't go to my room.

'Where are we going?'

'Don't worry about a thing, darling. Guess what? From now on you're going to have your very own new room.'

My new room was Caítlín's old room. The bedroom above the stain. They had made up a bed for me and drawn the curtains and there was a light on the table by the bed. The bedspread was green with furry ridges. The floorboards were still bare and the impala skin on the floor had a greasy feeling when you walked on it in bare feet. The dark cupboard also had feet, tiny feet which were balls, held in claws.

The bed was cold. I asked for a story.

Auntie Fee said: 'No story tonight, it's much too late and you're much too tired. But I'll leave the door open just a crack so the passage light shines in and you won't be frightened.'

I lay there for a while. The curtains were drawn, I couldn't see the hairy palm wagging its head outside the window. I was glad. I didn't want to see it, I didn't want to see anything. I buried my head in the pillow, pulled the rest of the pillow between my knees and lay there very quiet. I could smell beeswax and dust.

Outside in the dark, Gordon's people were still playing: I heard them shouting.

'Pass, man – *pass*. Here, man, over here. Shoot, man.
Oh, *shoot*!'

They were louder than the night-lions.

I wrapped the blankets round my ears. I didn't want
to hear. I wanted to cry, but I didn't because I thought
my tears might drip down from the bed and run into the
crack where Cousin Caítlín's tears had run, and if they
did that, my tears might change the map of Ireland and
I didn't want anything to change any more.

30. The Gay Gordon

My mom being married and somewhere else, and Grandpa gone to heaven, and Uncle Matt having failed to take the seat in Boksburg North, and my gran gone to run the hotel in Curzon – 'Because if I don't, who will?' – though she let me see her scar again before she went (it was still very beautiful), there was just me and Georgie left at the Villa Vanilla. Even Dr Verwoerd was somewhere else and his house was empty. Uncle Matt said he'd gone to be a senator in Cape Town.

Uncle Charlie said he was getting married and he wanted his navy kitbag back. It made me sad, I needed his kitbag. I didn't see why anyone would want to leave the Villa Vanilla. I went to my cupboard and lifted out the kitbag. I looked at my treasures lying on the floor, looking up at me. My father in his air force cap, winking at me, his box brownie with the ice-cube eye, his logbooks and the little picture of my dad's grave. They looked cold, like they didn't have any clothes on.

In my cupboard was an old dog. He had scratchy white hair and one brown eye. The other eye was lost.

He had a zip in his back. If you opened the zip there was a secret pocket. I opened him up and put in the pocket the picture of my dad, the picture of his grave, and his logbooks. The camera was too big. So I put it in the corner of the cupboard because no one really knew it belonged to my dad. Then I closed the zip tight and I put the dog in the other corner and he looked fine. He looked asleep.

I gave Charlie his kitbag. I hoped he'd say I could keep it but he didn't.

He said: 'Thanks, chief!' and showed me a trick with his elbow. He stood a shilling on his funny bone and it jumped right into his mouth, between his teeth. He gave me a kiss on the head. 'Take care of yourself, old chap.'

And then he went off to get married.

Uncle Jack and Auntie Fee came to stay. She went out to work at Anglo-Concrete every morning. Uncle Jack had a dark green Opel Kapitän. It was a free car. He was a traveller for Pretty Little Me Cosmetics. I didn't know how long my mom had been gone.

Auntie Fee said: 'Your mommy and Gordon will be back before you can say Jack Robinson.'

I tried saying 'Jack Robinson'. They didn't come back. I knew they would, one day, when I wasn't ready, when I wasn't looking. Once, I cried Asia Minor but it dried. I never saw Raymond again, though I always checked before I sat down in my secret place. A boy needs height . . . I spent a lot of time on Georgie's back or on the gatepost, looking down Sligo Road. I was up there, looking out, because I didn't want Gordon sneaking up on me. Sometimes I forgot they were coming back at all. When I missed my mom I only missed her for long enough to remember that if she came back then Gordon would come with her, and I'd stop missing her. Every day I forgot about my mom a little more.

I was on the gatepost when Mr Jinnah, the Snake Sammie, came by.

'Where's your grandpa, Martin?'

I didn't know what to say, so I didn't say anything.

'I came to say goodbye. You won't be seeing Mr Jinnah again. I'm off to Durban. I'm retiring there. I got a nice little house on the North Coast, near Tongaat. I got frangipani. I got avocados. I love avos. I couldn't go without saying goodbye to Mr Mac. And my friend here, he wants to say it too.'

He opened his basket and the long yellow cobra floated up into the air like smoke. Mr Jinnah took him by the back of the neck and the cobra moved his head this way and that.

'He's waving goodbye,' Mr Jinnah said.

I heard my gran saying: 'If one of those gets loose in my garden, I'll send Georgie after it with the garden fork.'

The Silk Sammie didn't come again, so I never bought his finest shantungs from the East for my mom. I was sorry. On the other hand, she was gone now. So I didn't really mind. The ice-cream man pedalled past. His cart creaked, he lifted his big brass bell and banged it down on the hot air like a hammer. He looked at me. But there was no one to give me a tickey. Behind me it was all empty, except for Georgie, snipping among the roses.

I rode Georgie's back down Sligo Road every day and Georgie still crossed over, even though Dr Verwoerd wasn't there.

I thought Georgie would be pleased but he wasn't. 'No, man. He's gone to be the government. We're in big trouble.'

At the lake I played a lot with Rosa Snippalipsky but she wouldn't go back to walking on her hands. I asked her why not and she just said: 'I did that, Martin, that's a thing I've *done*.' She gave me three cigarette cards: I got Bobby Osler, from Springbok Rugby, and a girl with gold hair and black pants, sitting on the back of a turtle, from a box of Flag Cigarettes. Rosa said it must be very hard for her to keep her balance. And a white rhino, from 'Our South African National Parks'. The white rhino had a very big horn that reminded me of Gordon's nose, and that was the only thing I didn't like about it. When I went to sleep I kept hearing Rosa Snippalipsky saying to me: 'I did that Martin, that's the thing I've done.' And I woke up screaming and Auntie Fee was there.

Auntie Fee said in her kindest, sweetest, most loving voice: 'Don't be frightened, Martin, I'm here . . .'

Auntie Fee said I was pining and she was going to cheer me up before my mom came home.

'We'll cheer you up,' Auntie Fee said, 'if it kills us. Your mom will be home soon, and if she sees you pining, I'll get it in the neck.'

I heard her whisper to Uncle Jack: 'It's missing its M-O-T-H-E-R.'

I wasn't. I was feeling something I'd never felt. Every day, when I woke up, I said: 'Please don't let her come home today.'

Uncle Jack winked. 'Ever been to Pagel's Circus? It's the best. Ever seen the Gay Gordons? I vote we go. They've got real live ligers. D'you ever see a liger? A liger's a cross between a tiger and lion.'

Auntie Fee wanted to see Shorty the clown. 'Shorty's not much bigger than you are, Martin. Two bricks and a tickey high. A tiny man, perfect in every respect.'

'Can Georgie come with us?'

'Course he can.'

We got on the tram in Erin Avenue, by the lake, it was very full but Uncle Jack said: 'Send Georgie upstairs. Put Robin Hood on your knee. Piece of cake.' Uncle Jack stood and held onto the strap. The driver wound his wheel and you could feel the tram grinding along the hard road underneath us.

The conductor came over and Uncle Jack said: 'Two of us for Ellis Park. And one whatever it is for the black chap. He's up in the rigging.'

Auntie Fee held me on her knee and when I got off because we were at the Circus she said: 'Careful of my nylons, Martin. They ladder if you look at them.'

The Circus was big, it smelt of hot fur. The ground was red dust, the tent was striped red and white. We went to a window in a caravan and bought our tickets. We sat on wooden benches almost at the front, and Auntie Fee fanned herself with her handbag.

Shorty the clown had red hair and big shoes. And he had two friends, Thick and Thin. They had yellow hair. They shouted a lot and hit each other with bats and fell over. Auntie Fee and Uncle Jack laughed, but Georgie and I didn't laugh.

'Shorty's tiny but he's perfect in every detail,' Auntie Fee said.

'Do you fancy him?' Uncle Jack said.

'He gives me the quivers,' Auntie Fee said.

The ligers came on. They roared a lot but their lion heads looked too big for their tiger bodies. The liger tamer had a long whip and black pants and black boots and there were big gold spangles all over his red shirt. He cracked his whip so loud I blinked, and the ligers jumped onto chairs. I remembered how the night-lions made my mom cry in her sleep when we still lived together.

Georgie bought us all popcorn.

'He's got a damn sight more cash than we have,' Uncle Jack said.

Georgie smiled. His cheeks were full of popcorn. His eyes were wide.

Auntie Fee said: 'Goodness, Georgie, eat any more and you'll pop yourself.'

I watched him, hoped he would – but he didn't.

After the ligers there was Alberta and her juggling act. She threw plates into the air and Auntie Fee said: 'Isn't she stupendous?'

'Meaning knockout, whopping, tremendous, heart-stopping,' Uncle Jack said.

'Please,' Auntie Fee said, 'no more words for him. Here come the Gay Gordons.'

I grabbed Uncle Jack's arm. 'They're ladies.'

Uncle Jack said: 'Certainly are. Scottish lassies. All the way from Bonnie Scotland and they wear the tartan to prove it. See what they have under their arms? Bagpipes. They're made from the stomachs of cows.'

'*Must* you?' Auntie Fee said.

The Gay Gordons squeezed the bags and blew hard. Their cheeks were red. Their leader was a woman with a silver stick; she threw it up and caught it, and everyone clapped. Their eyes popped, just like Georgie's when he ate the popcorn, and their skirts lifted.

Uncle Jack whistled. 'Nice bints. I can see their pants.'

Auntie Fee said: 'Don't be rude.'

Next came the St Moritz roller skaters, then two cowboys called Buck and Chuck. They did lariat-spinning, shooting and knife-throwing, then came the clowns, Thick and Thin, and then the Gay Gordons again. Then everyone stood up and sang 'God Save the King' and there were a lot of drums and then it was over.

Georgie gave me a shilling. 'Maybe you want to buy something? Don't tell anyone, Martin.'

Outside in the night it smelt of sawdust and ligers. We saw lots of caravans.

'You won't catch me on the open road,' Auntie Fee said. 'I like to sleep in my own bed.'

'It suits some folks,' Uncle Jack said.

'Who does it suit?'

'Circus-wallahs. They live here, they do everything out of caravans. Eat, sleep and boomps-a-daisies,' Uncle Jack said. 'Then, one morning early, they just up sticks, gone in a trice. Always on the move. That's what you get if you work for the Circus. Freedom. No one knows where you are. You never know where you'll wake up next. These buggers live for the open road.'

'Well, it wouldn't suit Auntie Fee, let me tell you. I like to sleep in my own bed.'

'No one's asking you, Finoonie.'

'Just as well, because I wouldn't.'

Uncle Jack said: 'Gordon and Monica will be back any day now.'

'That's what I tell Martin. Any day now,' Auntie Fee said.

I took a long time to go to sleep that night. The Gay Gordons went round and round in my dreams. '*Any day now . . . any day now . . .*' beat in my head like the bagpipe music.

31. Any Day Now

I woke up before morning. I got dressed very quietly and I put on my Robin Hood hat. I fetched my treasures and packed them all in the white dog's back and did up the zip, though I had to carry my dad's camera. I climbed over the gate. I went down to the lake. When the tram came, I had Georgie's shilling ready.

I said: 'One to Ellis Park.'

The conductor didn't say anything, he just gave me a ticket and that was fine. When I got to the Circus it was proper morning, there was a bit of mist around the place and the smell from the liger cage was very strong. I was glad I'd got there before they'd moved on. All the caravans were sleeping. So were the ligers. I knocked on the door of the caravan where they sold the tickets and a woman came, and she was the same woman with the shining stick who marched with the Gay Gordons, only she wasn't wearing her kilt, just an old pink dressing gown, and she said: 'What d'you want, little boy?'

'I want to come and work for you.'

She gave a big sigh. 'Oh God, not again.' She turned round. 'Wally, come here – we got another joiner.'

A man came out. He was the liger tamer, only he wasn't wearing his red shirt with the gold bits.

He said: 'What's your name, *boykie*?'

I didn't say anything.

The liger tamer said to the Gay Gordon: 'He's an odd little sod, isn't he? Look at the dog he's got there. Some sort of stuffed dog. Very stuffed. What's with the hat?'

'I was wondering about that hat. My God, Wally, do you think it's from one of those homes? Like Nazareth House. The ones they have for loonies.'

'Nazareth House isn't for loonies,' the liger man said. 'It's for unmarried mothers. Does the kid speak?'

'It did – a moment ago. It said it wanted to join the circus.'

I said: 'My name is Martin Donally. I live at 99 Sligo Road, Parkside.'

'It does speak,' the liger tamer said. 'OK, *boykie*, so you want to join the circus? Well, what does your mom say about that?'

'I lost her.'

'What about this place, in Sligo Road? You live there?'

'I live there but it's not my home.'

'You see,' the Gay Gordon said. 'He's cracked. He's from one of those bins. Wally, phone the cops. Where's your mommy gone, little boy?'

'Away.'

'Where's your daddy?'

'He bought the farm.'

'He's touched. Look, Wally, the dog's got a zip in his back,' the Gay Gordon said. 'What you got in the dog's back, little boy? Wally, ask him what he's got in the dog.'

The liger trainer wasn't listening to her. He was looking hard at me.

'Hey, just a minute. Listen, *boykie*, when did your dad buy the farm?'

'On 12 August 1944.'

The Gay Gordon said: 'For Pete's sake, don't encourage him, Wally. He's from a bin. For sure. The hat's probably part of the uniform.'

The liger trainer said: 'What did your daddy fly?'

'He could fly anything – Tigers, Ansons, Oxfords . . . Wellingtons.'

'Where did he buy it?'

'Up North. In Ramallah. It's in Palestine, which is Israel now.'

'Bugger me,' the liger trainer said. 'You know a thing or two, *boykie*.'

'When you two have *quite* finished,' the Gay Gordon said.

'What was your dad's name?' the liger man said.

'Dennis Hubert Donally – with two "L"s.'

'Two "L"s . . . Hey. That's important, is it?'

'Yes.'

'Why's it important?'

'Because on his grave they put the wrong spelling.'

'Is it, hey?'

'I'm going to fix it, one day.'

'Good for you, *boykie*. Writing on graves was done by base-wallahs and base-wallahs couldn't spell. Some of them couldn't even read without moving their lips. What's the dog for? You got something special in that dog? Want to show me what's in the dog, *boykie*?'

I pulled the dog against me.

'OK, OK. I'm not going to take the dog away from you. What was your dad flying when he bought the farm?'

'Wellington Tens.'

'*Ex-cuse* me,' the Gay Gordon said. 'Is this a private chat – or can anyone join in?'

'Did you know my dad?'

He shook his head. 'Different jobs. I was fighters. Number One Squadron. Spitties.'

There was a big hammering on the door then, and without anyone saying 'come in', or anything, Uncle Jack walked in. He smiled his pirate's smile at me.

'Here you are. You wily little bastard. Martin boy, if you go on doing this we're going to have to chain you to the table leg.'

The liger man looked at Uncle Jack and shouted right out loud: 'Well, I'll be buggered – it's Jumping Jack. Jacko, you old bastard.'

And Uncle Jack shouted right back: 'It's old Walter Basson. Wally, you prize pawpaw, long time no see.'

And they hugged each other and danced around the caravan so that it shook.

Uncle Jack said: 'God, it's years.'

'Shepheard's Hotel, Cairo, 1943.'

'Spot on. Shufti—'

'Shufti. Bints at three o'clock.'

They laughed and danced a bit more, and the Gay Gordon coughed softly, got up and touched her hair and wrapped her gown tightly round her.

'Excuse me for breathing. I'll just sit here, shall I? – until someone notices me.'

'Jacko, meet the missus,' the liger man said. 'Mandy, meet Jacko, my old oppo from Up North. We were both on Spitties, Number One Squadron.'

The Gay Gordon said: 'So the boy's yours?'

'No bloody fear.' Uncle Jack laughed. 'He's my nephew. Flighty little bastard. Turn your back for a second and he's over the fence. Last time he turned up in Anstey's. The missus wakes me this morning and says the bloody kid's gone AWOL. Again. Bloody panic stations. The wife's all for belling the cop shop. Then I had a thought. We saw your show last night, Wally. Keerist, I never knew it was you under all that bloody scrambled egg. A bloody liger tamer – Wally Basson . . . Who'd have believed it? That's life, isn't it?'

'A bugger,' the liger trainer said.

'A right royal one,' Uncle Jack said. 'Anyway, we were here last night. I caught a gleam in his eye. So this a.m., when the wife's all for getting in the cops, I said: "Hold on a sec – let me take a shufti at the Circus." And bingo.'

'Good old Jacko,' Wally said. 'Night vision – one hundred per cent.'

'Lots of carrots, right, you old bastard?'

'Dead right, you old bugger. We were still in bed when *boykie* here pitches up. He's carrying the dog. And he's got this camera, the box Brownie, only it doesn't work. He says it's dead. Mandy wondered if he was – you know – a bit touched. Anyway, we had a chat did *boykie* and me. He starts rabbiting on about Up North. And how his dad copped a packet. And I thought: "Christ, he's air force."'

'*Ja*. That's right. His dad was a mate of mine. Crazy bastard. Bombers. Western Desert. Never made it.'

'How come he wears those funny clothes, hey? That sailor suit. And that hat.'

'The sailor suit's from his mom. The hat's a hood, actually. His Robin Hood hat, see? Won't go anywhere without it. Hangs onto it for dear life. The dog . . .? I don't know about the dog. The dog's new. What's in your pooch, fellow?'

I undid the zip and showed them the logbooks and my dad's picture and his grave.

'Jeez,' the liger tamer said, 'he's got his old man's bumf in that bloody dog.'

'I gave them to him,' Uncle Jack said. 'I mean, why shouldn't he have something of his old man's?'

'Does he carry them around all the time?' the liger trainer said.

'Poor little chap,' the Gay Gordon said. 'Losing his mom too.'

Uncle Jack said: 'Who told you that?'

She flicked her eyes at me.

Uncle Jack laughed. 'That'll be the day. She's alive and kicking. She's just got married. She's on honeymoon at this very moment. In East London.'

The Gay Gordon turned to me. 'Why d'you say you lost your mommy? When she's only in East London? Your mom's only in East London, that's on the coast. It's not being dead.'

I didn't say anything. If you said anything you saw your words climbing like birds, higher and higher. But your words never got into their ears.

'You won't get any sense out of him,' Uncle Jack said. 'He's in a world of his own half the time. He lives in books. And things. Good flier, though, but loopy, like his old man.' He gave the liger trainer his card. 'Cheers, Wally. Give us a bell sometime, hey?'

'Will do, Jacko.'

He took my hand. 'OK, soldier, let's hit the road.

Your auntie Fee will be going bloody bananas. Goodbye, folks, and thanks.'

'Shame,' the Gay Gordon said.

The liger tamer waved. 'Bye-bye, *boykie*.'

We went home in Uncle Jack's Opel Kapitän, and he let me play with his perfume samples, which he kept in the cubbyhole. There were little pink tubs and bottles and boxes. My hands smelt of flowers. Uncle Jack talked about war. In the war what counted was a man's value. Life was cheap but if you bought it you were noble. In peacetime only the price counted. No one was noble. That was bloody hard to get used to.

'It's the same with scents and creams and such – they gotta be pricey. No one cares what they're really worth. Sheep fat and flowers. But if they don't cost a fortune people think they're just junk. Fancy bumping into old Wally. Bravest flier I ever knew. Look at him now – making ligers jump through hoops. Bloody pathetic, hey. You think you've put all that behind you. The war, I mean. You think you've escaped. But escaping's easier said than done. You think you're over the fence – and *wallop*.'

When we got back to Sligo Road my auntie Fee said: 'Where have you been? You gave us a real *skrik*. I woke up this morning and your bed was empty. We looked all over the garden for you. Georgie checked the park. The Snippalipskys hadn't seen you. We *even* thought of going to the cop shop. Then your uncle had a brainwave – did

Georgie give you any cash? Georgie said yes, only a bob. Jack said: "Wait a mo' – the little bugger's probably run off to join the circus." ' Auntie Fee laughed her rusty laugh. 'Hoo, boy. Thank your lucky stars your mother isn't here. It's dangerous, out in the world. Anything could happen. It's not full of people who love you to bits, like Auntie Fee. What if some old *dronkie* grabbed you? What if some loony decided to *gaps* you, and carried you off. To the back of beyond. To heaven knows where. The ends of the earth. Your mom would've had a cadenza. Let's not say anything when she gets home. OK?'

You think you're over the fence – then *wallop*. There were people who lived in the back of beyond, in the middle of nowhere. They were lucky.

I went out into the garden and it was dead still. Then I went to bed and cried, then I felt a bit better and it was still dead still.

32. The Bitch

Nothing happened, and nothing happened again.

'Any day now,' Auntie Fee said.

'Jack Robinson,' I said.

Ever since I showed the liger tamer what I kept in my white dog, I knew I had to find somewhere else for my things. I unzipped my dog and wrapped my things in tissue paper and put them into a hatbox from Le Chapeau, and put the box at the back of my mother's cupboard. I had a plan. If I went away I was going to carry the box by the string, like a suitcase.

Every morning I did my songs, I said my words, I sat in my secret place and I said: 'Gordon won't be coming home today – please.' And he didn't.

One morning I was in my secret place. I checked for Raymond. Nothing. I leaned back against the wall. I breathed in very slowly, listening to the words of the song in my head: '*He must know somethin', he don't say nothing, he just keeps rollin', he keeps on rollin' aloo-o-ng . . .*'

Everything was right. The sun was just there. The top

of the mulberry tree was just here. I shut my eyes. I sat exactly in the middle of the smooth old tree trunk, my feet were together, my ankles touched.

'. . . *Lift that bar, tote that bale – Get a little drunk and you land in j-ai-llll . . .*'

The sun was on my knees. I breathed out. I knew where I was. Somewhere Georgie's shears snipped another deadhead. I wanted the world to go on being like this. For ever and ever. World without end. Amen. Then, I did a bit of '*Mamm-ee, Mamm-ee, my dear old Mamm-eeee . . .*'

Then I got up, walked around the side of the house, saw Georgie bending his head among the roses and I thought: 'Why is he keeping his head down?' My senses were alert, my eyes were sharp, Robin's keen glance raked the greenwood for signs of intruders.

I saw why Georgie was keeping his head down.

Gordon was standing on the veranda. He was wearing khaki shorts and a white shirt. He was smoking a cigarette and whistling. I wanted to run. I wanted to slip effortlessly into the cool depths of Sherwood Forest and never, ever come back. I felt the hot breath of my pursuers on my neck. I felt cold, I felt sick. He had us surrounded.

Gordon saw me. 'How are you, Mor-ton?'

I didn't say anything.

'I see we've still got the old bahm-teckla to keep us warm. How the hell did you find it? That's what I'd like

to know. Hold onto it, my boy. Wouldn't want to lose
that again. Would we?'

My mom came onto the veranda then, and she hardly
looked the same because her legs were bare and her skirt
was yellow and she had a straw hat on that I'd never
seen before.

She saw me and held out her arms: 'Martin, darling,
come and kiss me. Come and tell your mom what you've
been up to while I've been away.'

I went to her slowly. Gordon was watching. I pushed
my face into her neck and took it out again and she said:
'Well, that wasn't much of a hug, was it? Don't I get a
kiss?'

I gave her a kiss but my head was so heavy and I
could hardly lift it up to her face.

'Look what we brought you.'

She gave me a round white cap, a bit like the cap my
uncle Charlie wore when he was a sailor. Only smaller.
And made of white paper.

'We know you like hats,' Gordon said, 'and this one's
got writing on it, see? It says there "I love East London".
They sell them on the beach.'

He said: 'bitch'.

My mom said: 'Martin knows what it says, don't you,
darling? His grandpa taught him to read. Can you tell
us what's on the hat, Martin? I'm sure Gordon would
like to hear you read.'

I didn't know why she did it. It hurt. My teeth were

closed tight, my head was going to jump off my shoulders.

Gordon laughed. 'I'd rather see him with a cricket ball. You any good with a cricket ball, Mor-ton? You any good with a rugby ball? You don't want to spend all your time with your nose stuck in books.' He said: 'boks'. 'Boks are all very well. But too many boks make a man namby.'

Namby.

'Gordon's got something else for you. Haven't you, sweetheart?'

'I might have. If he puts a smile on his face.'

'Smile, darling. It costs nothing.'

I tried to smile but it wouldn't come. I looked up at the sky, there were clouds and, suddenly, I loved those clouds. They were big and soft and easy and they floated away. Free. I felt I must be kinder to clouds. Next time I sat in my secret place I'd look at the clouds and say 'thank you' for being there, for being easy, for being full and soft and gentle and free, for saying that not all the world was like Gordon.

'What a face,' my mother said.

Gordon gave me a little walking stick, striped red and green and pink.

'Here you are, *boet*. To go with the hat. It's seaside rock. Watch your teeth, it's a jaw-breaker. Where's Jim Fish? We brought something for him too.'

Gordon went inside and came out with a bottle. It

was a Rose's Limewater bottle and it was full of water, with a bit of sand in the bottom. There was a piece of newspaper screwed in, where the cap should have been.

Georgie was down among the roses, stooping. Gordon didn't see him.

I pointed. 'He's there.'

Gordon and my mom walked over to him and looked down on him and Georgie crouched even more, going *snip, snip, snip,* as if he didn't know we were there.

Gordon said in a big loud voice, right down to him: 'Hello, my boy. We got a present for you. Here's a *bonsella*. From the seaside.'

He held out the bottle.

Georgie didn't look at it.

'Georgie, say thank you,' my mom said.

'Not necessary, Monica.' Gordon's voice was in his nose. 'There is no obligation on his part. None whatever. But if he doesn't want it, I know plenty of others who'd jump at it.'

He kept holding out the bottle. Georgie went on not looking at it.

Gordon didn't talk to Georgie, he talked to the bottle. 'It's a custom, isn't that so, my boy? Natives like drinking seawater, don't you, my boy? They knock it back because they believe it keeps them regular.'

Georgie went on not looking at the bottle.

'After they've knocked it back, it sends them to the *khasi*. Look, my boy, it has sand in it.' He shook the bottle and the sand swirled. 'There has to be some sand in the bottle, so they know it's the genuine article. Otherwise they won't touch it. We know this in PE. Yes, the Xhosa chaps down our way love the stuff. They dote on it. But it must have sand.'

I said: 'Georgie's a Zulu.'

'Don't get clever with me, Mor-ton. Unless you're looking for a thick ear. I don't care if he's a bloody Congo pygmy. They all love it, believe you me, *boet*. And I ought to know. I grew up on a farm. There's nothing you can tell me about our black brethren.'

He dropped the bottle near Georgie's foot and stood there, looking down at him. He was angry. You could hear him breathing. The waves were coming off him. I wondered if he was going to give Georgie a boot in the backside. Or a clip round the earhole. Or a bloody hiding. Or a good biff.

'Georgie, say thank you.' My mom sounded worried. 'It's not much to ask.'

'Thank you,' Georgie said. But he didn't look up. He left the bottle down on the ground, picked up his shears and went on snipping.

'There you are,' my mom said to Gordon. 'That's taken care of.'

Gordon went on looking down at Georgie.

'Don't stick this bottle under the madam's undies – hey, my boy. I don't want my seawater confiscated if the cops raid you again. Things are going to change around here. The sooner we get used to that the better. No more hooch under the frillies. You savvy?'

My mom got this flash in her voice.

'I've told you – umpteen times – it wasn't that kind of cupboard. I kept nothing there but empty boxes. Anyway, that's behind us. I'm sure it won't happen again. Will it, Georgie?'

Georgie looked at the ground. I looked at Georgie's neck. The muscles were squirming like Mr Jinnah's cobras.

Auntie Fee came in then and she said: 'Didn't I tell you your mom and dad would be back in two ticks.'

Gordon said: 'So what's he been up to while we've been gone?'

'Nothing,' Auntie Fee said. 'He's been as good as gold. Haven't you?'

She winked. I wished she wouldn't.

'Makes a change,' Gordon said.

'Shame on you, Gordon. Martin's been no trouble. We've been very happy, haven't we, Martin?'

'You're too soft on him, Fee.'

'I'm his favourite aunt.'

'Things are going to change now that we're home,' Gordon said.

My mom said: 'Well, isn't this just like old times?'

Then there was lunch. We had roast lamb and my mom said: 'Martin gets the knucklebone, because it's his favourite.'

It was true but I wished she hadn't said it because Gordon looked at me.

Uncle Jack said: 'Malan's a Nazi. His people are thugs, they're in for ever now. And they'll ruin us.'

'Better the devil you know,' my mom said.

'Why any devil at all?' Uncle Jack said.

'At least he's a rugby man,' Gordon said. 'That's a good mark – in my book.'

Uncle Jack was drinking a big glass of beer.

'I don't care if he plays rugby. Or lacrosse. I don't care if he plays with himself. The bastard stinks.'

'Well, Jack, you're entitled to your opinion, but I must beg to differ.'

Uncle Jack crashed his glass down on the table and said: 'Oh, you must, must you? Well, I couldn't give a stuff if you must beg, borrow, or steal, Gordon. Just loosen up, OK?'

'I am perfectly loose. Thanks very much. Though that may surprise you.'

'Surprised? Count me as A-fucking-A-mazed!' Uncle Jack said.

My mom said: 'Gordon brought Martin such a funny hat from East London. Why don't you run and fetch your hat, darling. And show us.'

I sat there. I didn't move.

Gordon said: 'See what I mean? Stubborn. Well, so am I. We'll sort him out. Say something, Mor-ton.'

I didn't say anything, I couldn't say anything. My ears

were hot. I just went into myself, to the quiet still place inside me, where I could block out everything. I listened to my breathing. I thought: 'Just let me live through this time – when I get out of here I'll go and sit in my corner, on my tree, and count to twenty-one and get calm again.'

Gordon said: 'I told you about that. In the army that's dumb insolence. You can be locked up for that.'

'Let's not talk about the army, let's talk about you lovebirds,' Auntie Fee said. 'Tell us what you did, Gordon, down at the coast.'

'We had everything that opens and shuts. Nahoon's a friendly little place. Good table.'

'We swam too,' my mom said.

'*You* swam, Monica. I sat on the bitch.'

He had these things he said a lot. Like tall people do. As if you can say them – and they're right, because you say them, because you say them all the time, because you say them with a sigh, because you're important, because you're tall, because you're you, because you forget you're saying them and everyone has heard them a hundred million times and wishes you wouldn't say them. Because you can't hear yourself, because you're deaf . . .

When no one was looking, I went round to the rubbish tip where Georgie put his dead flowers and all the grass he cut. I dug a hole and it smelt of the garden, and I pushed the rocky walking stick and the sailor's hat deep in the hole, covered them up again and stamped them down until you couldn't see anything was buried there.

33. Our War

Every morning my mom went to the Consolidated Insurance Company. Gordon went to the bank. His neck was black with hair that had been shaven there. He came home every afternoon on the tram with my mom.

I was between them. I felt like a knife, thin and turned sideways so there was no thickness to me.

My mom kept saying: 'I'll talk to your dad about that.'

'We'll have to see what your dad says . . .'

'Why don't you ask your dad?'

Gordon kept saying: 'We can get on, or we can fight. It's entirely up to you.'

'Yes.'

'Yes – who?'

'Yes, Dad.'

He looked at me with his grey glittery eyes. 'I'm on to you, my boy, I'm bloody well on to you.'

A boy had to watch his back.

My mom and Gordon slept in her room and when the night-lions tore up the night, I heard them but I was in

Cousin Caítlín's room and I didn't want to go through to her because if I did Gordon would be there.

Once, I was in their room, and he took out his teeth and put them in a glass and I saw them and he said: 'What's the matter? Never seen a pair of snappers before?'

The smile in the glass was part of my dreams.

I was really sorry I hadn't killed Gordon. One day I'd kill him, for sure. I would cut him up into a thousand pieces and bury him in the compost heap, under the grass, like I buried his sailor's hat from East London and his seaside rock. I wouldn't tell anyone, and no one would know and Gordon would be gone from the face of the earth.

'Where's Gordon?' people would say.

'Search me,' I'd say.

Hoo, boy. That was fine – for one fine day. But what to do about now?

I felt Gordon watching me. I took my treasures out of my mom's cupboard, wrapped them in plastic and hid them in a fork in the mulberry tree.

The wind blew in my head, it blew between my bones, it would blow me away. If I lost my treasures, I was lost. This was war. A boy needed all the help he could get, he needed height, fight, light, bangs. A battle to the death, no quarter given. Sword rang on sword in the greenwood; the feathered shaft flew true to its mark.

I lay in bed. I felt Gordon watching me, even when he

wasn't there. Outside the windows the moon was very bright, I had to close my eyes a bit to look at it. The shadows were climbing the walls, they were like black clouds, like black paint. I got out of bed and went outside to the mulberry tree. I pulled out the pictures of my father and his grave and took them back to bed and put them under my pillow. I left the logbooks in the tree. The logbooks were no use to anyone. What could anyone do with the logbooks?

I went to sleep talking to Them: 'Just you wait. When I'm big, you'll see. Just you wait.'

I didn't know what they'd see. I didn't know what I was waiting for, except it was something. And my Something was better than their Nothing.

Georgie was my nanny again.

'Did you like being the government, Georgie?'

He put his head on the side. 'I liked it, Martin.'

We walked down Sligo Road and at the bottom of the road was a shape, in oil, on the road. Nothing else.

'Where's the Café de Move On?'

'It was moved on,' Georgie said. 'It was the police.'

'Why?'

He shrugged. 'It could happen to anyone.'

'Could it happen to me?'

He touched the tip of my nose with the tip of his finger.

'Big, big changes coming. They going to move us all, Martin.'

Every morning I looked to see that my logbooks were still in the tree. And they were there, every day, until one day they weren't. I knew what had happened. They'd been moved on. It was the police.

Gordon was on the veranda, in a wicker chair, turning the pages of the *Reader's Digest*. He didn't look at me when I came and stood right next to him. He was reading a page called 'It Pays to Increase Your Word Power'. He didn't look up.

'Lost something, Mor-ton?'

It wasn't what he said; it was how he stared when he said it. Like Raymond when he got up on the wall and stared down at me. That's why Raymond got sent to me. He came to show me how Gordon would look when he said: 'Lost something, Mor-ton?'

He folded the *Reader's Digest* and put it down; I saw a picture of three men around a fire, they had short, shaved hair, like Gordon, and they were all wearing ties and drinking beer and eating steak and it said: 'Be Emphatic – Buy Monatic! It's a South African custom.'

Gordon stood up. ''Bout time we had a little chat, son. Sit down.'

He went inside. I sat down on the floor next to his chair. He came back with the logbooks and flipped through them. He knew where to go. He opened the second logbook first, the biscuit logbook, and turned the pages till he got to the end.

'These are your special books, aren't they?'

I didn't say anything.

'They were your father's.'

I still said nothing, but something was coming, I could hear it coming.

'Now you're a real little smart-arse. So you'll know how your father died, won't you?'

I couldn't stop myself. I let him have it.

'My father was in the Western Desert. Jerry was moving up his armour. The Wellingtons pasted the place. My father radioed he'd copped a bad one. They got his gunner. He was heading home. He didn't make it.'

Gordon said very flat and hard and in his nose: 'Indeed.'

'Yes.'

'Is that so?' Heavy words, one, two, three – Is-That-So?

'Yes, it is.'

'Says who?'

'My uncle Jack.'

'It's a lie.'

'But he saw it.'

'I beg to differ. It's a tissue of lies, a farrago of fabrication. The only bit of truth is that your father was flying a Wellington when he died.' Gordon flipped over the pages some more. 'And how do I know this? Simple. Because it's all written here. You can read, son, can't you? You've read these logbooks. Tell me – who was with your father when he died?'

'Lieutenant Beswick, Lieutenant Godlington, Sergeant Ballard . . .'

'That's right. Now, Martin, d'you see this big red line? Well, just under the red line there is some writing. Correct me if I'm wrong. What does it say just under the red line?'

'All killed.'

'That's right. All killed. And what does it say after "All killed"?'

'It says COTO.'

'Right again. We are firing on all cylinders today. COTO. But that's just the initials. What I'm asking you is: what do they stand for?'

Gordon was smiling, his teeth were wet. Like they were when he put them in the glass.

'Come on, Mor-ton, you must have an idea. Spit it out. What do you think COTO stands for?'

I said it slowly, I said it feeling a big wide hole opening up behind me. 'It means "Carry On Top-hole Officers".'

'Oh, it does, does it? Indeed. And who says so?'

'Auntie Fee.'

'She did – did she? Allow me to tell you what it means. Shall I?'

I didn't want him to tell me but I knew he would.

'It means "Crashed On Take-Off". And do you know

what that means? Shall I tell you? It means your father was a lousy flier.'

'He wasn't.'

'Oh, wasn't he? Look at the logbooks. He couldn't even bloody well take off.'

'He could fly Hornets, Avro Ansons, Oxfords, Tiger Moths, Hawker Harts and Wellingtons. He could do steep turns, side slippings, forced landings, aerobatics . . .'

'Your father didn't know up from down.'

'He could do Straight and Level flying. He could do Stalling, Climbing and Gliding, he could do Taking off into the Wind . . .'

'I don't care if he did walking on water. Read what it says here. *Crashed On Take-Off*. COTO. Smack into the bloody ground. That's the truth. Top-hole Officers my arse. Your father wrote himself off, and he's buried somewhere in Gyppoland.'

'It's not Gyppoland.'

'What difference does it make?'

'He's in Ramallah – in Israel.'

'OK – I stand corrected. He's buried in Israel.'

'Eight miles east of Jaffa.'

'Who cares if it's eight miles east of Brakpan? But have it your way. He's not in Gyppoland, he's in Jewland.' He leaned down and put his mouth right by my ear and he shouted: 'BUT HE STILL FLEW INTO THE FUCKING GROUND.'

He dropped the logbooks on the table.

'You MacBrides like shouting the odds. You don't like what's real. Show you what's real and you run in the other direction. Your father writes himself off – but he's a hero. Your granddad goes to Curzon. He thinks it's the coming Jo'burg, when anyone with half an eye can see it's just a one-horse *dorp*. He buys the Grange Hotel – it ruins him. He backs Smuts – Smuts gets thrashed. Your uncle Matt takes on the Nats in Boksburg – he gets hammered. And do you care? Not a damn. You just sail on regardless. You like talking. Singing. Going to the races. Shouting the odds. Playing politics. Always backing the wrong horse. Always telling stories. When something's right in front of your nose, you can't see it. When it comes to logic, you can't manage. When it comes down to the bottom line, you go blind. Your mother's the same. Sees what she wants to see. Bugger the rest. And Fee and Charlie and Matt. The same. You read COTO and it comes out Carry On Top-hole Officers. Fine. Except it isn't. It's killed on bloody take-off. That's what it is. But that doesn't suit – so you make up some bloody story. When something doesn't suit you just change it. You bury it, hide the evidence, run the other way. Well, life doesn't work like that. You got that, Mor-ton? Do we understand one another?'

'Yes.'

'Yes – WHO?'

'Yes, Dad.'

'That's better. I think we've got the makings of an understanding.'

His voice was in his nose again. He had this sad, shaking-head, sighing look he always got when he was really pleased. And he was really pleased, it leaked out of him, he was a right royal bugger. He'd won. Hands down.

'I'm on to you. So you choose. We see eye to eye – or I skin you alive. It's up to you.'

He got up and walked inside and didn't turn round.

I thought about my grandpa. About my family. About their stories. About Midnight, like liquid lightning. And how racing wasn't in Gordon's book, and how we sang all the way to Turffontein and all the way home to the Villa Vanilla. About the muscles like snakes in Georgie's neck. About COTO, and Lieutenant Farebrother, and my father flying into the ground.

Crashed On Take-Off ... Carry On Top-hole Officers ...

Gordon was right. I wouldn't face it. And he wasn't going to make me. I would take Auntie Fee's stories any day over anything he said. Anything Gordon did do, I wouldn't do. It was simple. Gordon was alive. The alive ones were the tall ones. You looked up and you saw their knees and then their belts and then their chins. They had terrible knees. White, dangerous poisonous round knees. They had big voices. They thought they were the bosses of everything. The dead ones were low down, they had very small voices. But if you listened, you could hear them and love them and speak to them.

I thought: 'Well, one day Gordon will also be dead – and then no one will speak to him.'

I picked up the logbooks. My ears were humming. I could hardly bear to go on holding them after Gordon's hands had held them and his eyes had read them. They had bits of him on them. I went to the compost heap and dug a hole, on the other side of the pile from where I'd dug a hole for Gordon's paper hat and his seaside rock, and I pushed the logbooks deep under the soft wet grass. They had to go. Out of my sight, out of my light, out of my air, out of my world.

I hated Gordon. The more I hated him, the more right he was.

34. How I Discovered Dynamite

My mother bought a wide yellow hat. My dad bought a pale green Vauxhall. 'It's a pretty little bus.' Each Sunday they went off in the car. I heard my mother talking about 'south facing' and 'servants' quarters' and 'parquet flooring'. She talked most of all about 'the move'.

If I kept down low, like Georgie, they might forget to take me with them. But it didn't really help. If they were moving, then I was moving, they wouldn't leave me behind, even if I asked, even if I said I'd be fine, really.

I built a house in the backyard, with red and yellow bricks. The walls stayed up and I even had a window. I asked Rosa to come and see my house and she wriggled in and we sat in the kitchen and she said: 'Gosh, you've got shelves.' She liked my bottles. I had Old Buck Gin and Grand Mousseux from Georgie, and Pretty Polly Floral Fragrance and Satin Bath Foam from Uncle Jack.

'It's like a chemist's shop. It's beautiful, your house.'

I said Crossly Hall had fifty-four rooms.

'I like yours better.'

'I know a man who lives at Crossly Hall and he had his affections alienated.'

'What's that?'

'That's when someone loves you, and then another person comes along and stops that person loving you.'

'Gosh, Martin.'

'I'm going away.'

'Where to?'

'Don't know.'

'Can't you ask?'

I couldn't ask – in case they told me.

We went to her house and Mr Snippalipsky was there. Rosa said: 'Martin's going away. Only he doesn't know where.'

I could hear in her voice how bad that was.

Mr Snips looked at me. 'Cheer up, Martin, it may never happen.'

But it was going to happen. Auntie Fee said so. 'What luck. A house at the end of the world, a brand-new place, with a brand-new garden, lots and lots of space to play in and lots of other children to play with. You're a lucky boy, aren't you? Any day now. Before you can say Jack Robinson.'

I said Jack Robinson, but nothing happened. I made kites with Georgie. We cut up tissue paper from my mother's boxes and stuck it down with flour and water glue. Every day Georgie got lower and lower in the garden, till he was almost out of sight. We walked down

Sligo Road, we crossed over the road when we passed Dr Verwoerd's house, even though it was empty. We passed the barbers snipping away under the bluegums. Amos waved. I climbed on the swings and Georgie pushed me for ages. Then he did something he hadn't done for a long time. He got on the swing next to me.

'My turn, Martin.'

We thought of the Ghost Squad, but we didn't care, we just laughed and I pushed him. Georgie kicked his legs out, he went high in the air. I ran to push him. I was still running to push him when the swing came back, very big, very quick, and banged into my head and I fell over.

I woke up and I was at Sligo Road and my auntie Fee was there. She looked very pleased.

'Have you been in the wars! Wait till your mom gets home, she'll have an absolute cadenza. You should see your face. You collected that swing smack in the kisser. Your bottom teeth have gone west.'

My mother came in. She put her hands up to her mouth and she looked flabbergasted.

'Honestly, Martin. How *could* you? Today of all days. And to think – I had a real surprise for you. You can't go now. Look at you. I turn my back for a second and this happens. What am I going to tell your dad?'

Auntie Fee said: 'Gordon needn't know.'

'Of course he'll know. He only has to look at the child.'

'Say he was building a house, say it fell on him.'

'Well, golly – I don't know.'

'*I'll* tell him,' Auntie Fee said.

When she told him, my dad said: 'I don't see why his mishaps should wreck our day. He can come with us. But he better not bleed on my new upholstery.'

'We're going for a quick look,' my mother said, 'at our new home.'

I sat in the back of the car and felt a bit sick. The car was green and the seats were green and the air was green. My lips felt rough and my tongue tasted funny and I kept licking my gums, they were sore.

My mother kept turning round every so often and saying: 'Keep your chin up, Martin – try not to drip.'

'Why doesn't he stick his head out of window? If he's dripping,' my dad said.

'Then he'll drip on the paint.'

'I can wash the paint.'

It was miles and miles. I kept saying: 'Are we there yet?' But we weren't. On and on we went. Somewhere behind me was Sligo Road. The Villa Vanilla.

My mother counted off the suburbs: 'Look, there's Cyrildene and oh, look, there's Orange Grove.' As if she'd never seen them before and this was a miracle.

And my dad said: 'Yes, that's Cyrildene, all right.' As if he had just made it happen.

The blood got dry on my lips and I could push my

tongue into the holes where my teeth had been. I counted four holes. Further and further. We passed a big muddy dam, and there were a lot of people round the dam, wearing white sheets and standing by the water.

'Black Zionists, that's who those bods are,' my dad said. 'You sometimes get them in PE. When they're going to be baptized, those chaps dunk themselves in the water. Think nothing of it. For your black Zionist, it's like going for a swim. Just jump in, and bob up and down like a bloody cork.'

'Goll-ee,' my mother said. 'You wouldn't catch me in that dam. No fear. It's bound to have bilharzia . . .'

'Those chaps don't mind a bit of bilharzia.'

On and on.

The road ran out of tarmac and turned to dirt, the grass stopped, the veldt was yellow, there were black trees, there was no more green. We drove down a sandy street and stopped outside a shining wire fence.

'End of the line. Here we are,' my dad said.

We got out and looked. There was a house with a tin roof and windows and a lot of sand.

'This is our new home,' Gordon said. 'The suburb's being developed for ex-servicemen.'

'Just *look* at those picture windows. Look at those chimneys. That's real face-brick,' my mother said.

'It's still in the early stages. But I've seen the plans and I must say I am pretty damn impressed. Going to be quite a place. High-grade materials, everything straight out of the box. There'll be a servant's room and a garage for the Vauxhall. I also want to put in a rockery.'

'My goll-ee.' My mother took my hand. 'Well, darling, what do you think?'

I tried to think. Nothing happened. 'What's it called?'

'It hasn't got a name, it's so new,' Gordon said.

'It must be called something,' my mother said.

'It's just called Extension Number Six. Names come later. I believe that they're thinking of royal names, Windsor or Balmoral. That sort of thing.'

'It looks a bit . . . bare,' my mother said. 'But it will come along fast when families settle. Won't it, Gordon?'

'It's come a long way already. Six months ago there was nothing here but red dust, shale and blackjacks, and that big muddy dam, where the black bods dunk themselves – and the dynamite factory.'

'Dynamite?' My mother spoke in the voice she kept for worrying about drunks and lions. 'My godfathers. A dynamite factory – right next door. Whatever will they think of next? I hope it's not a big one.'

Gordon got his steely-twinkly look, I knew what was coming.

'Big? Biggest dynamite factory in the southern hemisphere. Biggest one between here and Cairo. If that goes up we'll all be blown to smithereens.'

'Thanks very much. Who wants to get blown to smithereens?'

'Spoken in jest, Monica. That factory's run by wallahs who really know their onions. When it comes to high explosives there is nothing you or I could teach them.'

I said: 'Can Georgie come and live with us?'

My dad said: 'We're having a regular servant, not some shebeen-king-cum-barrack-room-lawyer-cum-banker.'

'Maybe Georgie will come and visit you, darling, now and then,' my mom said.

'Please God he doesn't,' Gordon said.

35. Iron in the Soul

The streets were called Henry and Elizabeth and Victoria because they were royal names and this was a royal suburb. The streets were dusty, and they ended in a big dip where there was a muddy little river, and after the river the ground climbed up to a hill, very hot and stony. I liked the river because there were lots of bluegums next to it and if you made your eyes very narrow it looked a bit like Park Lake, except there weren't any barbers. But my dad said there were lots of burglars in the bluegums, but I couldn't find them, even though I went there every day.

I had a room at the end of a long passage. I used to get up in the night, and walk in my sleep. My mother told me in the morning and asked me to stop.

'Lord's sakes, Martin, you gave me the fright of my life, standing there, right at my feet, holding your pillow, and I spoke to you but you didn't say anything. Just stood there, eyes wide open. It gave me the heebie-jeebies, I can tell you. Thank heavens your dad didn't wake up.'

The house smelt of new bricks. I didn't like bricks any more. There was no grass. Sometimes the dustbin men came and the dogs chased them. Sometimes the water truck came to sprinkle the sandy streets to keep down the dust. I lit a lot of fires, mostly in the garage, where there was nothing but boxes of Trotter's jellies. It was fun to see the flames getting higher, and to think just when I would jump on it, and if I got it wrong everything would burn in the house, and all the yellow face-brick and the red tin roof, and everyone inside too.

I killed off my mom and dad almost every day.

Number One – they drowned in the municipal lake, and I didn't mind. I lived on doorsteps and apricot jam.

Number Two – they were out driving somewhere, in the Vauxhall, and Gordon would be saying: 'That's Cyrildene, over there . . .' My mother would be saying: 'Goll-ee!' And *kee-rash!* Someone would come to the house and he'd say: 'Martin Stock, we have some bad news – your dad and mom have been killed in a terrible smash . . .' And I'd say: 'Does that mean I'm an orphan?' And they'd say: 'It does. Don't be sad.' And I'd try to keep my face as sad as I could.

Number Three – they were driving past the dynamite factory and *ka-pow!* They were blown to smithereens. There was not a piece left, not even anything to say who they were, so no one came to tell me, because every tiny bit had been blown away, but I heard the bang, and when they didn't come back I got on a tram and went

back to 99 Sligo Road and Georgie was there and he
bent down and said: 'Hop on, Martin, hold tight.'

I was sorry the dynamite factory was run by chaps
who knew their onions. Still, there was a chance, wasn't
there? Something to hope for? I went to bed at night
and I prayed for a miracle. In a war, a boy needs some
elevation, he needs to watch his back. He needs big
bangs. High explosive, cordite, gelignite . . . dynamite.

I ran away so often my dad said: 'Why don't you
pack him sandwiches, Monica? And if he gets carried
off by the burglars, who live down by the river in the
bluegums, it serves him bloody well right.'

One morning I heard my mother calling me. She had
on her old voice, the kind voice, the voice before
Gordon.

'In the kitchen. Quick. Come and see who's here.'

And there was Georgie. He was wearing my grandpa's
salt-and-pepper suit and he had a watch chain on his
tummy.

'Georgie, show Martin what you found.'

He held out his fist and when he opened it, there, in
his hand, were my teeth. Then he hugged me. Then he
cried and I cried.

'He went and looked all over the grass, under the
swing. Take them. Don't show your dad.'

My dad came in then. 'Hells' bells, a bladdy tearfest
in my own kitchen. Put a sock in it, won't you?'

Georgie and I cried some more.

Gordon said to my mother: 'Can't you do something?'

'What can I do? Don't look at me. I didn't *ask* them to cry.'

'Well, at least get them to do it away from the window. What happens if people see them like that? They might get the wrong end of the stick.'

'Do you want to play something?' I said to Georgie.

'Oh my God,' my dad said.

My mother closed the curtains. 'Why don't you take Georgie down Henry Avenue to the bluegums and play there?'

I didn't ride on his back. We walked down to the bluegums where the shadows were like black water and the dust got up your nose and you could hear the little rusty river running in the thin red sand. There I sat and Georgie picked up a bit of white tree branch and said to me: 'Watch this, Martin.' And he put the stick on his shoulder and said: 'Parade, a-tten-shun!' and he started to march, left and right and left, like Gordon, only better, and I didn't know what to say. When he marched he was someone else. When he started I couldn't see why he was someone else and then I could – he was taller when he marched.

He said: 'What can you tell me, Martin?'

I told him about the dynamite factory. 'One day it might blow us all to smithereens.'

He liked that. 'Dynamite, that was what Boss Mac wanted.'

We walked home up Henry Avenue and I wanted Georgie to come inside but he said he had to go.

'Will you come back?'

Georgie hugged me and he said: 'I'll see you again, Martin.'

I knew he wouldn't.

I took my teeth and put them with my picture of my father, in the bottom of my cupboard. I was glad to have my teeth back, though I wasn't sure what to do with them. They were part of me. I thought they might come in useful, one day.

My dad went on worrying about Georgie coming back.

'What happens if he makes a habit of dropping in when the mood takes him? A lot of effing munts, togged up to the nines, knocking on our back door. What'll people think?'

And my mother said: 'There's no need to swear. I didn't ask him to come here, did I? I didn't know he was coming. I suppose he thought Martin better have his teeth back.'

'What for? Little bugger'll go and grow new ones. Why bring his bloody teeth back?'

'Don't ask me, Gordon. Who knows how their minds work? I'm not a native psychiatrist.'

His eyes went all hurt. He didn't know her. I was even sorry for him, but only once; this was war to the death. A boy needs bangs, and my mother was dynamite.

I was dynamite. Down the road was more dynamite. I didn't know how to get it but knowing it was there made me feel good. It wasn't much, but it was something.

Carry on Top-hole Officers . . . left, right, left . . .

I lay in bed at night and thought about the past. Putting things in place. Making it like I wanted it. Back to when there was my mom and me, and we had a deal. When things were fine. When we lived at the Villa Vanilla in Sligo Road. I could make pictures of it in my head. There was the long red wall, and there was the gatepost where I used to sit and wait for my mom, and there was the shaggy palm tree, sticking its head over the wall. It was quiet. I could hear Georgie snipping away at the deadheads. I was outside the wall. But somewhere in the garden there was me too. In my corner, behind the mulberry tree, singing in my head:

> 'Sure, I've got rings on my fingers, bells on my toes,
> Elephants to ride upon, my little Irish Rose,
> So come to your Nabob, and next Patrick's Day,
> Be Mistress Mumbo Jumbo Jij-ji-boo J. O' Shea.'

But the big wooden gate was closed, the palm tree turned its hairy head this way and that and wouldn't let me in.

Acknowledgements

'My Mammy'
Words by Samuel Lewis and Joseph Young, music by Walter Donaldson.
© 1920 Donaldson Publishing Co./Bourne Co./Redwood Music Ltd/Warock Corp., USA
Reproduced by permission of EMI Music Publishing Ltd/Francis Day & Hunter Ltd/
International Music Publications Ltd, London.
All rights reserved.

'Wild West Show'
Words and music by Cy Coleman, Betty Comden and Adolphe Green.
© 1992 Notable Music Co. Inc. and Betdolph Music Inc., USA
Warner/Chappell Music Ltd, London.
Reproduced by permission of International Music Publications Ltd.
All rights reserved.

'White Christmas'
Words and music by Irving Berlin.
© 1940 and 1942 Irving Berlin Music Corp., USA
Warner/Chappell Music Ltd, London.
Reproduced by permission of International Music Publications Ltd.
All rights reserved.

'If You Knew Susie'
Words and music by Joseph Meyer and Buddy Desylva.
© 1925 Shapiro Bernstein & Co. Inc., USA
Reproduced by permission of Keith Prowse Music Publishing Co. Ltd, London.

'Mona Lisa'
Words and music by Jay Livingston and Ray Evans.
© 1949 Famous Music Corporation, USA
Used by permission of Music Sales Ltd.
All rights reserved. International copyright secured.

'Ol' Man River'
Music by Jerome Kern, words by Oscar Hammerstein II
© 1927 T. B. Harms and Co. Inc., USA
Universal Music Publishing Ltd, London.
Used by permission of Music Sales Ltd.
All rights reserved. International copyright secured.